The Quest for Juice

Jonathan-David Jackson

This is a work of fiction, but any similarity between persons living or dead is intentional. If this book reminds you of yourself or events in your life, it's because it was written about you.

ISBN-13: 978-0615826820
ISBN-10: 0615826822

Books by Jonathan-David Jackson:

The Quest for Juice (Paranoia #1)
The Quest for Truth (Paranoia #2)
The Quest for Nothing in Particular (Paranoia #3)

Also,
Not Quite the End of the World,
a post-apocalyptic novel.

For my father, Jack.
Without you, this book
would never have been written.

Part 1

Chapter 1

MY KEY STUCK in the lock. I turned it away, and then back again. This was okay, no need to be worried. I jiggled it, looking for the correct angle for it to fit against the tumblers of the lock, but still the door would not open. My heart beat faster. They had trapped me. I was out in the open, and defenseless. I rammed the key into the lock and twisted it as hard as I could. Nothing. I flicked my eyes side to side. Nobody was there—but someone was watching me. I looked over my shoulder. Did a curtain move in a window across the street? I wiped my hand over my mouth. *Breathe. Slow and deep*. I flexed my hands, closed my eyes, and let my fingers find the key on their own. The cold metal brushed against my skin. Once more, I turned the key away, and then back again, gently, feeling the tumblers engage with it as much as I heard them. And once again it stuck before the final *click.* I slammed my palm against the door, rattling the windows. For a moment I decided I would smash the windows, but then I remembered the bars that reinforced them from the other side.

"Let me in!" I shouted. It was my house. I had as much right as anyone to be there—more of a right! Where else could I go? There was nowhere. If they could get to my keys, they could do anything.

"Please," I whispered, "let me in." I turned the key feebly. Back and forth, back and forth. It would not open. Even if it turned all the way, it would not open.

Tears dripped down my face. Was it too much to ask, for a bed to sleep in, a roof over your head, a fridge to keep your juice in? I would have to live on the street, and under bridges. I would depend on the charity of soup kitchens, and my willingness to sell my body. I shivered through my tears, feeling the touch of strangers on my smooth flesh, hearing their words—their commands, as they paid me to do their bidding. I heard myself burst into a sob, and I could not control it. The neighbors heard me weeping. If my head had not ached so much, I would have been able to hear their voices. They judged me. Hated me. I could not even get into my own house; I was worthless and they knew it the same as I did. Nobody would even pay for the use of my body.

I dropped to my knees on the front step and turned my face, beseechingly, heavenward. But there was no help from there—there was no help from anywhere. I let my head drop forward, and my forehead pressed against the door.

The floor smashed into my face as the door swung open. Eyes wide, I pushed myself up and blinked at the key. It had turned after all, without me realizing. I scrambled inside and threw the door shut behind me. The deadbolt slammed into place. My ragged breath slowed down. I was home.

With hands still shaking, I poured myself a glass of Sunshine Juice orange juice. I downed it in one gulp and then poured another. I had been right.

The changes were small, at first. When the doorbell rang, it was always a dear friend you'd love to see or a

Girl Scout selling cookies you'd love to eat. But then, suddenly and without warning, on Tuesday maybe once a month or every two months, it might instead be someone trying to tell you the benefits of converting to Mormonism, and you'd have to listen for several minutes before you closed the door because you didn't want to seem rude. It was very inconvenient, because maybe you were cooking something and you only answered the door because it needed a little while to cool, but then it needed to be stirred, and you know it's in there waiting for you, congealing while you stand at the door.

There were more things. After I had a shower, the door to the bathroom sometimes wouldn't shut properly. Now, ostensibly, this was because the heat and steam from my shower had caused the wood fibers to swell so it would not fit in the doorframe. Ostensibly.

I wasn't employed, for reasons which will soon be made clear, but I knew of people who were employed and when their paycheck direct deposit was due to come through on a Thursday night, often it wouldn't actually come through until Friday morning or even Monday, meaning they'd have to put off vital purchases or perhaps pay a thirty dollar overdraft fee because their bills somehow made it through while their paycheck didn't.

Who was behind all of these things? I felt certain that it was *someone*; someone with access to Mormons, wood, banks—and now, keys. My name is Oscar, and I decided it was up to me to find out who. This is the story of how.

I started small. I'm not going to recount my entire life for you though, so I'll just spare you the suspense and tell you that I did grow to a regular adult size over a period of many years.

I began my investigation with small actions. I wrote a letter to the editor of one of my local newspapers, explaining and complaining about everything changing. I kept writing the letters, until eventually they published one in the *Letters to the Editor* section. There was no investigation, though, and much to my disappointment, nobody went to prison. Not yet, anyway; that happens later.

After that letter was published, I began to get the impression that I was being followed[1]. For most of my life I'd had that impression, actually, but now I started to get it more, and not just when I was walking out late at night and the sound of my own footsteps would frighten me.

The kind of inconvenient changes I'm talking about started happening all the time. Other people didn't see it and so they went on about their regular business like nothing was changing, but it was clear to me; I have a good head for changes that nobody else can see, and I'm always alert. Some might say *too* alert, but they will be the first ones to be eaten by a bear while I would be straight into my bear-proof safe room to wait for rescue.

---

[1] You'd think the letter would have scared them off, but these guys were tough.

When I went to the store for my weekly shopping, they no longer carried my favorite brand of orange juice, Sunshine Juice. The only brand which they had in stock was Sunlight OJ, which has '*50% more real orange pulp.*' I hate orange pulp, and I'm not ashamed to say so.

I'd always been loyal to that store, even though there were other stores closer, partly because they had all the brands that I loved, but mostly because they were one of the few stores that hadn't banned me from shopping there (bans mostly based on unfounded accusations, I assure you). So I made an effort to enjoy their new juice, but after a few days of closing the curtains to hide myself before straining the juice through a paper towel—just so I could enjoy a cold drink with my breakfast such as any free man is entitled to—I decided it was time to take my business elsewhere. It wasn't really my decision, because those two glasses I'd poured myself were the last of my final carton of Sunshine Juice.

For the first time in years, I went to a different store. While I was driving there, my head began to ache. I imagined what it would be like if someone got there first and took all my juice. I could almost see it happening; I saw the villain pushing me to the ground and taking the juice from me. I saw him standing over my broken body and pouring the juice—*my juice*—into his own mouth. The more I thought about it, the more my head ached. I knew there was nothing I could do about it until I got there, though, so I did my best to ignore the thoughts. That's not an easy thing to do when your mind insists on showing you them over and over. Headaches like that had been increasing along with the inconveniences. Usually the headache would come, and then the inconvenience. Not all the time, but enough that I'd sometimes scream into a pillow from the combined injustice and physical pain of it all. My head had been hurting for hours on the night my screaming pillow lost a few of its feathers. Not all of them, but enough that I had to get rid of the pillow, because when they took the feathers out who knows what they could've put in. After that, I tried my best to keep it in instead of screaming—it was better if they didn't know how the things they did affected me.

Even though the store was a new place, I didn't feel nervous once I arrived. There were cameras watching, and if someone was following me then the cameras would catch the follower. Theirs was an organization based on secrecy, so it seemed unlikely that they would be so bold as to follow me into the eyes of a network of cameras. I got about halfway through the store—right to the middle of their small clothing section—before I realized that if whoever was following me had the sort of connections I suspected, they wouldn't need to follow me in person; they could just as easily watch me through the store's cameras.

I crawled under the racks of pants and shirts. When there was no more cover available above me, I pressed myself as close to the shelving as I could, to avoid the cameras, and made my way towards the back of the store where the juice and tea were stocked.

I was pleased to see that this store still carried my

favorite, Sunshine Juice, and there wasn't a single carton of the pulp-heavy Sunlight OJ in sight. Sadly—for someone else—they only had one carton left, and I was going to have that carton all to myself.

I began formulating a vague plan to pour the juice all over my naked body when I got it back home, but when I opened the refrigerator door and reached for the bottle, it took a step away from me towards the back of the shelf. I held still, since I didn't want to spook the juice further. If it got away, who knows where it would have gone to? Nobody knows what goes through the mind of an orange juice carton, or what they do when not under the watchful gaze of humanity (although I have often had certain suspicions about it).

As I waited, planning my next move in this game of cat and juice, I saw that there was a red glove gripping the back of the orange juice carton. My gaze followed the glove up an arm and to the face of the man who had come to take my Sunshine away. The man stood in shadow behind rows of juice cartons, but I thought I could make out a blank face with dark glasses, which I imagined covered cruel eyes[1]. Then I saw the name 'Ron' was printed on his green stockboy's smock, and I realized that he was simply a store employee checking and changing stock, and he probably wore dark glasses because he had trouble with fluorescent lights. I relaxed and closed the door.

---

[1] Maybe they were friendly eyes, who can say? I admit it; he was taking my juice, so I judged him.

I waited patiently while he filled the shelf full of juice again. When I looked back, I saw to my horror that the whole shelf was full of Sunlight OJ and my coveted carton of juice was gone.

I peered behind the cartons into the stocking area, but there was no sign of the stockboy, so I went to the customer service desk to have the orange juice situation rectified. Behind the desk, a short, beetle-like man with a '100% satisfaction guaranteed' button on his vest eyed me nervously, looking worried about the prospect of me approaching him and asking a question.

As I walked up to the counter and he saw that there was no escape, he gave a heavy sigh, rose to his feet, and asked, "Is there anything I can help you with?"

I saw a sign on the wall behind him that promised service with a smile, and I wondered if his training in that area had perhaps been neglected. It was no matter to me; I was not after smiles.

"Yes," I said, "I believe you can. I've come to lodge a complaint." My confidence grew as I spoke. I knew I was in a position of power. I, the customer, was surely right. "I came here to buy my favorite brand of juice, Sunshine Juice. There was one carton of it left, but when I reached for it, a stockboy named Ron took it away and filled the shelf with Sunlight OJ."

He opened his bloodshot eyes enough that I felt pretty sure he was almost definitely awake. "You've got a complaint about juice?" he asked. Then he looked like he remembered something from long ago, and adjusted his demeanor. I think maybe he smiled, and then said, "Um, you must be mistaken... sir. Ron isn't at work today; he's taken a sick day."

"And besides, sir," he went on, speaking livelier, "juice isn't my department, but I'm sure we don't even carry Sunshine Juice."

I wasn't getting anywhere with this guy, who seemed eager to just get back to sitting down comfortably again and thinking about what sort of condiments he might have on his fries that night; he would say anything to get rid of me. But I wasn't going to give up my juice without a fight just because of this guy's French-fried potatoes though, so I said, "Alright, maybe it is as you say, and maybe I didn't see what I saw. That remains to be seen." I put my hand palm down on the counter, to show that I meant business. "But I want satisfaction, *sir*, as that button on your vest has been promising me the entire time I've been standing here, so if it wouldn't be too much trouble for you to check your stock records, I'd like to know when you last carried Sunshine Juice." I wasn't normally that assertive, but routine kept me calm, and not having my juice for several days, coming to a different store, and having to have a conversation with a stranger were all great deviations from my regular routine.

"That's not something we're allowed to do..." Then he seemed to consider how long it might be before he'd be able to sit again if perhaps I wanted to speak to his supervisor. He sighed. "But of course I want you to be satisfied, sir. Now, let me just access the records," he said, and began typing. I knew I had him then; the records would expose his lies about the juice, and all I'd had to do was put my palm on a counter.

The keyboard was one of the quiet models that make hardly any sound at all when you type, so I made the keyboard sounds in my head while I watched his fingers on the keyboard.

Tap. Tippity-tippity tap. Tappity. The noise grated in my head. *Tippity-tap.* Still he typed, and each key press slammed into my brain. I covered my ears, but it made no difference. *Tap, tap, tap,* on and on. I had almost reached the point where I couldn't take it anymore and would be forced to flee the store, when he turned the monitor in my direction and touched his finger to the screen.

"You can see here that we had a shipment of Sunlight OJ just yesterday and we haven't sold very much of it since then, so the shelf has been fully stocked. And here," he slid his finger down the screen, "you can see that Sunshine Juice was discontinued."

I looked at him. He looked at me. We had reached an impasse. I knew, and he knew that I did, but he wasn't going to let on that there was anything unusual, which was why he was showing me fake stock records. I thanked him for his time, which is the polite thing to do even when someone is actively working against you.

As I turned away, he stopped me by saying, "Sir?"

I turned around. Perhaps he'd changed his mind and was going to tell all of his secrets—or at least the juice-related ones.

"We haven't had Sunshine Juice for months now," he said. He looked at me with something like understanding in his sleepy eyes that wanted nothing more than to not be seeing. "Maybe you need some rest, sir."

Rest. Now that was an idea. I supposed I did need sleep, after the stress of the juice and just anybody knocking on my door and when my key didn't quite fit in the lock at first but then it did. That kind of thing builds up. Maybe it had made me confused about the juice. I left the store, passing the cash register where a cashier was bagging up several cartons of Sunlight OJ for a customer. I felt a surge of anger at that stranger who was offering financial assistance to my enemy, but just as quickly as it had come, the anger went away. He was probably just a guy like me, making do with what he could, and so I did not go over to him and hurl his juice to the floor.

It was late when I got home from my juice journey, so I went to bed without drinking anything at all. I laid there, eyes open in the dark. Did I really see the juice I wanted, or did I just think I had because I wanted it so badly? Why did Ron take it away from me? I felt restless, and I couldn't get to sleep, but then I woke up, so I guess I could, as is often the case when you tell yourself you can't do something.

Chapter 2

That morning I called my good friend—my only friend—Winslow, who was always able to help me figure out something that I couldn't puzzle through on my own. He would wear a problem like a dog with a bone, until he was licking at the marrow of it. When you have a broken leg, perhaps that's not such a good quality, but in all other problems he was always a great help to me.

Before I called him, I first sat and stared at the phone for a while, because I'm never quite sure how to start a phone conversation. In the movies, you'll sometimes see a lady in a bathtub with flower petals floating around her while she calls her friends 'just to talk.' I can't call without a purpose, though, and sometimes even when you dial with a purpose you forget what it was by the time the call connects, which is how I came to find myself saying:

"Oh hi, Winslow, I just called to talk." I giggled a little, like I was in a bath surrounded by flower petals. I fumbled around the conversation for a little while, until I remembered that I'd wanted to ask him if he'd come over because I really needed his help with something I'd feel more comfortable discussing in person.

Later, my thoughts about the way things were

changing for the worse were interrupted by a knock at the door. I looked out the peephole even though I was expecting Winslow, because you never know, but of course it was him. He entered the door eyebrows first, as I liked to say about him.

"Winslow, things seem to be changing," I began. Right away, I saw recognition on his face as he raised his hands up to stop me, and I felt relieved because I had worried he would think I was crazy when I told him what I suspected; I had even prepared a story about how much sleeping I'd done already if he happened to tell me I just needed some rest.

"Oscar, stop there. I know what you're going to say," he said. "I know I've been distant lately; it's probably been weeks since we talked."

"Months," I clarified. Although I knew it was the fault of my nearly-crippling social anxiety and growing paranoia that we hadn't talked in so long, I was prepared to let him think it was his fault and I was willing to accept his apology for it too.

"Months, then," he said. "It's just been so inconvenient to get around to see you. The bus timetable has changed, so that I'd have to get up way earlier in the morning to come here, and then the bus takes me through all the suburbs so everyone else can go out for their shopping; the trip takes hours now. I've got my car, of course, but you know I switched to electric recently—you didn't?—well, I switched, but the battery needs some kind of tune-up because it only holds enough charge for short trips—"

"That's just it," I said, stopping him before he could

really get started with the apology. It wasn't important anyway. "That's the thing I wanted to talk about. It's inconvenient to not have your car holding a good charge, right? And the bus timetable, that's pretty inconvenient too?"

"Yes, it's quite inconvenient, that's what I've been saying," he said, with one eyebrow rising in the direction of wariness.

"Well, that's not all, just listen. Everything is inconvenient lately. For example, the other day my key wouldn't fit in the door."

"That is pretty inconvenient." Now you would certainly have described his eyebrow as 'perched'.

"The keys did fit right afterwards, but that's not all, that's not all." I sprang to my feet and began to pace. Now I would convince him, I could feel it. Winslow's other eyebrow had heard the call of duty and began its march to higher on his brow, but I didn't let up. "A few days ago the store I usually shop at stopped carrying the Sunshine Juice that I like; they only carry Sunlight OJ now. Sunlight OJ has fifty percent more pulp than before."

"And you hate pulp," he offered.

"Yes, I hate it. I can't imagine why they thought it needed fifty percent more than whatever it had before, because now it's like putting a solid orange in a glass with the skin still on. I could do *that* on my own. What I cannot do is produce a delicious and reasonably priced pulp-free, free-range orange juice. I've been pulling the curtains closed and crouching down behind the counter like an animal—not that an animal would be in my house drinking orange juice, not while I'm alive—just so I can filter out the pulp without my neighbors looking in, as they might do."

I felt my eye twitching as I waited for a response from Winslow. I wondered if he could see it; I knew what he would think if he could.

"Oscar, man, there's no need to come unhinged about it," Winslow said, as his brow furrowed under the effort of keeping his eyebrows aloft. "Sometimes companies stop selling products, or they switch one product for another that they think might sell better. They had a contract with the maker of Sunshine, the contract ran out, and they didn't renew it; whatever. Just relax about it; it's only juice. Go buy it at another store."

"I wish I could," I said mournfully. "I went to Jack's Grocery Mart, and I nearly had a carton of it, but then a stockboy took it out of my hand, pushed me down, and filled the shelf with that twenty-oranges-in-a-carton Sunlight stuff."

I stopped pacing and looked Winslow squarely in the eye, but he wasn't backing down. I shifted from one foot to the other and back again, and then admitted, "Alright, he didn't push me down. But it was on the shelf, and I had already claimed it, and he took it away from me just the same as if he'd broken into my house, taken it out of my refrigerator, then weeks later sent me an envelope in the mail which held only a ransom note made from letters cut out of magazines and a single photograph of his genitals resting on the carton."

"But he didn't actually push you down, right?"

Winslow had an annoying habit of bringing up absolutely irrelevant details in the middle of an important conversation. It was best just to ignore him when he was like that. "So, considering his genitals on my juice," I continued, "I went to customer service to report him, since I'd seen his nametag even though he was hiding in the shadows, and they told me he was out sick. Had been all day, they said! 'Dead for a week, sorry,' I bet they'd say if I went back now and asked."

"If that wasn't enough," I went on, "I got the customer service guy to check stock and he said they hadn't had any Sunshine Juice in stock at all, yet I had seen it right there on the shelf and nearly held it in my hand. He told me I needed *rest*! As if not having enough sleep could cause you to hallucinate a juice theft." I gave a short laugh, to show that the very idea was ludicrous.

"Don't you see what this means?" I asked. His eyebrows told me that he didn't, so I took it upon myself to explain. "It's proof, Winslow! All the time there are inconvenient things happening to you, things that you just shrug off as being a part of life. You miss the bus by ten seconds and then have to wait ten minutes for the next one, which happens to be a bus just for bus company staff and they won't let you on. So you walk home, and on the way a car splashes through a puddle and soaks you, because today—quite inconveniently, by the way—it happens to be raining. Who drove that car? Who made it rain? You reach for an apple in your fruit bowl and find that it's full of Gala apples, which you only kind of like, and you're pretty sure that this time you had only bought Granny Smith apples; where then did the Gala apples come from?"

"What does all of this have to do with the orange juice?" he asked, trying to divert me.

"I'll tell you where the apples came from," I said. "*They* put them there."

"Who—"

"And don't ask me who; I don't know who. But they're doing it, just as sure as I'm sitting here talking to you. The orange juice is the key; it's the first time I've seen it happening, the first time I've had proof. When I held the carton in my hand..." I saw his eyebrows marshaling for another assault against his forehead, and corrected myself, "or at least nearly in my hand, I held proof of it. The man in the shadows is one of them, or he's working for them."

His eyebrows came back down and he closed his eyes briefly, before opening them and saying, "Oscar, you know you're being paranoid again. I can see your eye twitching." Crap. I had tried my best to hide it. "When you miss the bus, it's because you didn't leave early enough. If you get wet on a rainy day, it's because you didn't carry an umbrella. And if a company stops selling orange juice, it's not because they're out to get you. Have you been taking your Psylocybin?" He asked, directing an enquiring look at me from beneath his eyebrows. I looked away and fidgeted with books on a shelf, but he persisted. "*Have* you?"

"Alright, no," I relented. "I haven't been taking them. I don't feel like myself when I do. I felt calmer, sure, and I didn't feel the desire to fasten all the locks on the door or keep a knife under my pillow when I go to sleep, but it's not me. This is me," I said, lifting up one of the couch cushions to reveal a ball-peen hammer underneath. "That's in case they come while I'm watching TV."

"You always get this way when you don't take your pills." He sighed. "Remember when you felt sure the milkman was going to steal your girlfriend, so you attacked that guy with a shattered milk bottle like it was some kind of child's bar fight? And you didn't even have a milkman."

I remembered it.

"You barely even got this house, because you were afraid to go to the county clerk's office and file the paperwork. I had to go for you!"

It was true, but could anyone blame me? The county clerk had a look in his eyes like he would use you and then throw you to the ground like a crumpled tissue. He was the sort of man who killed children and buried their finely-ground bones in plant pots around the garden—I could see it in him. I started to tell Winslow about the rational grounds for my fear of the county clerk, but he was already talking again.

"And then, after that, in the institution, when you refused to eat for weeks because there might have been leprosy-infected armadillo meat in your food—"

"Armadillos are the only wild animals which carry the bacteria that cause leprosy."

"You nearly died of starvation," Winslow said,

unconcerned about how near I came to contracting leprosy. "I can go on, but I don't think you need to be reminded that you've only recently been allowed a provisional driver's license or that the District of Colombia has forbidden you to go within a hundred feet of the Museum of Natural History."

I heard a noise in the kitchen.

"Do you hear that?" I asked.

"I didn't hear anything," he said, "and I want to see you take your pills."

I put my finger to my lips and pulled the hammer out from under the cushion. Winslow stood up from the couch and I took a step towards him with the hammer in my hand.

"Ron is in the kitchen," I whispered to Winslow, with my mouth right beside his ear. I pointed to myself, then to the kitchen, and put my finger to my lips again, indicating that I was going in there quietly. He moved so that he was on the other side of the coffee table from me.

I walked quickly to the kitchen entrance, and pressed myself flat against the wall. Ron was in there, rummaging through my things. What did he hope to find in the kitchen? Or was he tampering with my food? Perhaps cocaine planted in my sugar bowl, and an anonymous tip to the police. I didn't intend to give him the chance to carry out his plan, whatever it might be. I was acutely aware of the weight of the hammer in my hand, the solid wooden handle topped by the metal head. I had practiced many times with it, first painting little faces on the heads of nails and then pounding them into wood. My experience with that taught me that a hammer is very good at smashing heads.

I steadied my breathing and spun around into the doorway with the hammer held ready at my side. Nobody was there. The window was open. I went to it and looked out. I didn't remember opening the window, but nobody was outside. I knew I had heard someone. How had Ron escaped so quickly, without giving himself away?

Winslow came up behind me, snatched the hammer from my hand and then backed away, holding it in front of himself.

"There is nobody in there," he said to me from the living room. "I can't handle it when you're like this. Take your medicine, Oscar. Let me see you take them."

I looked at him. I looked at the hammer. I flexed my hand, where the hammer had just been.

"That's my hammer," I said, and moved towards him. He moved back, raising the hammer along with his eyebrows, and I stopped. I reconsidered. I knew what that hammer did to heads.

After I had taken my pills to his satisfaction, and I had assured him that I would continue taking them, he left. When the door shut, I opened my hand and looked at the pills I had palmed. They didn't seem like much: two centimeters, white, oblong. They certainly didn't seem like something I needed. They did get rid of my paranoia, but it left me feeling cloudy and vague, with essential parts of me hidden away.

I knew I wouldn't have been able to hear whoever was in my kitchen if my mind had been coated by the chemicals in those pills; who knows what they would have done to me and Winslow if I hadn't been ready with my hammer and my months of training. All the pills were actually good for was getting rid of my headaches, which I was definitely having a lot more of recently, but the tradeoff wasn't worth it. I turned my hand upside down over the trash can and let them fall into it.

Winslow had taken the hammer with him, so I got another one from my box of hammers and placed it under the couch cushion. The next time they were in my kitchen, I would be ready.

Chapter 3

I sat in my bedroom, looking at the wall. This was the sort of thing I knew people might call crazy, so I had my house locked up tight. I had my bedroom door locked too, so just in case somebody happened to drop by and peek in through the letterbox, the most they'd be able to do is look at the closed door to my bedroom and imagine that I might have the wall covered with pictures and notes relating to longer waits for tables at restaurants, gloves that shrank in the washing machine, missing juice, and all manner of inconvenience. They'd never know for sure, though, and no court could force me to testify against myself.

I looked at 'Ron,' represented by a crude drawing of a man in green. Since I felt he was at the center of it all, I had placed him literally at the center of it, in the middle of the wall with a circle drawn around him in red marker. It wasn't my best idea to draw directly on the wall, but I could always put a poster up to cover that later.

Around Ron, I had taped pictures of orange juice, bus timetables, and my house keys. These were the things I felt for sure Ron was somehow involved with.

I'd felt like I was being watched when my keys wouldn't work, and the more I thought about it the more it seemed I was being watched by cruel eyes from behind dark glasses. Winslow might sometimes have felt as if his words fell on deaf ears, but I had taken what he said into consideration. It was true, coincidence does occur. The juice might have been coincidence. His car battery troubles might be coincidence. Any manner of things might be. How could my ill-fitting keys be something that just happened, though, without outside interference? Moreover, since the evidence convincingly showed that there was a third party involved, how could anyone have had access to my keys to alter them?

It would have to be a very fine, precise alteration; it couldn't be so much that they wouldn't work at all, but only just enough so they'd usually still work and would only occasionally stick for a moment so I'd have to turn them slightly one way and then slightly the other several times, with the whole world watching me, judging me as an idiot not able to get into his own house. I kept my keys next to the knife under my pillow at night, and in my zipped pocket during the day, there's no way anybody would be able to get to them.

As I turned my brain upside down and shook it for a solution, I heard the mail dropping through the letterbox in my front door. That was it. My business mail always came to my post office box, and when I last took my key ring out to open that, Ron or an accomplice must have taken my house keys, altered them, and replaced them while I was reading through my mail. I licked a stamp and stuck it near the drawing of Ron to remind myself of the new connection I had made, untaped my keys from the wall, and headed to the post office. Someone there would have seen what happened, and if not then I knew they had a security camera that was always watching from its perch in the corner of the ceiling and blinking redly at me.

I got in line at the post office, and immediately the clerk at the counter left his position. He passed another clerk and said, "Going on lunch, the counter is all yours."

"No problem, Ron, I gotcha," came the reply from his colleague. The hair on my neck stood up; the clerk's name was Ron, just like the stockboy who had removed my juice. He cast a backward glance at me as he donned his hat and exited the counter area. What could it mean? Where was he going? Were he and the Ron from the supermarket partners? Was he even now on his way to my house to look at my wall of information and glean what I had been able to piece together about their partnership while I stayed at the post office on a fool's errand[1] of getting a surveillance tape that would be mysteriously missing or erased if they even allowed me access to it?

Never one to wait around and find out for sure when I could make a rash decision instead, I left the post office right away to follow Ron. I saw him hurrying away down the street; his hat marked him out among the crowd. He didn't look back, and he walked with a limp, making him easy to follow.

When he got to my house, I planned to take him by

---

[1] Yes, it was an errand I had assigned myself, but it's impolite of you to point that out.

surprise and force him to reveal his plan. The specifics weren't quite clear in my mind, but I'd recently bought some things at the flea market which I was pretty sure were thumbscrews and I was eager to try them out. Instead of going down the street to my house, though, he passed it and carried on further away from town.

That was unexpected. Maybe he was going to meet the Ron from the supermarket. Or maybe he was going to pass a message on to someone; that's how these things are done. Always through middlemen, with no faces seen and no names exchanged, only a whispered message or a scrap of paper slipped from one hand to another hand (a hand belonging to someone else, he wouldn't just be juggling the paper around like some sort of clandestine jester[1]).

Ron passed a bus stop. There was a man waiting for the bus, huddled in the corner of the shelter, reading a newspaper with the collar of his heavy coat up around his neck. Was he huddled for warmth, or as protection against being identified? I looked again and saw that he was wearing dark glasses, as Ron at the supermarket had been.

Perhaps the message was to be exchanged here, so I walked fast to catch the whisper or snatch the paper as it was being passed. As I got closer, I noticed for the first time the gray hair under Ron's hat. I had only seen him briefly in the post office so I hadn't realized, but now I saw that he was an old man—the perfect cover,

---

[1] Or would he?

since nobody would suspect an old man of being involved in this. As he walked past the man waiting for the bus, Ron tugged on his ear and sniffed. That was it: the signal sent, the message conveyed. But what did it mean? The bus pulled up and I had to make a decision; should I follow Ron, or should I go after the man in the heavy coat?

I thought quickly about the decision, which was made more difficult because I felt the beginning of one of my headaches. Suddenly, in my mind flashed a picture of the man waiting at the bus station meeting others in a dark, smoky room, huddled around a table covered with pictures of me. I knew he was the one, and I got on the bus after him.

The door to the bus closed as I settled into my seat. We drove past Ron and I got a clear look at his face. His eyes were tired and watery, and I knew I had made the right choice. He probably only wanted to finish his part of the mission and then go home to a dinner of Salisbury steak in front of a TV showing The Price is Right and I hoped that no harm would come to him when they realized it was due to his carelessness that I had found the man at the bus stop.

It was clear to me now that the Ron from the post office wasn't the mastermind behind the plot against me, but the man in the coat on the bus was the link which would lead me to the anchor at the end of the chain. When I saw that he was looking straight ahead instead of reading his newspaper, I looked out the window and confirmed my suspicion that he had left his newspaper at the bus stop, proof that he was only posted there to receive a message and now he would be the one passing it on.

I kept a good watch on the man in the heavy coat. When he looked out the window, I looked out as well to see what he was looking at. When he napped, I napped. When he got off the bus, I got off the bus. When he went to his house, I went to his house. When he became part of a vast underground network dedicated to making my life and the lives of others less convenient for some as yet unknown reason… well, I had to draw the line somewhere, and that was really going directly against my mission. So I made some plans to apply for membership, but without serious intent.

At his house, I crouched behind the evergreen bushes outside his living room, looking over the tops of the leaves and watching him. So far, there had been nothing unusual to see. The man in the heavy coat, who was no longer the man in the heavy coat and was instead now the man in cats'-paw-print pajamas, talked on the phone as he made his dinner. I imagined the things that he might be saying to whoever was on the other end of the line: passing on the information that I wasn't in my house and that it was free for breaking in and ransacking; discussing why I had been at the post office and probably arriving at the conclusion that I must have figured out their plot to make my keys sometimes almost not quite fit in the lock; planning the next move, like replacing my mouse with one slightly less ergonomic so that after several years I would develop carpel tunnel syndrome and be unable to publish my findings on the internet.

After what he was saying to whoever, I imagined who that whoever might be. Could it be Ron from the supermarket? Ron from the post office? I even briefly entertained the outlandish notion that he might not be talking to anyone sinister at all, that he could be talking to a good friend and relating how pleased he was with the way his dinner was going—General Tso's chicken[1] over a bed of white rice, which did look as if it was going to be delicious. I moved around the bushes and pressed my ear against the window to hear the conversation of the man in the pajamas.

"It's turning out really well," I heard him say. My heart beat faster; I now knew for sure that they were talking about me. He paused to listen to a question from the other end of the line and, with a laugh, replied, "Yes, it's actually much easier than I expected it would be."

I sat down below the window and leaned against the house to collect my thoughts. They were mocking me. I had thought I was figuring out their plan, perhaps even getting one step ahead, but apparently they considered their operation against me to be easy. Easier than expected even; maybe they'd done it to hundreds or thousands of people and they'd all put up more of a fight than me.

---

[1] I did wonder, briefly, why General Tso seems to have been the only general ever to create his own recipe. The military should do more to encourage their officers in the culinary arts; the propaganda value of a Chinese buffet should not be underestimated. There is that Colonel, of course, but I really think the movement needs to come from higher up than that.

I felt ashamed that they felt they had so little to worry about from me, but I also felt my determination grow; I would get to the very core of their organization, the head of it, then I would get them to leave me alone and force them to set right all the slight wrongs they had done.

Determination and shame combined to make me warm, and I was tired from the chase earlier; I drifted off to sleep.

I dreamed of a giant red fist closing around me and squeezing me until I popped with a loud bang. I was suddenly conscious of a door slamming and my eyes opened wide to the bright light of the morning sun. I shut them immediately, because for some reason a hundred thousand years of evolution has still not properly equipped us for living on a planet which orbits an unimaginably huge ball of nuclear fire. My skull throbbed from a dream-induced headache.

I climbed to my feet and looked around the corner of the house. The man in the gray pinstripe suit had just closed his front door and was heading for his car.

I knew I wouldn't be able to follow him in the car, so I stepped out from behind the wall without thinking. Then, with thinking, I thought what a stupid idea that had been. Now he would see me, he would know that I had followed him; he would report me, call his co-conspirators, and it would go beyond mere inconvenience—they would trap me, capture me, torture me, even kill me.

The cruel eyes of Ron from the supermarket seemed to be glaring at me from behind the surprised eyes of the man in the pinstripe suit as he saw me, a disheveled and unkempt man with sleep-heavy and bloodshot eyes, leaping from behind his house and staggering towards him.

"What do you want with me?" I shouted at him, grabbing him by the shoulders and shaking him even as I shook myself out of sleep. "All I want is peace, I want to be left alone with my own things and my own thoughts, like any man deserves!"

"I don't know—" he started, but the rest of what he said was cut off by a piercing increase in the pain of my headache and a powerful impression in my mind that this man meant to do me harm and would do it, incongruous as that may have seemed to anyone observing the situation and seeing who was shouting at who.

"Don't spit your lies at me," I said to him through teeth clenched against the pain of my headache. He tried to push me away, but I was stronger. I felt the blood pounding in my head and I exulted in the power I had over them as I held him in my grasp.

They had toyed with me. They had thought me impotent against them. They had mocked me, laughed at me, derided me and considered me low. They had experimented on me like a rat in a cage, but I was no longer blind to their experiments. I wasn't content to press the lever and receive a treat any longer, I wasn't going to scamper around and let the small inconveniences build up until they crushed me under their weight. At last I was fighting back, and he seemed shocked by it. What incredible naiveté he must've had, to have not expected this would happen. Or maybe it was incredible confidence; perhaps he and his cohorts had been acting with impunity for decades or even longer. I had no way of knowing for sure how long they had been acting even in my own life.

He struggled more in my grip, trying to wriggle out of his coat, and I pushed him back towards his house. He tripped and fell, and I heard the knock of his head against the brick of the wall. I advanced, standing tall over him and blocking his escape.

I demanded answers from him, names and information, but he only gave me a blank stare. Then I saw the red stain smeared onto the wall where his head had hit and spreading to the shoulders of his suit, and I stepped back. I had killed him. I looked around and saw for the first time the people on the street who had been watching us, all standing as if they were frozen.

"He's been following me," I said to the people around. "So I followed him, and watched him, and now… he fell…"

I turned to point to him to show them just what had happened, but everything went dark. The voices from the crowd sounded fuzzy, and far off. I stumbled in the darkness and fell to the ground. I hit my head, which is never pleasant, but you should've seen the other guy. Someone picked me up and carried me. Walls seemed to close in.

Eventually, I came out of the darkness. I was looking up at a fluorescent bulb on a concrete ceiling. When I sat up I saw that the walls which had closed in on me were the walls of a jail cell lined with bars.

Chapter 4

This was decidedly inconvenient. My body had chosen a terrible moment to betray me. My senses had deserted me and my locomotive control had left me at the precise moment when I needed to locomote. Now I was in jail. I had a lot of information to add to my wall at home after the previous day's adventures, but that wall was outside of the jail, so I had no way to get to it. Nobody would even give me orange juice.

Winslow visited me on the first day, which I was informed of by a guard coming to my cell, announcing, "Visitor," and motioning for me to follow him.

The visiting room was the kind where they separated you from your visitors by thick plastic and you had to talk to them through a phone even though you're several inches away, which I thought must have taken some incredible marketing gymnastics from the phone company to convince the prison administration it was necessary.

I grinned triumphantly at Winslow and said, "I guess you've reconsidered what you said yesterday now, haven't you?"

He looked a little taken aback, like perhaps he was reconsidering his reconsideration. "Oscar, do you know what you did?" he asked.

"I know what they want everyone to think I did. Even I thought I did it at first." I'd had time to think about it quite a lot, since jail cells weren't particularly busy places.

"It was very convincing," I said, "with the hollow sound of his head hitting the wall—that was my first clue to the deception, since obviously heads aren't hollow—and the little smear of blood, which was a nice touch, but all it took was a few ketchup packets taped to the back of his head."

Winslow closed his eyes and pinched the bridge of his nose between his thumb and forefinger. His eyebrows were sympathetic to the task, and bunched in close together over his fingers. He wasn't ready to admit I was right, so I continued.

"Don't you see? I was this close to discovering the nature of their organization," I said, and made a gesture in the air with my own thumb and forefinger indicating a very small distance indeed, "and they got scared. They'd tried to shut me up with the threat of me not being able to get into my house occasionally and very briefly, and of course the implied threat that in the future one of my boots might turn up smaller than the other boot in the pair."

When he spoke, Winslow's voice was calm and steady, though he kept his eyes closed and his fingers pinched to the bridge of his nose. "I don't think you understand. You killed a man. I saw the corpse being taken away; they hadn't yet covered his face and it was as white as the sheet over his body." He opened his eyes, and they glistened in the fluorescent light. "That man is in the morgue right now. They don't take you there unless you're dead. You haven't really started back on your medicine, have you?"

"I haven't, and I won't," I said, raising my voice. "I threw them in the trash. I was only able to penetrate this far towards the center of their circle because my head was clear. I followed one of them from the post office on the lunch break because his name was Ron like the man in the supermarket who stole my juice, and he led me to another man who I knew was in with it all because of his heavy coat, then I realized that Ron from the post office wasn't very high up and also the man in the heavy coat left his paper at the bus stop; I saw him in some kind of meeting about me in a dark room and later he changed into pajamas with cat prints on them—I saw because I watched him through his window." I had got up off the stool and now stood over Winslow, looking down on him through the plastic divider. "He talked on the phone and I couldn't hear most of the conversation but his lips were practically dripping glee about all the things they'd done to me, then he tried to escape while I was still asleep and I only grabbed him to get him to help me find the next man and I pushed him a little, only a little, so I know he couldn't be dead."

"They planned it all out," I went on, after a brief pause for breath, "they must have had someone following me while I was following him, and probably someone following the man following me so they could rub him out if it all went south, or maybe just to tie up loose ends. Then they saw me asleep in the bushes and told the man in the gray pinstripe suit to put the bag of ketchup in his hair, close his door loud enough to wake me up, and then provoke me to violence by acting confused and frightened when I confronted him." I was talking fast, and perhaps saying too much for Winslow to take in all at once, but I couldn't slow down until I had said it all. "Then he'd pretend to trip, pretend to hit his head, and pretend to be dead long enough for me to be put in jail. The investigation will sort it all out once they realize his body has hopped off the morgue table and left town, but of course it'll take weeks for me to be cleared because of all the witnesses, including you, who think they saw me kill a man, so by then the whole crew will have regrouped with different names and different faces, and all my work in tracking them down will be for nothing." I stopped talking and returned to active respiration.

I needn't have worried about Winslow's understanding. He opened his eyes and I saw that he had tears in them because he was so moved by my thorough investigation into and passionate explanation of the workings of this shady gang, and by my modesty and good-heartedness because I hadn't even reprimanded him for being such a fool and falling for their simple tricks.

I was about to comfort him and tell him it was all right, they were very clever and he didn't have the same information I had, when I became aware of a little noise from my phone handset, like a click or maybe a buzz. That noise had been there all along, but I realized, too late, why prison visits included phones even though you were only inches apart: the whole conversation was being recorded, maybe it was even being listened to at that very moment. Winslow, by being concerned for me, had unwittingly caused me to open up to him and reveal everything I knew to the people listening in. Now it would all change; they wouldn't just have different names and different faces, but they would also have different hats; maybe they would be disguised as shrubbery, which would make hiding behind shrubbery very risky for me.

"So, as I was saying, I'm sure this will all be over with soon, and there's no reason for me to continue trying to uncover any secret organization which doesn't exist," I said loudly into the mouthpiece. "Ha ha, what was I thinking, sleeping in bushes and following elderly postal employees on their lunch break? I guess you're right, maybe I have been working too hard, and I did forget to take my medication once or twice, I'll be sure to take it every day now, I surely will. Alright, well I've got to go now; I have a whole wall in my cell where I haven't counted the blocks yet. It was nice speaking with you."

I returned the handset to the wall cradle and winked at Winslow, who was still holding his handset and had forgotten to close his mouth after having been amazed at my cleverness and sharp mind which led me to discovering that they were monitoring our conversation.

I had forgotten that the visiting area was sealed on both sides by a door which was only unlocked after the visitation period of an hour was over, and on my side there was a guard who didn't look like he was going to bend any rules for me, so I settled down to wait.

Winslow talked to the guard on his side, pointing to me and looking worried. I waved to them and smiled, to show that I didn't mind waiting and there was nothing to worry about. Winslow took a prescription pill bottle out of his pocket and offered it to the guard—maybe the guard had a headache; Winslow was always considerate—but he must have changed his mind about needing the pills right then because he just nodded to Winslow and put the bottle in his pocket.

Back in my cell, I sat down to think. I had figured out they were listening on the phone, but not before I told Winslow things I knew about them and how I had tracked them down the day before. They might have been thrown off by me ending the phone conversation and pretending that I agreed with Winslow, but they would probably change the way they operated just to be sure. Men waiting at bus stops would no longer leave their newspapers behind, and messengers would be sure they were not followed when they left the post office.

The changes would make it more difficult to track them, but after having done it already I felt pretty sure I could do it again; I would recognize the man in cats'-paw-print pajamas even if he changed his disguise to dogs'-paw-print pajamas. And the next time I would change my methods as well. I would be more careful. I wouldn't fall asleep in bushes, for one thing. Or at least I would have a blanket with me if I did, and some coffee for in the morning, so I wouldn't be so easily framed for a fake murder. Planning, that was the key.

Several times each day, I would have visitors

directly in the cell. At first, they were men in suits with names like Brown or Johnson, asking me questions about what I had done. Since it had mostly all been recorded already when I was walking to Winslow, I told them a lot of things.

After a few days, it seemed like they weren't really taking what I said seriously ('But then—let me be clear—the keys *did* fit?'), and shook their heads in a way I didn't appreciate when they took notes in their little notebooks, so I stopped answering their questions; then the men in suits stopped coming, and nobody came for a week. I knew it was a week because I'd carved the days into the wall, like I knew you were supposed to do in jail. That is, I tried to, except it's actually quite hard to carve anything substantial without proper tools, so I gave in after a few minutes and just used the actual calendar the county jail administration produced, and marked off the days using a marker they provided as well. This lessened the dramatic incarceration atmosphere somewhat.

On the seventh day with no visitors, a plump female nurse came to check my pulse, take a sample of my blood, and ask me a few questions about my medical history. I sort of objected at first, but she was much more pleasant than the men in suits, so I only objected in a routine kind of way, like I thought might be expected of me—I didn't want to appear easy.

Different doctors visited me, checking my eyes, poking in my ears, and sometimes asking me questions such as, "When was the first time, as an adult, that you cowered under a blanket for no discernible reason?"

They seemed pleased with the results of their poking and questioning. One of them said that my condition was unique, and that I would be out of there in no time at all, which was exactly what I had been telling Winslow.

Chapter 5

They came for me, not in the night under cover of darkness as you might expect, but during the day, and very politely. I was handcuffed and led to the back of a van, where they took off my handcuffs and seated me on a comfortable seat with two men—my liberators—on either side of me.

My jailing had served its purpose. They wanted to scare me; they wanted me to know that they had the power to manipulate the justice system and imprison me. Now that I had received the message, they were taking me to the courthouse, where the prosecution would have misplaced the names and addresses of all the witnesses, or some evidence would have been stolen, or the jury was tampered with. The judge would declare a mistrial, issue a summary judgment of twenty days incarceration—already served—and then the prosecution would object for the sake of appearances, but the judge would overrule them and order my immediate release.

Already I had a plan for what I would do once I was free again. I had to go back to Jack's Grocery Mart and confront the Ron who had stolen my orange juice. He had been the most brazen, committing the act right in front of me as he looked into my eyes, daring me to do something about it. At least he was probably looking into my eyes; his dark glasses had made it hard to tell.

He would have answers, and I would demand them from him.

I was so busy planning what I would say to him that I didn't notice we had passed the road to the city courthouse until I looked out the window some time later and saw that all the scenery was unfamiliar. The van's engine strained as it climbed up a steep hill, through an area wooded with maple trees and into a clearing filled with large, boxy buildings made of stone, which stood in front of a mountainous ridge. The buildings had vines growing up their sides to dark windows, which made it all look quite ominous; my muscles tensed, but then a sign at the entrance said *No Parking*, which seemed safe enough, so I relaxed my grip on the seat. Then another, larger sign said *Welcome to Maple Ridge Psychiatric Hospital*, and I knew the first sign had only been a trick to lull me into a false sense of security.

I shifted my eyes to the left and right, checking on the men who I now recognized as my captors instead of my liberators, and saw that they were staring absent-mindedly out the windows. Seizing the opportunity, I jumped up, but to my surprise found myself pulled back down and pinned to the seat by the strong grips of my captors. Their absent-minded stares, too, had been a trick, and I had been well and truly lulled.

"Calm down," one of them said. "We're almost there."

I ignored him and raged inside about the injustice of their deceit. I had trusted them as my friends and they had betrayed me. Why had they even taken off my handcuffs, if they still intended to keep me as a prisoner? They had to be in league with the dark group that had taken such pains to slowly and slightly ruin my life. With all my strength, I broke free of their grips and leapt for the door. Somehow, (perhaps by using the handle, but my recollection is hazy) I managed to open the door and get out of the van, and I ran back down the road towards freedom, towards my appointment at the courthouse.

I looked over my shoulder just in time to see that one of the men had caught up with me. He leapt to tackle me, and I spun around and pushed my legs up under him so he was unbalanced and his momentum carried him up and over me as we rolled on the ground.

To my surprise, I ended up on top of him. I felt myself possessed of an unusual strength that allowed me to hold him so that he could not throw me off. Even though I felt strong enough to hold him down, when I tried to hit him my arms felt as heavy as lead and moved slowly, like I was punching through molasses. I felt frustrated that I couldn't make him understand, I couldn't make him leave me alone, and I couldn't even hurt him because my arms were so heavy, slow, and weak.

With a slowness that would have been comical in any other situation, my fist pressed against his nose and a dark red liquid squirted out, which I recognized as the same liquid from the head of the man in the gray pinstripe suit. I knew it was another trick; I wasn't able to hit him hard enough to hurt him or make him bleed.

My arms moved wildly and ineffectually, like the arms of a newborn, and the cries I heard matched.

The flesh around one of his eyes began to swell; how had they managed to fake that? My eyes flowed with hot tears. If I couldn't even stop this one man in broad daylight, how would I have any hope of stopping an entire gang of men who operated always in the shadows? Here I had one of their agents in my grip and could do nothing, how much less would I do when I couldn't even see them or grasp them? Because my tears blurred my vision, the man's face looked to me like a mass of red and purple.

Strong arms reached around me and pulled me back, the other man from the van had finally reached us. What had taken him so long? It felt like I had been holding his partner on the ground for several minutes. Perhaps he had been standing and watching me, laughing at the silly way I tried to hit the man on the ground, and only came to intervene when he saw that I was crying, like a parent whose children are playing at fighting and have taken it too far.

I struggled to free myself at first, but my whole body was weak and shaky as the adrenaline drained out of me, and I had to stop. I saw that the red liquid from his face stained my hands; my fists were red, like in the dream when I had slept in the bushes. I was carried backwards up the stairs to the main building. The other man still lay on the ground, resting after the joke he had played on me.

I was so weary that when they placed me into a wheelchair my body slumped forward and my head hung down. For a long time while they pushed me down the corridor, I could only stare at my knees and the floor, until they strapped me upright.

I looked into the open doors we passed. Here there was a man sitting and staring at the wall but his face held an expression like he was staring at a beautiful landscape. A woman stood in a doorway, moaning and looking outwards at us. In another room with a larger doorway I saw two orderlies holding a man down by his shoulders and thighs while a doctor prepared a syringe; as I passed by, I saw the doctor's nametag and all of my muscles pulled taut so that the wheelchair jumped out of the hands of the man pushing it. The doctor's name was Ron!

Then I looked again, and saw that it was only a trick of the light and my excited blood; the nametag read 'Dr. Roy'. I relaxed again and my eyes met the doctor's; he held my gaze for a moment as he slid his needle into the arm of the struggling man, who immediately became the non-struggling man.

The doctor's eyes were still watching me as I rolled past the doorway in my wheelchair. It was like an amusement park ride ('*step right up to The Asylum, you'd have to be crazy not to*'), one where the cart moved past animatronic patients with inhuman faces, and every person in uniform slowly turned on its creaking base and looked at me. The ride stopped at a room with the number 20 above the door, and a nearby orderly came over to help in unstrapping me and guiding me to the bed. They left the room, closing the door behind them, and I heard the bolt of the lock snap into place. My thoughts turned to how I could escape, but the mattress was soft and the sunlight shining through the slats in the metal window blinds had warmed the covers, and so I soon fell asleep; it was my worst escape attempt ever.

Cold fingers touched me and turned my head from side to side. I was afraid what I might see if I opened my eyes. I felt a tapping on my skull and heard a voice saying, "Here." Another voice responded, but it was muted, like the whole conversation was from another room, and I could not make out the words. Then I tried to open my eyes, but I could not; they were taped shut. When I tried to move my wrists, I found that thick leather straps restrained them, and my feet were likewise restrained. I heard the high-pitched, mechanical whine of a saw and the clattering of tools. With great effort, I forced my eyes open and broke the tape with my eyelashes, and then I woke up from the dream. There was a film of cool sweat on my brow. A woman was in my room, carrying a tray with food and a cup that clattered. I recognized her as the nurse who had visited me in the jail after the men in suits, and from the nametag she was wearing this time I saw that her name was Penelope. Her body strained against the confines of her scrubs.

"Good morning," she said. "Have you had a good rest?"

I blinked at her in lieu of a response. I wasn't quite sure if I'd had a good rest, because since the sunlight from the window looked the same as when I had first arrived, it could have been only several minutes that I'd been asleep or it could be that I had slept many hours and it was already the next day. That seemed like a lot to say though, and most people are only making conversation when they ask if you've slept well, they don't really want to know[1], and I also wanted to make a good impression on her now that I was no longer in prison and had more capacity to flirt, so I finally just answered, "Yes."

"I'm glad to hear that, Oscar. Here's your breakfast, and I'll be back in a few hours to check on you again." She set the tray down on the bedside table and left the room. I heard the bolt slide home like before; I was apparently to be locked in this room at all times. I got up and looked out the window through the metal blinds, but the early morning sunlight was too bright for me to see anything. I paced my room out and found that it was perfectly square: six paces by six paces from one cream-colored wall to another. The door was in one corner, my bed was in the opposite corner, and in the corner next to the door was a tiny shower and toilet. I paced more. I read once that prisoners and others confined to small spaces soon learn to pace in a certain method, turning opposite ways at each end of the room so that they don't get dizzy. Left at the

[1] Try it next time someone asks you if you slept well. Just say, "No, I pooped myself and spent an hour cleaning it up using your socks," and see if they don't just leave to check on their socks instead of consoling you for your lack of sleep.

window, right at the door, that kind of thing. I'm not one to be taken in by just anything I read, though, so I paced in one direction.

Escape was out of the question; the door was always locked, the window blinds were made of metal and fixed to the frame, and everything else in the room was plastic, including the furniture and fixtures. The bed was more comfortable, but was this any less a prison than the cell I had been in only the day before, and was I any less a prisoner? I continued pacing. I felt a little dizzy from the pacing, and sat down to think.

Something had gone wrong; this wasn't how it was supposed to be. I should have been freed already, and I should have been back at my house picking up my search where I left off. What had happened to the lost evidence, to the prosecutor who would object halfheartedly? Somehow, the nefarious men who arranged to have me framed and imprisoned had planned a further scheme and put me here, in this hospital for lunatics. The phone recording had made it obvious that they were involved in the operation of the prison, now it seemed they could also arrange to have someone put in a mental hospital; how far and how deeply did their tentacles penetrate, and why did they even have tentacles? Were they some race of winged octopus-men, risen from beneath the sea, from some lost sunken city, back to claim the dry land they lost many centuries ago? I slapped myself to clear my head of those thoughts; I knew that I had just imagined the word 'tentacles' in my silent monologue to give a more exciting picture to how their influence reached, but even with that knowledge I had moved off on an inner tangent about men who are also flying cephalopods. I found it difficult to concentrate in that insane asylum; it was difficult even to feel that I was still sane. Did sane people have thoughts like that? Do you?

Then I saw clearly why they had arranged to have me removed from prison and put in the mental hospital. As soon as I told someone about how I had been followed, harassed, framed, and inconvenienced within an inch of my life, they would pat me gently and condescendingly on the head while thinking to themselves, *The poor fool, he's been in Maple Ridge,* and leave as quickly as possible after dropping a few coins at my feet. Now even if I were to find the heart of their organization, nobody would believe me. They had underestimated me though, because that would not stop me. I would still find them, and break them apart from the inside. There would be no glory in it for me because nobody would believe me, but I did not care about glory; I only wanted to be able to drink a glass of orange juice in peace.

The door opened and a doctor stepped through with a plastic chair and a clipboard; he unfolded the chair, sat, and asked, "How are you feeling, Oscar?"

"I'm fine," I answered, without looking at him. I didn't want to play any games, I just wanted to wait patiently until I was released, since I knew I wouldn't be staying here very long once they found out I was perfectly sane. Then, realizing I should encourage that line of thought with this doctor, I met his eyes and said, "I'm sane." Then I looked away.

The doctor's pen made a scratching noise on his clipboard of papers; he must have been making a check in the 'Sane' box, below the question 'Is the patient sane or insane?' This was encouragingly quick progress.

"Oscar, how long have you had violent tendencies?" he asked.

That was a trick question in the same style as 'When did you stop having sex with horses?' It was the sort of question where they try to trick you into incriminating yourself because you can't answer it directly or simply. Unless you actually have been having sex with horses, then you can give the approximate date you stopped, or if you never stopped then you can just say you're still doing it. In my case, I had never done it, and could not directly answer the question. I didn't blame him for trying, though, I knew all doctors like this had an insanity quota to meet; the more psychopaths he found, the sooner he'd be able to go home for the day. The hospital's income from the state also depended on a steady flow of mentally ill patients, so he had plenty of incentive to find many people to be in need of mental care and treatment.

In any case, instead of falling for his trap, I answered, "I've never had violent tendencies, doctor. In fact, my friends used to say I wouldn't hurt a fly. That's actually an exaggeration—you know how friends are—because I've killed many flies, but at least I wouldn't go out of my way to hurt a fly, it would have to come to me." He didn't say anything, and seemed to be expecting something more, so I leaned closer to say,

"Sometimes they do come, you know. They've got a score to settle."

As I spoke, the doctor took notes. Maybe to remind himself to check the story with my friends, or maybe to put up a sign outside my door warning staff to exercise caution because I was a homicidal maniac. Then, seeing that he wasn't going to have an easy time of tricking me into a quick diagnosis, he changed his questions.

"I understand that you have a prescription of Psylocybin for paranoid schizophrenia. Is that correct, Oscar?"

"Yes, I take them regularly," I said, nodding.

He took a bottle of pills from his pocket and placed them on the bed. It was full, and the name on the label read 'WELL, O.R.,' which was the same name it had on it when I got them from the pharmacy several months before. "Are you sure you take them regularly?"

So the jail definitely was in on it. The guard there had not had a headache after all; he had tricked Winslow into giving him the pills for use as evidence against me. I decided not to tell the doctor that, because I wasn't yet sure where he stood in the grand conspiracy of things.

"Alright, I haven't taken them in a while," I said. "But they're not good for me. I can't think clearly with them. Without the pills, I can see things as they really are. Since I've stopped taking them, I nearly…" I stopped when I saw that his eyebrows were raised in the style of Winslow. He saw that I was looking at them, and slowly lowered them back down to a reasonable altitude. "If only you could see the evidence

I've accumulated, you'd understand. I've got it all on the wall in my house. It's like the sort of wall a detective or a really dedicated person would have, not like a serial killer would have. They changed my keys and they took my juice, that's in your report isn't it, all the terrible things they've done to me?"

"Oscar," the doctor replied, adjusting his glasses, "let's put aside the juice for a minute. I'd like to ask you about a few other things." He had avoided my question, but I dutifully put aside the cup of juice I had been drinking and feigned interest in what he had to say.

He produced a stack of photographs and laid them next to the bottle of pills. "Do you recognize this man?" he asked. I did recognize the man as I looked through several of the pictures; he was the man in the gray pinstripe suit, the man in the cat's-paw-print pajamas, and in the heavy coat. In these pictures, he was the man in jeans and a t-shirt at an outdoor party with friends, and my interest was no longer feigned.

"Doctor, this is proof! Incontrovertible proof, proof they'll never be able to deny. This is the man they say I've killed, the man they put me in jail for, probably the reason they were able to put me in this… this…" I realized I was about to go too far, and chose my words carefully, "…in this fine medical establishment, which so far I'm enjoying very much and have been treated very well by all the staff. And that's what I'll say, that's what I'll tell them, there won't be any trouble for you or the nurses or anyone, I swear. Just let me have the pictures, or come with me and we'll show them to the judge back at the courthouse, and I can be free again." Breathing hadn't been a priority as I said all that, and now I was panting for breath and my heart was racing; I shook with excitement. With those pictures, I could expose everything!

The doctor was shaking his head; my fingers tightened on the bed sheets and my jaw shifted. He was in on it. Even now, seeing that the man who they had said I killed was actually alive, he wasn't going to help me.

"Oscar, these pictures were taken roughly a month ago, at a community barbecue," he said. He pulled a few photos from the bottom of the stack and fanned them out. "These are the most recent pictures of him, taken at different times over the past three weeks as the investigation progressed." In these pictures, he was the man on the cold, metal table; the man in the body bag; the man with blood pooled on the ground under him—or rather, I reminded myself, a clever facsimile of a man with blood pooled on the ground under him, since I knew it was not blood at all. It looked very realistic, and I wondered how they had done it. Perhaps sugar water at just the right consistency, mixed with red dye. In these pictures, and to the casual observer, the man did look very dead. His eyes had the sort of blank stare you might expect from eyes that no longer had any consciousness behind them, and his skin was an incredible shade of white.

"Dr. Boggs, please," I said, addressing him by the name on his tag, "you don't really believe this, do you?" His expression told me that he did, or that he wanted me to think he did. "Well, at least you don't expect me to believe it, do you?" His expression stayed the same. "Of course the pictures *look* real, but that's not the point; I didn't kill him, they just arranged the whole thing to make it look like I killed him. I pushed him, but he fell back on purpose and made sure that his head struck at just the right angle, loud enough for the people across the street to hear, but not enough to hurt. Then all he had to do was lie still with a blank look long enough to horrify all onlookers and be zipped up in a body bag. A child could have engineered it just the same—not that I would surprise a child outside of his own home and push him into a wall."

The doctor reached into his bag and pulled out several more photographs. Numbers written on the photos in black marker showed that they had been taken earlier that morning. "Could a child have engineered this as well?" he asked. The pictures showed a man's face; it was a misshapen mass of swollen flesh, purple bruises, and split skin. The eyebrows and upper cheeks had swollen in around the eyes to close them. The lips were split and swollen like a caricature. "This is the man you attacked outside yesterday, after he brought you here. He's in a coma."

That couldn't be true. He'd been fine when we had left him. He had been lying peacefully on the ground, resting, looking up at the clouds. "That's not the same guy," I said. "I didn't even hurt him."

"It's not uncommon for someone in your state of mind to not want to accept responsibility when you've done something terrible, Oscar. We'll work on that, but first you must at least admit it to yourself." He held up one of the pictures in front of me. "Why did you do this?"

"Stop it," I said, and clapped my hands over my ears. The doctor was one of them. He wanted to trick me into thinking I had beaten one man into a coma and killed another man. They'd get me to sign a confession, they'd put me in chains, and they'd leave me in here forever, pretending to be 'treating' me, but really just keeping me out of the way, so they could go on inconveniencing everyone with impunity. I wouldn't play their games; I wouldn't give them what they wanted. I snatched the picture from his hand, ripped it in half, and threw the pieces onto his clipboard. "I don't want to see any more of your lies."

"Oscar," he said, in a soothing voice, "let's talk about this some more." As he spoke, I got up, moved to the other side of the bed and faced away from him. He tried again. "You don't have to look at any more pictures; I'd just like to talk to you." I did not respond, and I would not. Already I had probably said too much, given him too much information to use against me. Eventually he gave up, saying we would talk about it later. I knew he had left when I heard the door close and the bolt click.

I lay in bed, staring at the wall. Several hours later, I heard him come back into my room. "I already told you, I'm not going to answer your questions," I said. "Go away."

A woman's voice said, "Alright, but I was just going to ask if you might have a peanut allergy or if this cake with your lunch would be ok."

I looked over my shoulder and saw that it was Penelope, the nurse from earlier. Not having made many friends in the hospital so far, I decided it was best not to make an enemy out of her.

"Sorry, I thought you were the doctor," I said. She still had an expectant look on her face, and I remembered the cake. "Also, I'm not allergic to peanuts. I'm not allergic to anything."

"What happened with Dr. Boggs?" she asked in a low voice, while she removed the empty breakfast tray and replaced it with the lunch tray.

"I don't really want to talk about it," I replied. So far, everyone had turned out to be one of *them*. It was hard for me to believe, but maybe even Winslow was in on it. When I spoke to him about it weeks ago, he seemed simply not to believe me, but he could have been putting on a one-man production of *Good Ol' Winslow* and playing all the parts beautifully. Yes, I saw it now. They expected me at the house of the man in the cats'-paw-print pajamas; it fit that Winslow had tipped them off when I told him that I was onto them, giving them time to prepare the elaborate sham of murder and insanity that had ended up with me in a mental hospital, unable to stop them or even reach them. I could see now that Ron at the post office had not tried to hide himself when I followed him, and the newspaper was intentionally left at the bus stop so I would know I was on the right trail. Then they had me right where they wanted: just a little knock of a head against the wall followed by a pool of fake blood, and

I'd be out of the way for weeks or months—maybe forever. When I was released—or if I was not to be released, when I escaped—I would start with Winslow.

The door bolt exclaimed loudly that it had slid into the locked position; while I had been piecing together the puzzle of Winslow, Penelope had left the room without me noticing. She was apparently not interested in asking me any further questions, and had known to leave me alone with the cake. I liked her.

Chapter 6

Lunch was plain, but good. There was the cake, of course. There was a humble ham sandwich, which is not worth describing further. There was also a cold, buttered bread bun, which is a simple food I have always loved. I lay back on the bed and partly closed my eyes, with one hand behind my head and one hand holding the bread, occasionally bringing it to my mouth. When I was a child, my brother, Benjamin, who was eight years older than me, often attempted to steal food from me at mealtimes or snack times. He would never do it directly, since if he had I would simply tell my mother about it; then he would be punished and I would get my food back. Instead, he devised elaborate schemes of food-thievery. The first time I can remember it happening is when I was a baby; I'm not sure how old I was, but I was sitting in a baby's highchair, with food on the tray in front of me—I only recall it as being orange and green, which I imagine probably means that it was mashed up carrots and peas. My brother, and others, would sometimes play what *they* called a game with me where they would ask me where they were, briefly wink out of existence, and then reappear, shouting, "Here I am!" and making horrible gurning faces. It was frightening, but I could not yet speak and knew no expressions to convey my fear, so I only laughed nervously hoping that the moment would soon pass. In my fear, my laughter would turn hysterical and too loud, which they mistook for my extreme enjoyment. There was no way to make them stop. It was a terrible time in my life, one that I have never related to anybody before this writing. I only hope that such a thing never happens to you.

Benjamin chose one of these 'game' sessions as the first time to try stealing my food. He asked me where my food had gone. I knew it was a silly question, because my food was on the tray right in front of me, and always had been for as long as I could remember, but I thought perhaps it was just him testing my ability to look around, as people sometimes did[1]; so to please him, I looked down and was astonished to find that my food had disappeared from the universe; the tray in front of me was empty and spotlessly clean. I had never been a baby who was fussy about my food, instead enjoying everything that was fed to me, and angrily I looked up at my brother to complain about my non-existent meal, only to discover that he was also gone! Moments later, I heard the clunk of my plastic plate on the tray below. I looked down at it as my brother came back into existence and shouted, "Here it is!"

I paid no attention to him and instead eyed my food

[1] "Look over there," they would say, pointing at my uncle who I knew very well. "Who's that? Is that your uncle?" Luckily for them, I was not yet able to speak and insult them for their condescension, but even so I was barely able to hide my contempt behind the veil of innocent youth.

suspiciously. Where had it gone? Had it gone some place with Benjamin? I was chilled by the realization that I had no way of telling if this was even the same food as before; I hadn't thought to take a picture of every meal I ate in the unlikely event that somebody caused it to no longer be corporeal, and now I did not have a picture to compare against this probable imposter on my tray. The safest and most plausible explanation was that he had replaced my lunch with an entirely different—but identical in appearance—meal. Who knows why he did that, or what could have been put in the vegetables by him or some other party before they reached my plate.

I didn't think all of that at the time, of course—that would be ludicrous, because, after all, I was only a baby. It wasn't until much later, when I was well into my teenage years and had gained knowledge of the world, that I was able to unravel my thoughts and figure out what had truly happened. What I did do, though, which I think supports that I understood the basic principles of what I'm writing here, is throw my plate upwards onto him so that he was covered in mashed peas and carrots. And obviously, all these years later, I now understand the concept of object permanence much better than a baby does, yet to this day I am always careful to keep a close eye on my food until I have eaten it.

I finished my meal and fell asleep. Later, I was partly woken by the noise of the food tray being removed and the door closing. When I woke even later, I noticed that the light from the window was still the same as when I had come in the night before. There was no clock in the room, so I could not tell the time. I didn't know how long I had been asleep, but it felt like several hours. The light from my window never seemed to change. I had never seen it dim with dusk or brighten at dawn, so it was impossible for me to know even the approximate part of the day I was in. It could be a sophisticated artificial light behind the window, always set at the same sunny brightness, to make me think it was daylight outside, when really I was being held in a dungeon miles belowground, and all that was beyond the glass was a light bulb with ten thousand feet of solid earth packed on top of it.

There was no way for me to be sure; it was fully possible that I really had been falling asleep in the afternoon and only waking up the next day after the darkness of night had gone and the sunlight returned. The suspicion that there could be a billion tons of dirt just above caused me to feel uneasy. I sat on the cool toilet, tried to relax and forget the light, forget the dirt, but it was all around me and above me, and then my head began to hurt. Suddenly the image of the ceiling pressing down and sagging under the weight of all that soil flashed into my mind. I got off the toilet and saw that the walls were pressing in towards me. Some outer set of joists must have buckled due to disrepair combined with the incredible pressure of the earth. Cracks appeared around the window, and I backed against the wall nearest the hallway. I banged on the door and shouted for help. Soon the wall would collapse completely. A worm made his way through a crack around the window frame, and as I crouched down in the corner, my mind calmed and I marveled that the worm could survive on its own, so far below the surface and outside of any stable structure, while I, a far more advanced being, would easily die. Of course, worms only have a lifespan of a few weeks, but that was better than dying right there in my room. This worm was the humble harbinger of death. How would it happen? I would suffocate. Oh God, I would suffocate! Of all deaths, what a horrible way to die was suffocation. The wall would burst open and the mantle of Earth would pour through onto me, pinning me against the wall. First, the room would fill with dirt, and then in the same instant my lungs would fill with dirt. If it didn't crush me right away, I would gasp for air, but there would only be more dirt, piling up in my lungs like dirt shoveled into a grave. From dust I had come, and now that dust was returning for me, I desperately did not want to go back to it.

"Help me, please, help me!" I shouted, and banged on the door again. I did not hope for any response; no doubt they had already all left when they first knew the joist had snapped. How many other patients were also left locked in their rooms like me to meet this hellish fate so far beneath the surface of the earth, away from any kind words or friendly faces, away even from the notice of a society that might spare a mention in the newspaper obituaries?

Since I could not force the door open, I pressed my body flat against it in the hope that the lateral pressure of the earth as it poured into the room might press my body into the door and force it open. If that didn't kill me, I might still be able to make it into the hallway and escape with my life. Several sharp cracks like gunshots sounded, starting out low, far away and rising in intensity as they came closer. The guards were shooting other patients—or prisoners, as I was now certain they should be properly called—who tried to escape. The sounds came closer, and then were so close that it could not be gunshots; it was the sound of further building supports snapping, and the end for me was near.

I braced myself for a wall of earth to slam against me, almost able to believe that I could protect my soft internal organs from harm just by the power of my tightly straining muscles. The door swung open from the pressure and my body flew forward through the doorway. I briefly waited, and realized that because I was still able to wait, even briefly, I was alive. I felt no pain, except where my face had landed against the hard tile of the floor, and saw no soil in the corridor, so dirt could not have slammed me through the doorway. Looking up, I saw my savior dressed all in white and wearing shoes with sensible heels: Penelope! She had come back for me, against her orders, even risking her own life to save me from a terrible last meal of choking earth. I wasn't going to let her gift be wasted, and I sprang to my feet, kicking the door shut behind me as I did so, to buy us precious seconds for our escape.

"Quickly, get to the ladder. I'll follow you, just go!" I said to her.

She only looked at me. She didn't know!

"It's in my room," I said, "that's where it's starting. The wall is collapsing right in there, and when that wall caves in the rest of the building will follow. We have to get out."

Then I remembered the others, who were also trapped in their rooms. I couldn't abandon them, those others who were just like me. "Give me the key and I'll try to get out as many of the other prisoners if I can. You've spared me, now let me spare them." She still didn't display any of the urgency you might expect someone standing in a soon-to-be-collapsed building to have. "Please," I said, "hurry!

At last I saw the two stocky men standing with her. One of them barred my way when I tried to go past, so I stepped back and felt myself once again pressed against the door, but now from the hallway side. Suddenly I didn't feel especially spared; she had pulled me from the frying pan into the fire, and there happened to be two large, rough-looking men already in the fire waiting for me. There was nowhere to go; they blocked my way forward, and the door behind me was by now tightly packed shut with dirt. The frame of the door wouldn't hold very long, soon the earth would burst through and we would all be buried in the deepest grave ever dug.

"Oscar," Penelope said, "don't you think you should be in your room?" I didn't understand why she would say that. Hadn't she heard me?

"I can't go in there; the walls have already caved in!" After I spoke, she nodded to one of the men, and then it hit me—not the wall of dirt, or even a fist, like I might have expected, but the realization that she wanted me back in the room buried under ten tons of dirt. She hadn't come to rescue me at all, then; she was only there to check that the job was finished. I was to be buried here, a secret victim of an unfortunate accident. It was a cruel thing to know that even the bringer of peanut butter cake could be against me.

Now that I knew where she stood, I wasn't going to waste any more time. I ducked under the arm of the man she had nodded to, but immediately I felt a powerful hand on my neck. I twisted my neck painfully to slip away, and then I spun around and swung my fist into his face with the full weight of my body behind it. He staggered back for a moment, causing my body to thrill with triumph, but then he recovered and circled his thick arms around me. The other man grabbed me from the side as well, twisting me around, and they both held me still. I struggled until I was exhausted, but I would have been powerless to wriggle free from the grasp of even one of them holding me like that; there was no chance I could get away from both.

Penelope reached for the door. Had she gone insane? She turned the handle and pulled the door back slightly, but as she opened it the first centimeter, I summoned my strength to lift my legs and kick it back shut with a resounding slam. The men pulled me out of reach of the door, with hands as solid as iron shackles.

Penelope put her hand to the doorknob again, and I shrieked with fear. They were denying me the most basic right of all living creatures, the right of struggle for life. "Even that worm is free!" I would have shouted, if my terror and exhaustion hadn't reduced any sounds coming from my throat to moans and whimpering. I could not beg or plead. My chest heaved. As she turned the handle, I felt my inner self shrink back away from the door. Then the door was open, and I closed my eyes tightly.

Nothing happened. The light on my eyelids was warm and bright. I opened my eyes and saw that there was no dirt coming through the doorway, only sunlight. I had gone insane along with Penelope. Was this how my mind reacted to the extreme terror of dying in this way? Perhaps I had died so suddenly I didn't realize it was happening, and this is what comes after death: an inviting, open door, and warm sunlight shining through onto my skin. The bonds around my arms were loosed, and I moved through the doorway almost as if floating on air. Then everything was all wrong. The room was just like the room I had been in before the wall collapsed and it was filled with dirt. Penelope was in the room with me, and so were the two men who had held me. I was not dead, and I felt someone owed me an explanation for why.

"The walls…" I began, but stopped when I saw that the walls were unblemished. There were no cracks. There was no dirt. I ran my hands around the frame of the window where the worm had come in, but there was no hole where a worm could have slipped through. I dropped to my knees and ran my hands over the ground.

"The worm!" I said to no one in particular. "It came

in through the window, through the crack that's not there anymore." *How unjust,* I had thought, just a minute before, *that the worm should live while I should die.* But I was alive; it seemed that there was no worm in my room, and considering the way that Penelope had looked at me it was hard to tell if there had ever been a worm at all.

"What's happening to me?" I asked her. I moved to sit down on the bed, but I kept my face turned away, lest I look at her face and see cracks appearing there as well. I felt her sit down next to me.

"Why don't you start by telling me what you think is happening?" she said, gently.

The different feelings of confusion, shock, fear, and anger battled inside me, but none was victorious, so my voice emerged as emotionless and monotone, the opposite of how I felt.

"I was in my room, and I was thinking about the window here," I said. "Do you see the light coming through it now?" She must have nodded, though I still didn't look at her. "Since I've been here, I've never seen any other kind of light coming through, no other shade or any variation in brightness. I suddenly realized, or I guess I should say 'felt', because I'm not really sure right now, that there was an artificial light behind the window. There's also no clock in my room, so I could never be sure what time it is. Even right now it could be nighttime and I wouldn't know it, because there could be an artificial light shining in and no clock to say otherwise. And the only reason for an artificial light is that we're somewhere deep down underground because Ron doesn't want me getting in the way of his plans."

I heard the door click shut, but I still felt Penelope on the bed beside me. The two men had left us alone.

"When I thought about being so far underground—miles, probably—the ceiling started to press down and the wall cracked and the worm came through, flaunting its carefree worm lifestyle right in front of me while I faced death. I banged on the door and cried out for help, then you know the rest because you're the one who came to what I thought was my rescue."

She was quiet for a few moments, and I looked over just to be sure she was still there. I was surprised to find myself looking into her eyes because she had been watching me closely. I nearly blushed under her intense gaze, so I looked away again. Then she said, "I'm not a doctor, Oscar, but I think you just experienced claustrophobia. I've worked with other patients here who are claustrophobic and this sounds very similar. It can be a very powerful feeling."

"Why did it only happen today," I asked, "since I've been here for days in this same room? And why has it never happened to me before?"

"Well, I think for the past few days you haven't felt confined. You were just in a reasonably spacious room with sunlight coming through the window and the entire open world only several feet away. It was only once you started to think of yourself as being miles underground that you felt trapped. The idea of a trillion tons of dirt on top of your head is probably enough to make anyone feel claustrophobic, even people who've never had trouble with it." She thought for a moment, and then her face brightened. "I've got an idea that should help. I'll have to get the doctor's permission, but why don't I just take you out of your room and we go outside? That way you'll see you aren't a character in a real-life *Journey to the Center of the Earth*, you're just safe in our hospital." Then, she added, "Our *above-ground* hospital."

It seemed like a good idea to me, so before she left me in the room we agreed that she would discuss it with Dr. Boggs, and the next day she would take me outside to alleviate my fears. If nothing else, it would be nice to see the sun unfiltered through my frosted window.

While I sat and thought, I looked around my room. I noticed that there was no food tray. I was sure that there had been one before I left the room and was brought back in by the muscular orderlies, and I hadn't heard anyone take it. Always before, there had been a noise when someone took the tray, some clattering or clinking—enough to wake me up, even. I briefly thought that actually it would have been possible to put me in a different room to my original one, especially since the struggle in the hallway had disoriented me. It was even possible that my room *had* collapsed, and they had just moved me to this nearly identical room to convince me otherwise. The more reasonable explanation, I knew, was just that one of the orderlies had taken the tray away while I was distracted by talking with Penelope, and so I hadn't heard it. Although, I *had* still heard the door clicking shut. I didn't entertain those thoughts for very long, anyway; Penelope had seemed genuine in her offer of help, and I had agreed to try things her way, at least for a day. I focused on just being a regular patient in a mental hospital, and not being imprisoned underground.

The sheet was slightly rumpled where Penelope had sat on the bed beside me, and when I put my hand there I felt the warmth of her body lingering. She had shown me only kindness in the time I had been here, and though she had not rescued me (because, perhaps, there was nothing for me to be rescued from) she had certainly improved my mood from that of one facing certain death to one who was at least looking forward to tomorrow.

Chapter 7

Tomorrow came, and with it came Penelope. And with Penelope came the two men from the day before, "just as a precaution; the doctor insisted." One of the men ("Steven," according to his nametag, which he wore but the other man did not, and which he himself had not worn the day before) produced a pair of handcuffs, which the doctor had also apparently insisted upon. I asked why, and Steven said it was because I was a flight risk, so I was going to be handcuffed to him and I was going to like it, whereupon Penelope shushed him. I refused to be handcuffed to him, and sat back down on the bed, which is what a small child might do if you try to make it wear one of those child leash-harness things made to look like a monkey where the leash was an extremely long tail, but you'd have done the same if you saw this guy who I was supposed to be handcuffed to. You didn't see him though, and so you're probably judging me as petulant and sulky, but then you've probably never had to be handcuffed to Steven in a mental hospital—and if you have, then just pretend you didn't read the last couple of sentences, because they're not directed at you and I apologize.

At last, Penelope presented a compromise, wherein she would handcuff me to herself instead of to Steven, and Steven and his colleague would flank us on either side. Steven grumbled to Penelope about it being against the rules, but he handcuffed my wrist to hers.

The handcuffs had a long chain between the cuffs to allow two people to be more comfortably cuffed together, but I wouldn't have minded being cuffed a little closer to Penelope. It was hopeless to think something like that; she was a nurse, and I was a patient; she was professional and I was in her care. Even so, I walked slightly closer to her than I had to.

Once we were attached, we left the room. The back of my head began to hurt and I felt compelled to look down the hallway behind us. When I looked, I saw a man in dirty overalls exiting a room just down from mine with a wheelbarrow full of dirt. He glanced in my direction and hurriedly withdrew back into the room with his wheelbarrow when he saw me. I opened my mouth to say something to Penelope, but he was gone, and I wasn't quite sure which room he had gone into. Had he been there at all? I decided to say nothing, but as we walked down the hallway in the opposite direction, I furtively looked back and saw where dirt had been scattered on the floor. I opened my mouth again to point out this evidence to Penelope, but we were already most of the way down the corridor; could I really have clearly seen a few bits of dirt at this distance? I looked again, and I couldn't see anything at all on the clean floor.

We got into the elevator, and it began its humming journey up to the next floor. I read once that the average time for a non-express elevator between floors was four seconds, with a further four seconds each for starting and stopping, so that to go from one floor directly to the next should take about twelve seconds. Like elsewhere I'd been in the hospital, the elevator had no clock, so I couldn't be sure of the time, but I had at least enough time to count every one of the hairs in Steven's left ear. I'm not going to tell you how many there were, because this story isn't about the hair in Steven's left ear (or his right, before you ask, you always trying to find out what's happening before it happens), so I'm not going to waste valuable space going on and on telling you all the details about those hairs and perhaps arranging them on a color scale from dark to light shades—which I could do, because we were on the elevator long enough for it—but I can assure you that there were enough hairs so that it'd take a lot more than twelve seconds to count them all.

One hundred and thirty-three hairs, alright? That's how many. And more, actually, but that's all I counted up to before I couldn't take the waiting anymore and I asked nobody in particular why the elevator was taking so long. Steven looked at me, with an expression that seemed to say, 'I know you've been counting the hairs in my ear,' then raised his hand and used his knuckles to tap a sign on the elevator wall behind me. *This elevator travels slowly for your safety,* the sign said, *thank you for your patience*. Steven went back to staring straight ahead. I thought about it, and figured that several centimeters per second *was* pretty safe. It was probably safer even than air travel, which I've heard is the safest way to travel.

I didn't remember even coming down an elevator

the first day I was here, but I was pretty upset that day so maybe I'd just forgotten it, or maybe they had moved me using the elevator while I was asleep. It would be easy for them to use me as their guinea pig[1] for whatever bizarre psychological experiments they wished; while I was asleep they could have moved me to any other part of the hospital, or even to another building entirely. They could put me on the moon in a place with artificial gravity. As long as the room and the few people I interacted with looked the same then I wouldn't know at all. My room could be like a movie set, and if I looked behind some of the other doors in the hallway I'd just find bare wood frames and makeup artists putting foundation on Steven to cover up a mole, which they haven't done very well because I could still see a large mole just to the left of his mouth. They could put me underground and leave the artificial lights on all the time and tell me it was the sun, just to find out what happens to a human when it thinks the earth's rotation has messed up so that it orbits the sun with the same side always facing it and the other side is in never-ending darkness. I turned to ask Penelope if I

---

1 Why do we use this expression? Does anyone even experiment on guinea pigs? I thought it was rats. Maybe hundreds of years ago guinea pigs were the animal of choice, but then it was discovered that they were extremely emotionally sensitive and it offended their dignity to be experimented on, or perhaps that they had photographic memories and would keep records of all they had seen so that competing research companies could capture them and pull out their little toenails until they gave up all their secrets. So now we use rats, who prefer to keep secrets because they know what's good for them. Push a button, pull a lever, keep a secret, get some cheese—it's a job, anyway, no shame in a job. Better than being dressed up in little hats and dresses by young girls, like what happens to guinea pigs now.

had ever been moved to another room without being told and also if the man without the nametag was named Ron, but just then the elevator jerked to a sudden halt and I lost my balance, knocking my head against the *this elevator travels slowly for your safety* sign. The elevator doors opened with a ding, and we stepped off.

Steven led the way past a security checkpoint where a guard waved us through, down another hallway, and towards double doors beyond which I could see the outside. He pushed the doors open and we walked through, into the cool, fresh air. I was free, out in nature on a warm summer day with a beautiful companion. Does it get any better? Well, perhaps without the handcuffs and the guards it might have been better, and if my beautiful companion had not been a nurse watching over my mental health. But who can say for sure?

"Oscar," Penelope asked, after we had been outside for a while, "do you see now? We're still here in the same place; you're not being kept in some underground dungeon." Her expression changed, like she'd thought of something new, and she said, "Come with me." We walked around the side of the building, with Steven and his nameless friend following, and the ground sloped away, to reveal another floor below the first floor—the hospital was built into a hill at the front. She led me by the cuffed hand to a window that was low to the ground, and she bent at the waist in front of me to reach it, and tapped her fingers on the window. "This is your room right here," she said. "This is your window. When you see light through your window, it's just the sun shining in."

I looked at the window, but that wasn't all I was looking at. When she straightened up, she lost her balance and bumped into me. Her soft body pressed against mine, and I put my hands on her shoulders to steady her. I apologized for being in her way; she assured me that it wasn't a problem. I felt conscious that we were standing close together, close enough that I could hear her breathing, and I stepped away a little bit so as not to make her uncomfortable. I was still close enough that I would have been able to see down her top perfectly if she wasn't wearing hospital scrubs. The very idea made me start to sweat, and I couldn't take my eyes away from the section of her top where I would've been able to see her cleavage if that fabric wasn't there. It was more tantalizing than if I *had* been able to see. None of that mattered, anyway. She was a nurse, and she wasn't interested in me. And even if she had been interested—which she definitely was not—it didn't mean I had to stare at her as if she was a bowl of cheerios and I was a jug of milk. "Get ahold of yourself," I whispered to myself through clenched teeth.

"What?" she asked.

"Nothing," I said, and tore my eyes away before she could see that I'd been looking at her not-cleavage. I looked at the window she'd pointed out instead. Since it was made of frosted glass, which keeps people from looking in (and also works just as well to keep people from looking out, although that fact is only incidental),

I couldn't see what the room was like inside. The window did seem the same though, and it seemed about the right position in the building to be my room. It didn't seem impossible that I really could just be in a mental hospital, staying there in that room. And a mental hospital was actually a good place to be, because sometimes it felt like I was truly losing my mind. I looked out on the forest of maples and sighed inwardly; maybe that was it, maybe I was just going crazy. It wouldn't hurt to let them try; the worst that could happen is I'd still feel crazy. Maybe they could help, though, and maybe they'd get me to a point where I could get through a day without thinking the stockboy at the grocery store was out to get me, or feeling worried about talking on the phone to my mother about how her garden was doing, because they might have the line tapped. Feeling like the earth was going to collapse on me the day before was terrifying, and I didn't want to have to go through that kind of thing again.

"Ok, you win," I said to her. "You might be right; I'll cooperate with treatment. I think there might be something wrong with me, maybe you guys can fix it. Or maybe not, but I'm going to let you try. I'm tired of looking over my shoulder because I think I'm being followed, and I'm tired of feeling like I have to follow the people who are following me. I don't want to spend the rest of my life being unable to make friends with guys named Ron."

"Why guys named Ron?"

"It's a long story," I said, and smiled. "Maybe I'll tell

you tomorrow night, over some psychiatric checklists and a bottle of pills."

"It's a date," she replied. She probably had occasion later to worry that using language like 'it's a date' was giving me the wrong idea. It wasn't giving me the wrong idea though; I'm not socially inept. I've taken girls on dates before; only a few have brought psychiatric checklists, and never on the first date.

We stayed outside for a while, making conversation about my family and my past. There were no 'Were you jealous of your mother's love for your siblings,' types of questions, so it didn't feel like treatment, and it was just good to be outside in the sun and in the fresh air, after being inside for so long. I still wasn't sure how long I'd actually been inside, but I didn't want to spoil my time outside by asking questions which might make it seem like I wasn't seriously on board with accepting treatment, or like I was faking it. It was a pleasant afternoon.

Chapter 8

Penelope came the next day, with a clipboard of the sort you'd keep a psychiatric checklist clipped to. She brought her own guest chair and I sat on my bed.

"I'm glad you're doing this," she began. "It makes it a lot easier and faster when a patient is willing to help with his own treatment. We always get better results. I know some of the experiences you've had have been very frightening for you, but I think that with your help we'll be able to get you past it all. Then you won't have to go through that kind of thing anymore."

She pulled a bottle of Psylocybin from her pocket and placed it in my hand. She closed my fingers over it. I looked down at her hand closed over mine.

"This is an important step," she said. "You've admitted that you have a problem, and the things you've said to me make it clear that you really do believe that. We're helping you to get better, and now you need to show that you're willing to help yourself."

She moved her hand away, and I looked at the bottle in my hand. "What does it do, exactly?" I asked. I'd had these pills before, but it was really only to placate Winslow because he was worried I might hurt myself or somebody else[1] if I didn't get mental treatment, and he threatened to call the police; I had barely listened to

---

[1] Oops.

the doctor's instructions.

"In your brain, the amygdaloidal nucleus—or amygdala—is responsible for emotions like fear, anxiety, and other basic, negative emotions. So, for example, if someone is breathing right over your shoulder while you're drinking orange juice, you might feel socially anxious because of their proximity, and you'd probably move away a few feet. That's normal. Scientists think it's an evolutionary protection, because fifty-thousand years ago someone standing that close to you might be trying to steal your delicious juice, and to do so they might smash your head open with a rock, or a stick, or a piece of metal, or a bone, or… you get the idea, they'd use whatever they could do the smashing."

"Now, that's great for most people, but," she said, raising her hand palm-outward, "in some cases, like in your case, the amygdala has grown too large, and the rest of your brain gets the impression that signals from the amygdala are more important than they actually are, purely due to the size and strength of them. So you're drinking juice you got from a vending machine, and just to be safe, your amygdala suggests that because other people also think juice is delicious that it's probably a good idea to go in your house, lock the doors and close the blinds before you have a drink."

My cheeks warmed and I looked away from her—many times I had bought a drink from a vending machine only to have to hide it protectively in my coat and rush home, and by the time I got there the cold refreshing drink I was promised by the billboard would be warm and unappetizing. I would drink it still, but it would only taste of shame.

"And while you're at it," she continued, not noticing my discomfort, "why not get under a blanket, too, in case somebody can see through walls. Then they'll just see a lump under a blanket instead of a guy drinking juice, and since lumps aren't delicious you'd have nothing to worry about then. It's actually a bit more complicated than that, but I'm not a neuroscientist myself, so all I can give you is the basics, which is good enough for me and you."

"For most of human history, that's what people with your condition were stuck with: irrational and unreasonable emotions, fearful reactions and frankly absurd behavior, all just to reassure the tiny (yet still oversized), nervous, tyrant Amygdala. A decade ago, researchers at the pharmaceutical company NorCorp," and here she paused to remove a pamphlet from a deep pocket and place it on the bedside table, "discovered an enzyme which can control or limit undesirable signals from any specific part of your brain. This enzyme was trademarked as Psylocybin. As you probably remember from the newspapers at the time, a lucrative market sprang up among the newly invented sport of bare-knuckle bear fighters, who used a version of Psylocybin to suppress their wholly rational fear of boxing against a six-hundred pound carnivore that doesn't understand the gentlemanly rules of boxing. That kind of thing is self-correcting though, and so soon the bare-knuckle bear fighting market for Psylocybin dried up and the sport died off—along with the human competitors. The only parties who cared about this event were NorCorp, which had to search out new markets for its drug, and certain species of bear which had grown accustomed to their dinner running calmly, fearlessly, and directly into their jaws, and now were loathe to return to the effort of chasing…"

My shame faded. After all, at least I've never tried to fight a bear, and I prided myself in keeping track of all bear sightings at *bearbeware.net* before vacations so that I didn't accidentally holiday in an area where a bear or someone in a bear suit might have been looked at once. I was feeling so pleased with myself for being sensible and safe that I'd forgotten to take in what Penelope was saying, but I caught the trailing thread of her Psylocybin history lesson.

"… mental diseases such as manic depression, paranoid personality disorder, and schizophrenia were beginning to lose some of their social stigma. NorCorp was excellently positioned to address the problems, and Psylocybin went on the fast track for FDA approval. Within a year, it was approved for use in treating a wide variety of mental disorders, and now it's available to help you."

"Does it really work?" I asked. "Is it really going to make me like everyone else, not worried and afraid of everything?"

"It works—" she broke off her sentence, and I could see her considering her words carefully.

"It works," she said again. "I know, because I use it myself. A lot of the staff here have Psylocybin prescriptions for different disorders. It's why many of us were chosen to work in Maple Ridge, since it specializes in mental disorders. We have intimate knowledge of the way these conditions can affect a person's life, so we're better able to help patients like you. I know what you're going through; I've been through the same things myself."

She couldn't have had the same irrational worries and fears as me; she was so professional and in control. My face must have betrayed my disbelief, since she said, "It's true, it really is. I know it seems unbelievable, since now I'm professional and in control, but there's been more than one night before where I've stayed up until six in the morning with my ear pressed to the side of a windowless van parked outside my apartment, listening for the sounds—sounds that never came—of somebody inside talking about me. I wasn't able to work—I was hardly able to eat for fear they would hear—and when I got fired for never showing up to my job at the hospital I convinced myself it was a conspiracy to leave me penniless and powerless so I wouldn't be able to do anything about the man in the van. I was living in a homeless women's shelter and sleeping with three pillows over my head at night, when a doctor at the free clinic recommended me to a friend of his who was running the first experimental trials of Psylocybin for paranoid people."

She reached into her pocket and took out another pill bottle. She held it up to me and I read the name on the label: 'HOPE, P.' Penelope Hope. "I take one of these every morning, and since I started I've been able to lead a normal life again. It's so good to have a nondescript van pass me in the street these days and not feel anything. Not that I'm numb; I do feel things. I just don't feel worried that every van has it out for me. I was lucky that a hospital like Maple Ridge exists with the unique mission they have, to give me a second chance."

I turned the bottle in my hand and listened to the pills tumbling over each other. "When I used this before, I felt like it changed me. Not just my thoughts, but it changed *me*. It changed who I was."

Penelope nodded. "The paranoia you have feels like a part of you. You're used to the constant worrying, and you don't feel whole without breaking into a cold sweat whenever you see someone hidden halfway behind a dumpster in the shadows of an alley as you're walking down the street, when really that man hidden in the shadows is just having a smoke break, peeing against the wall, or conducting business with a prostitute who is hidden lower down behind the dumpster. If anything, he's the one who should feel nervous or ashamed because you've seen him."

"Feeling like you're being watched makes you feel important, though; just like anybody else, you want to feel cared for, you want attention. Your brain makes up that attention for you, and it can become an almost addictive feeling. When you're on Psylocybin it's hard to get used to the fact that really, you're not more interesting than everyone else in the world and nobody has popped out of your shower drain to go through your drawers the moment you leave the house every day."

"When your dysfunctional amygdala is no longer creating those feelings of importance and attention, you miss it, but you learn to fill your life with more meaningful things, like I've done by working at this hospital. I've made myself important to the patients here and to my employers; that's real importance, not just something that exists in your head," she said, tapping me on the temple.

"This is something you have to consciously accept; you have to *want* to change, or your brain is going to reject the chemicals in Psylocybin and it won't have any effect. I'm going to leave you on your own to think about it more, and maybe you should read through this pamphlet to see if it can help put you at ease. I hope you come to the same conclusion I did, it really is much better this way." She smiled at me, took her hand off my knee, and left the room.

Once she was gone, it was just me and the pamphlet; *mano a folleto.* The cover of it had only this lengthy title over a plain background of a solid color: 'Further information on the usage of Psylocybin and its effects on the overactive amygdaloidal nucleus of certain individuals.'

My hand hesitated over it—could it really hold information so powerful that it would answer all my questions? Make me feel fully comfortable with taking Psylocybin? Even comfortable with letting the drug change the way my mind worked? Maybe I didn't want to be rationally convinced into giving up my paranoia, that familiar friend of my mind. My head swam among a school of conflicting thoughts; Penelope had said this friend could be an enemy, that she had found it to be a false friend; I had found it to be the same, if I was honest with myself. I had killed a man under the influence of my paranoia—an innocent man. The pictures Dr. Boggs had shown me were not faked.

I stared at the pamphlet, unmoving. Anyone watching the scene—if anyone was so bored as to spend their evening watching a mental patient's internal conflict over looking inside an informative pamphlet—would have thought I had gone catatonic. I had not, though; I was only lulling the pamphlet into a false sense of security, letting it think that it could lie there unmolested until the end of time, with nothing to worry about from me. When I judged that it had relaxed sufficiently and would not expect it, I steeled my resolve, and quickly moved my hand to the corner of the glossy paper[1]. Before I could talk myself out of it, I had opened the pamphlet fully and its contents stared out at me.

It was one A4-sized sheet, folded into three sections. The left section depicted a dark, frightening scene of a man bearing a fearful expression, who was carefully peering from behind the corner of a dirty brick building, watching several men with heavy coats and hats. Their coat collars were turned up and their hats

---

[1] This is not *literally* what happened, it's only a way of representing in text form how I wrestled internally with the idea of accepting treatment for my mental illness. In actual fact, I knew that most pamphlets are far too clever to be duped by such an infantile ruse.

were pulled low; combined with the bright moon high in the sky behind them, this put their faces in shadow so that you could only see their narrow eyes. They huddled around a collection of papers and photographs, and in one of the photographs could clearly be seen the face of the man who was hiding around the corner of the wall. Other photographs had titles such as 'his house', 'his toothbrush', and 'his middle-school crush.' Among the papers were maps marked 'route to work', 'route to the store on Thursdays', and others. These men were well equipped to follow their prey—the nervous man around the corner who was dripping with sweat—and they knew a good deal about him.

I saw another detail I had missed at first: at the other corner of the building, opposite the sweating man who was watching, was another dark man in a heavy coat with a sinister bulge under the arm, and he was watching the first man with his narrow eyes. The intent of the scene was clear; the nervous man was watching those who were watching him, and staying one step ahead of them, but unbeknownst to him he was caught in an invisible trap—he was being watched, even while he watched those who he thought were the watchers; while he thought he was safe and out of sight he was under the eye of their frightful microscope.

The scene frightened me not because it was drawn realistically or in any kind of horrifying manner, for it was not; it was drawn in an abstract, cartoonish manner, like a parody or caricature of life. It frightened me because it could have been a direct snapshot of my mind at any given time in the past ten years. How many times had I felt I was being watched, and done my best to escape and evade, and even sometimes felt like I was successful in my escape so that I was able to hide and watch *them* from my hiding place; yet even in my safe place I had worried that I was still being watched, and doubted my safety?

The middle section showed the same worried man, sitting on a bed. A picture on the wall showed an older man with his eyes and an older woman with his nose—his parents[1], so he was in his bedroom at home. The clock showed 12:01AM, so either his clock had recently lost power or he was up quite late, and the darkness from the window indicated the latter. A set of narrow eyes pierced the darkness of the window—the eyes of a dark man in a heavy coat. The worried man on the bed had dark circles under his bloodshot eyes, and thick lines in his forehead like a piece of dough flattened and then pressed together from each end. It was like looking into a mirror that reflected the way I felt; inside as well as outside, I was always the man sitting up until midnight with stomach ulcers forming due to the stress from excessive worry.

I looked away from the pamphlet to think, and caught myself reflected in the acrylic safety covering of a picture on the wall. It was only a thin, blurry reflection, because that safety covering was not intended as a mirror, but still I saw a face that looked

---

[1] Or perhaps a male-female team of eye and nose thieves.

far older than I had imagined my face to look, with gray skin and haggard eyes. My body was thin; emaciated, even, because eating was a low priority when they were after you. A clump of my hair was missing; had it fallen out naturally from the stress of the situations I found myself in, or had I pulled it out in a paranoid fit without realizing?

I looked back at the pamphlet, and saw that a copy of the same pamphlet lay on his bedside table, and in his hand the man held a prescription pill bottle, with 'NorCorp' in large, bright letters on the label, and 'Psylocybin' below that. In his other hand he held a small pill, and was raising it towards his mouth.

The left section had been labeled 'Denial,' the middle section had been labeled 'Acceptance,' and the right and final section was labeled 'Joy.' The sun shone high and bright in a clear, blue sky, lighting up the scene. This section showed the same man, but he looked in much better health. Gone were the bags, the lines, the bloodshot eyes, the pale complexion, the harried, hunted look. His face bore a calm, satisfied, self-assured smile. He was sat at a table in the alley from the Denial section, and sat at the table with him were several men wearing heavy coats, the men from the other sections. Their heads were thrown back in laughter—perhaps at a funny joke the formerly-worried man had told. One man was pulling something out from his coat, but instead of an instrument of death such as a knife or gun—as you might expect due to the sinister bulge under his arm from Denial—he was pulling out a gift, wrapped in foil paper with handsome, muscular unicorns printed on it. Since it was now clear that these men were not kidnappers or murderers or hooligans of any sort but rather were friends of his simply bringing him a birthday present, I became aware of a new element to the smile of the no-longer-worried man; I saw that it showed a measure of self-deprecation because he now realized how silly he had been to experience such worry over such a benign situation. I thought of how perfectly ashamed he should be—how perfectly ashamed I should be, in fact, for it was very clear that I was the same as this man—for behaving the way he had towards those who only wished to do him good.

The message of the pamphlet was crude, but it still had a precise effect on me. The pamphlet fell from my hands. I had been a fool. How many days of my life had I wasted being in denial about my condition? How many years? But it wasn't too late; there was still time to turn things around. I could start on this medication I had been given. I could apologize to Winslow and to my other friends who I had wronged along the way, who I had suspected of treachery towards me or conspiracy against me for some innocuous reason.

Maybe I'd even be able to get back my old job as a candy tester, this time without breaking into a cold sweat every time a new flavor of M&M was brought to me because I was worried this might at last be the one which was poisoned so they could replace me with a man who had been surgically made similar to me in every way except for an overlooked mole on the back of his upper thigh, the significance of which could never be realized by anybody other than my mother, and then not even her because at my age it's very rare for your mother to see the back of your upper thigh[1], unless she's looking at faded Polaroid photos of you from when you were a baby playing in a metal washtub.

My mother hadn't heard from me in perhaps a year—for her protection, so that they couldn't connect her to me—and I missed her deeply. She called sometimes, less than at first, but still every month or so, and I just let the phone ring when I saw her number on the caller ID. Once she had called from someone else's phone, so I answered, but when I heard her voice I didn't say anything else. I heard her voice then in my head as I thought back.

"Oscar? Oscar, are you there? It's your mother. Please answer me, Oscar, why," her voice caught in her throat, punctuating her sentences in odd places, "won't you talk to me? I came over last week and knocked on your door for a while. I knew you were in there, I saw the curtain move at the side. Pick up the phone, Oscar."

---

[1] I wouldn't put it past this imposter to seduce my mother, and then she'd eventually have occasion to see the mole, but she'd probably just think I/he was getting skin cancer and suggest that he see a doctor. There's a slim chance that she'd realize that it wasn't me, put her clothes on and call the police (not that the police would do any good, you know how it goes), but it's probably just as likely that they'd remove the mole from him before he replaced me. In any case, at around this time in my life I was no longer thinking that the Mars Corporation had hired me in order to poison me with candy and replace me with a lightly moled man. It wouldn't really make much sense, even just from a financial perspective.

Even as she pleaded with me to just talk to her, I thought I was being protective and brave, shielding her from the bad people who were following me and might use her as a weapon against me[1], so I walled myself up inside and pushed my emotions down deep. But instead of being brave, I had actually been the world's worst son[2] for the mountains of grief and worry that I had caused to my mother for no real reason, when all she wanted was to be in contact with me.

The way I had treated my mother was just one example of what my friends and family had been through, and not even the worst example, which is why I told you about it. My former girlfriend was probably still mourning me after I had faked my own death and then left a dead pheasant in her mailbox to throw her off the trail, and I would tell the full story of that but it's rather embarrassing, so instead you only get a footnote[3] which leaves your questions tantalizingly unanswered. I'm sorry for being so difficult.

---

[1] A gun or even a knife are arguably more effective weapons, but these people preferred subtlety.

[2] Technically that guy who killed and ate his parents was far, far worse, but I'm not trying to weasel out of what I did. Not speaking to your mother even when she's done nothing wrong (or even when she has, because, considering all the times she didn't sell you or turn you in to the police for all the terrible things you did as a small child, she should be allowed a few wrong things) is pretty bad anyway.

[3] Some who know me well might say that I simply lack the courage to break up a relationship face-to-face, and that's true, but I'd also like to think I did it for her protection, and also a bit for my protection: Captain Scott, the famed 20th century Arctic explorer, was reportedly shocked by the penguins who practiced what he called "depraved" sexual acts – in fact, he was so shocked that he recorded his accounts of them in Greek instead of English, to protect

I felt the weight of the Psylocybin in my hand. The list of people I had wronged, neglected, or just confused by my behavior was nearly endless. If what Penelope had told me was true, inside that bottle was a way to shorten the list, to right the wrongs, to erase some of the names and perhaps in time get them to erase my name off their own list of weirdos[1]. I opened the bottle, poured several of the pills into my hand, and then set them down because I remembered you were supposed to have them with food. I waited impatiently until dinner time several hours later, when a nurse I hadn't seen before knocked on the door and came in, holding a tray of food for me. I thanked her, took several bites of my ham and cheese sandwich and took the pills. I didn't feel any different at first, so I finished the sandwich and settled down on my bed to await the effects. Gradually, for the first time since I had been inside Maple Ridge Psychiatric Hospital, the light from the window dimmed, and by the time I fell asleep that day it was dark outside my window and in my room.

---

the delicate sensibilities of the public at the time. My former girlfriend who I last contacted by way of dead pheasant was very penguin-like in that respect, and frankly I was frightened of her. At least I'm not writing this in Greek now, though, because I know your sensibilities are not as delicate as the public of Captain Scott's time. In fact, there's a good chance that you're pretty depraved yourself. Shame on you. Unless shame is one of the things that gives you sexual pleasure, in which case please experience the opposite of shame.

[1] Though you really have to question who's the real weirdo: the weirdo, or the one who keeps a list of weirdos. Both, I guess, but I still very much wanted to be off that list.

Part 2
Chapter 9

A SUNBEAM FROM the morning sky snuck in through my window and gently warmed me into consciousness like a breakfast burrito[1]. I sat up on the side of the bed and stretched; I felt good. For nearly as long as I could remember, I had dreamt terrible foreboding dreams every night, dreams which abruptly ended in a clammy early morning wakefulness. I had forgotten what it was like to just feel *good,* to have properly rested and be ready to face the day. Did my muscles really not ache from midnight tensing during paranoid dreams? Was my back really not sore? These are rhetorical questions; my muscles did not ache, and my back was not sore.

In the mirror, and in my head, my eyes were clear and free from encroaching red veins. For a moment, I thought I might be dreaming, but a quick look around the room revealed a distinct lack of malicious surveillance, so it seemed unlikely that it could be one

---

[1] I'm sorry if this has spoiled the story for anyone who up until this point had hoped the big reveal at the end would be that I was actually a breakfast burrito; I was only like a breakfast burrito in this specific instance. Also, there's not actually a big reveal at the end. Or is there?

of *my* dreams. A knock came at the door and for the first time since I had been in that room I didn't briefly worry that perhaps this knock would be the one which heralded a gun held by red gloves, with the silenced barrel aimed at my actually quite delicate head. Gloves did come through the door, but they were white, and on the hands of a nurse bringing my breakfast.

"You're up early," she noted, and she was right; this was the first time I had been up before the breakfast knock, and always before it had woken me up tired and irritable since I hadn't slept well the night before.

"I am," I replied, accepting the tray from her and giving a smile in return, "Thank you."

That's what a normal exchange of words could be like. I didn't have to accuse someone of poisoning my sausage and eggs at all, I could simply be polite and thankful for the food. What a relief that was. I devoured my breakfast, not once stopping to wonder whether the delicious flavor was a natural characteristic of the food, or something added to conceal the taste of the memory-wiping chemical. I spooned the last of the sawmill gravy into my mouth, and licked the spoon clean—what a rapturous feeling you could experience just from the combination of flour, milk, pepper, and fat. I felt a brief twinge of envy for all the people who lived every day of their life like this, but it went away quickly, because now I was living the same way, and if I was lucky I would be living every day like it from then on. Two Psylocybin tablets were supposed to be taken with breakfast as well as with dinner, so I got two from the bottle and swallowed them down.

Once, Winslow had told me that he felt sorry for me, that he couldn't imagine feeling restless, anxious, worried, mistrusting and unhappy—just to name a few—every day. When I asked him what made him feel good—because I had tried the usual things before and found that while they did remove the negative feelings, they didn't replace them with anything, and I felt used up and empty afterwards—he said it wasn't anything, that he just woke up and felt good every day. I couldn't believe it, and I even felt a little angry with him for making jokes at my expense, but he said that a peaceful happiness or contentment was the normal way to be. Now I was feeling what he had meant.

I could be normal. I could experience joy, unfettered by worry or fear. In the past, even in times where most people experienced pure joy, such as in the moment of orgasm or when winning an instant-win prize from the inside of a candy bar wrapper[1], I was still trying to figure out what new angle the world had planned to trap me. Contentment was definitely something I could get used to, and if I could feel it over breakfast and a back that didn't ache, what might I feel over the things

---

[1] Once I opened a bottle of soda and the underside of the cap declared "Instant Win—Free Drink." I took it to the store clerk, exchanged it, and the underside of the cap on the free bottle also said "Instant Win—Free Drink." I exchanged that cap as well, but by that time I was no longer able to experience any pleasure at my good fortune because I was consumed with misgiving at what might be in these drinks that they were so eager to give away. I went outside, poured the bottles down a street drain, and hid under a blanket back at home with only my tears to slake my thirst, although I could not cry enough for that purpose.

that normal people actually considered to be worthy of joy? I stretched out on the bed and contemplated the ceiling. Since the time when I had thought the walls and ceiling were about to collapse in on me, I hadn't been able to look up. I spent most of the time in my room looking towards the door, or with my face planted in a pillow. Now I was able to appreciate the molded decoration of the ceiling, how the light and shadows played at creating mountain peaks and valleys over my head, and I had no worries that those mountains would fall on me.

Several anxiety-free hours later, Penelope knocked and entered my room. I sprang out of bed and encircled her in a hug. Her whole body tensed and she pressed her hands against me to push me away, but then she seemed to realize I wasn't insane—or at least not the kind of insane that would eat you or squeeze you to death, which in my opinion are definitely probably two of the worst kinds—and she relaxed.

"Thank you, Penelope," I said. "I feel great. I mean really, really great. I don't even know what words to say. I feel good. I woke up and I didn't hurt, I didn't ache, I felt happy. For the first time I felt happy without anything happening to make me feel that way. It feels like it was just my natural state, to wake up and feel good. Thank you, thank you for your help." I felt the shoulder of her uniform blouse wet against my cheek, and when I lifted my head I realized I had been crying against her as I spoke. I apologized in a whisper and felt embarrassed, and it was my turn to try to pull away, but now her arms were around me too and she pulled me into her and held me tight. She held me as I pressed my face into her and wept. It felt like each tear contained a fear, an anxiety, a mental torment, all held in until then, because I never realized that I could let them go, that they didn't have to take over my life, and that they weren't really even a part of me; nobody had ever told me that.

"It's all right," she whispered to me, "Everybody hurts. Everybody worries."

I knew it was true. Everybody worries. Even Winslow worried about me, but he didn't let his worry define him, he was able to let it go. As each vexatious thing came into my head, I recognized it and turned it over in my mind before releasing it. I let go my fears that one day I would be walking down the street and a windowless van would pull up, the door would slide open, and they would pull me inside to torture me by the slow drip of a leaky tap in the next room until I broke down and told them what they wanted. I let go my feeling that every person in the world was set against me. I cried for a long time with Penelope, but I let every single paranoid thought go; I released them all, no matter how truly frightening or how completely absurd, and then there were no more tears. When I stopped crying, I sat down on the bed, mentally and physically exhausted but elated because I finally felt free.

"For the first time this morning, when the other nurse knocked—" I began, but she stopped me.

"I know how you felt. For the first time, you didn't worry who or what might be on the other side of the door, because you finally realized: why wouldn't it just be your breakfast being brought to you at the regular breakfast time? I had the same experience when I started using Psylocybin. Even when I'm not paranoid, I'm still very shy, but that first night, I gathered up the courage to order a pizza, and when the delivery guy brought it, I didn't look through the peephole to check; I didn't even ask who it was. I paid for my pizza, and when I set the box on the table I no longer felt like I needed to slowly open the box *just in case*, as I had always done before. Just in case of what? Just in case of *pizza*?" She tilted her head back and closed her eyes. "I ate that magnificent pizza, covered in pepperoni and olives and cheese, and it was the most delicious thing I had ever tasted." She opened her eyes and indicated the bottle on the table. "I had been changed by those little pills, just like you have."

I asked when I'd be able to leave the hospital now that I was feeling better, and she said that the doctor would like to keep me under observation for two weeks, just to be sure that the medicine was working and that there were no especially bad side effects (as with most medicines there were rare side effects like kidney failure, heart attack, and hair loss, plus the common and benign ones like sweaty palms), but if everything looked good after that time then I'd be able to return to my home with a clean bill of mental health.

Most of the next two weeks passed quickly and pleasantly, with two Psylocybin every morning and evening. Any time a cloud of worry passed over me, it was always blown away by the fresh, clean winds of optimism and rationality. I did develop the side effect of occasional sweaty palms, but it was nothing compared to before, when I would often wake up from a horrible paranoid nightmare, drenched in sweat.

Dr. Boggs visited me once more in my room. I told him about my sweaty palms, and he said that was easily taken care of; all I had to do was carry a discreet cloth with me at all times so I could wipe my palms before I shook someone's hand, or touched a doorknob, or stroked a baby's tiny sweat-free face. At first, I protested about the inconvenience of carrying a cloth with me everywhere I went, but I soon agreed with him that compared to a life of living in fear that the mailman (or my cat[1]) may be bringing a bomb to me, carrying a cloth for my newly sweaty palms was a small cross to bear indeed.

He asked me how I had been feeling since I started taking the Psylocybin regularly, and I was amazed by how different this conversation felt when I thought back to conversations I'd had with him in the previous weeks. Without realizing it, I had been cagey and reserved in my answers to even the simplest of questions before, anxious that I might give too much away and paranoid that he might be in league with the mysterious powers who wanted me to have a proper diagnosis along with state-of-the-art medical treatment.

---

[1] Which I had to give away for precisely this reason, and for several months after I constantly worried that the cat might still blow up in the arms of the new family I had given it to. After that amount of time, though, when he had not destroyed the adoptive family, I figured either the cat meant no harm, or he was a dud. Better safe than sorry.

Now my answers flowed easily, because we were partners on my journey back to mental health, and I knew he wanted me to be better just as much as I wanted it.

"Oscar, in a few days you'll be out of here and on your own," he said. "You'll be on your own in a way you never have before. You won't have phantoms and shadows tagging along in your mind. It's a lot quieter in the real world without them, and that's something you're not used to. If you have any concerns at all, you can always come back here," he paused in mid-sentence to adjust his glasses, "for a counseling session with me."

I smiled. "It's hard to imagine having any concerns, but I'll definitely come to you if I do."

"I can't tell you how pleased I am by your reaction. We were very concerned that your mind might reject the medication."

"How else could I react?" I said. "It's a great feeling. I have my life back now, thanks to you."

He hesitated, and pushed his glasses up before they had even slipped down. I didn't think he was going to continue, but then he said, "A small number of patients have reacted violently to even the suggestion that they take Psylocybin, and they're now in hospitals for the criminally insane. They'll spend the rest of their lives there. Their paranoia makes them a danger to society, as you no doubt remember."

I lowered my eyes and looked away from him, recalling the photographs of a bloody face and bruised body, all caused by me, but he held up his hand.

"I'm not blaming you for your past behavior, Oscar." he said. "A kleptomaniac isn't to blame for stealing. Someone with summer allergies can't help sneezing when there's pollen in the air. The amygdala is a powerful part of the brain, and can be impossible to resist, especially when it reaches the size we find in your condition." He stood up, clapped me on the shoulder, and finished with, "In any case, you're doing very well now; a nurse will be along shortly to show you to your new room."

I owed so much to Penelope. I wouldn't have agreed to take the medication on my own without her help, and without my agreement my mind would have rejected it. She was all that had stood between me and confinement in a maximum-security insanity prison. If she hadn't helped me, then I'd be locked up forever, thinking it was all a trap designed to keep me locked up and unable to investigate the shady goings-on of I-couldn't-even-remember-who. I'd always felt like I was doing the right thing. and I didn't *feel* insane, not even right up to the moment of the first Psylocybin pill sliding down my throat.

I guess nobody ever does feel actually insane; the way they are feels right, and it's everyone else who is insane. Normal people feel a little crazy sometimes, of course, but then they calm down after rationally considering the consequences of eating the face off the bus driver for being rude, or they get help. It was so strange that a part of my brain so small and evolutionarily primitive could have such a big effect on my life; it had made me insane and at the same time made me think I was the only normal one among millions of lunatics who just couldn't see the truth.

The nurse came to get me, and asked if there was anything I needed to bring along. I duly looked the room over, even though I had nothing there. I was leaving behind only the paranoid part of my past in that room, like a skin I had shed and crawled out of to emerge clean and new and slightly moist with mucous. As we walked away, I looked back for the penultimate time at room 21, and for a moment it seemed to me like it wasn't actually my room, like room 20 was the room they had put me in when I first came to the hospital. But as we walked away from the room which had been my home for weeks, I put that thought and the room out of my mind.

Chapter 10

My new room was like the Waldorf-Astoria compared to my previous room, which had been like a hole in the ground with only an empty turnip can for company, except without the turnip can because the sharp edges at the top might have been dangerous.

This room was still colored mainly cream, but there was a horizontal strip of blue that went all the way around the center of the wallpaper. I felt a slight shiver of pleasure at the new color.

There was a coat hook on the wall, which you could use to pluck somebody's eye out (not that I wanted to). The soap dispenser on the sink was made of metal, and you could crush someone's skull with it (not that I would). It was a validation of my progress so far that my nurses and doctors thought I'd be unlikely to either kill myself or kill someone else using common household objects. I tapped the window to check: it was glass; and through the potentially dangerous glass, I could see everything: grass, trees, the sun, a bird in a tree. It was actually good that the window in my previous room was frosted—if I'd seen that bird before Psylocybin was fixing my brain, I'd have worried that it was actually a hidden camera spying on me and I'd have been unable to look out the window anyway.

On the bedside table (wood, pointed edges) was a stack of neatly folded clothes and various accoutrements that looked very familiar, because they were my own possessions from before. My shoes were there, and they had the laces in them still, which was high praise for my mental state. I shrugged my hospital gown forward over my shoulders, letting it pile up on the floor, and stood naked in front of the mirror. I hadn't been taking Psylocybin for more than two weeks at that point, but I had already changed physically. My eyes were clear and bright, like the man in the third section of the NorCorp Psylocybin pamphlet. The patch of missing hair on my head had taken a few short steps towards regrowth. My face had the color a face should have, and the flesh had filled out around my previously sunken cheekbones and eyes. My body was still thin, but I looked less like someone who was kept up every night by eyes that refused to shut and a mouth that skipped potentially-tampered-with meals. I dressed in my old clothes, and put on my old shoes; in the mirror, I looked at me, but instead of me from a few weeks past I could have been looking at myself ten years before, looking healthy and happy. I put on my watch and checked the time, an unexpected luxury.

The door had clicked shut when the nurse left, but the handle turned easily; it was unlocked. I opened it a little and peered out into the hallway. No alarm went off, so I stepped out beyond the threshold. No burly orderlies came running, so my other foot came to join the more adventurous one. There were other open doors in the hallway, and I saw people lying on their beds reading books, writing letters at their desks, and talking with one another. It was impossible to tell that I was in a mental hospital.

I followed the hallway to the end and found myself in a communal area, with couches, chairs, tables, bookshelves, and other patients gathered around those things. I sat down at a nearly full table that had a single empty chair left, and listened in to their conversation. I soon learned that the people I was sitting with had also been recently moved to this area of the hospital and had just met each other that day, and it made me feel like less of a stranger to know that we were all strangers to each other. The conversation naturally drifted to the reasons each of us were there.

"Well, that's just the thing," one of my tablemates was saying, in response to a question from another, "the supermarket called in animal control because of the bags with holes gnawed in them, but when they followed the trail of dropped Cheese Snax to the maintenance closet they found only me, and I got passed from organization to institution until I ended up here. They said I had attachment disorder, but all I knew is that even after I lost my job there, the supermarket had seemed like the best place for me, and it felt impossible for me to leave."

The man who had asked the question nodded and said, "I understand what you mean, Dave. I had attachment disorder, but of a different kind, and I think mixed with some other kind of disorder, but I've tried to distance myself from it now that I'm getting better, so I don't even recall everything the doctor said. There was this hedgehog I found in the city—"

"In the city?" Dave interrupted, "But don't they need hedges?"

"You'd think so," the other man said, paused for a second and then changed his mind about further discussion on what habitats a hedgehog may or may not require, "but, look, I'm not a zoologist, I'm just saying I found this hedgehog. It's integral to the story, ok?" Dave nodded, and the other man continued. "So I found the hedgehog, and over time I came to feel that the hedgehog was a good friend. Eventually, I came to feel that the hedgehog was my best friend—it didn't go any farther than that because the hedgehog didn't find me attractive. I took the hedgehog into my house, it lived with me, and it went with me everywhere. It rode on my shoulder on the bus, that kind of thing. After many months, an unusual connection developed between me and the hedgehog, and it whispered things—or, I guess I should say now, I *thought* it whispered things—to me, sort of giving me advice, you know?"

"What kind of advice?" another man at the table asked. "What do hedgehogs know about? It's not as if it could give you advice about what stocks to pick, Jim, or which coats will be slimming to your figure," he said, giving Jim a friendly poke in the ribs. "Did you ask it for advice on which types of grass were the most delicious when on a long journey under the hedges?"

"Stanley, I've had enough of your friendly pokes," Jim said, edging away from Stanley and rubbing his sore ribs. "You know as well as any of us how serious this kind of thing is, even if it does sound funny. As it happens, it *did* give me advice on stocks, and it was good advice. But more importantly, I started to feel like it was giving me advice on what streets to go down, who was a good person, who to avoid."

"That hedgehog might have told you to sit on the other side of the table from Stanley," Dave put in with a grin.

"What's the deal with hedgehogs anyway?" Stanley asked. "Why don't they just share the hedge?"

Jim's face took on the look of a thin cardboard box left out in the rain. "Don't make fun about it, please," he said. "I know it sounds silly even when I try to talk about it seriously, and I know I'm better this way now, but I do miss Mr. Hodge. He was a friend to me through all things. He was very different from any friend I've ever had before or since." He looked back and forth between Stanley and Dave. "I guess that's the difference, that's why it was a crazy thing, because real friends aren't like that, they can be selfish, or… mean… I, uh, I think I'd better go to my room," he finished in a quiet voice and stood up from his chair.

"Now come on Jim, he didn't mean anything by it," Dave said, "sit back down, we'll talk about something else, won't we Stan?"

"Leave him be." Stanley held his hand out towards Dave to stop him. "We all need time sometimes to be alone and think; let him go to his room if he needs to."

I sat and listened to Dave and Stanley talk for a while, but I wanted to hear more about Mr. Hodge, so I went to find Jim. The central communal room had several long hallways leading off from it, and I walked partly down one of them before realizing that it would take a long time to find Jim that way, because many of the doors were closed and there were no names on the doors to show whose was whose. I went back to the central room and asked another patient if he knew which room was Jim's. He shrugged his shoulders, but when I said I was looking for the hedgehog guy he pointed me down one of the hallways to room 12. I knocked on the door to room 12 but there was no answer.

"Jim?" I called out, but there was still no answer. I turned the handle and found it unlocked, so I went in to see if Jim was home. When I opened the door, I saw Jim leaning away from the wall with shoelaces tied around his neck at one end and around a coat hook at the other end. His eyes turned to me and his mouth opened and closed a little, but no sound came out. Later, when I thought back to it, it seemed to me that he'd had the expression of a fish out of water, and I recalled that his face had been the color of beetroot humous. Memory can be a funny thing, sometimes, with what it decides is worth keeping. There are other things I should have remembered.

I went over to him, supported his weight with one of my arms and loosened the knots in the shoelaces with my free hand. I leaned him back against the wall, and he slid down to the floor until he was sitting, like standing was something he had simply given up on. A man came to the open doorway and said a brief, "Hey Jim, do you think—" before I closed the door in the middle of his question, being considerate of the lace marks on Jim's throat and the color of his face, things which most people would like to be kept private.

I'd heard enough of the conversation at the table to know he was missing his good friend, the hedgehog, who had probably been a better friend to him than I had ever had in my life. I didn't try to help, because only time could help with a loss like that; I just sat on the bed next to him to keep him company as he sat on the floor staring ahead through the opposite wall. The color of his face returned to normal after a couple minutes, and the marks on his neck faded a little, but he still didn't speak. I'm not sure exactly how long we sat like that, but after a while there was a knock at the door, and when I went to answer it, it was an orderly carrying two trays of food.

"One of the guys said you were in here too when I was bringing Jim's lunch, so I brought another tray for you," he said. He looked over my shoulder at Jim sat on the floor, but didn't say anything about him. I thanked the orderly, for more than the lunch, and though I knew that neither of us was hungry I set the trays on Jim's bedside table anyway. After a while, he did speak.

"Nobody knows—" he started, but a cough stopped him. His voice was a dry whisper because of how the laces of his shoes had compressed his windpipe. He took a glass of water from one of the trays and drank. He coughed again and massaged his throat as the water moistened it, and then he started to speak once more.

"Nobody knows what it's like. A lot of people in

here have lost friends, but they've lost them because of their condition. Now that they're better, they can get those friends back."

Even though he didn't know my circumstances, I felt guilty, because my lost friendships were ones I planned to be getting back as soon as I left the hospital.

"But for me," he said, "my friend *was* my condition, and now that I'm better I've lost the best friend I ever had." He continued talking but still sat looking straight ahead at the wall, or through the wall, like he'd be saying the same things even if I wasn't there. "It's a hard road for me to walk. Even though I know Mr. Hodge wasn't real—and I do know it, really, thanks to my medication—a big part of me just wants him back. So what if he's not real? They say that ignorance is bliss, and he made me *happy*. That was real happiness."

Jim smiled the shadow of a smile, and reminisced, "He had this way of pressing his paws down on my shoulder to comfort me whenever I was feeling sad—"

I looked at him when he stopped, and saw that a silent grimace of grief contorted his face. He leaned his head back and thin streams of sadness trickled from the corners of his eyes. He needed his best friend to comfort him, but he couldn't have that ever again, and that knowledge was pure pain. His face and his voice were like those of mourners at a funeral, and his friend was just as dead as the ones they mourned, killed by the medicine he needed.

I didn't know what to say, and I don't think there was anything I could have said that would help. I didn't know what he was feeling, and it would have been insulting to him and to the memory of Mr. Hodge if I'd tried. I stayed with him though, because just the presence of another being is enough to make you feel less lonely, even if it's not the presence of the one you're lonely for.

Jim's tears stopped flowing, as tears do, and he looked ahead once more, with red-rimmed eyes.

"What am I going to do once I'm outside?" he asked. "I'm going back in a few days, and I'm going to my brother's house where me and Mr. Hodge used to live together." The sadness in his voice was gone, but nothing had replaced it, so his voice was empty. "It's not that he's gone; he's still there. My brother's been taking care of him while I've been in here, so he'll be fine, but he's just a hedgehog. He'll probably put his little paws up against the glass and wiggle his nose at me, but he's just a hedgehog. That's what any animal would do with a human it recognized, one that brought it food and water and took it for walks; I won't see his eyes light up now, it won't be the recognition of a friend. He's just a hedgehog."

"You know," he said, looking at me for the first time, "they say even if I stopped taking Psylocybin, other parts of my brain would have compensated by now, so most likely Mr. Hodge wouldn't come back anyway; I'd just develop an attachment to something new, like a *cat*." He spat the word 'cat' out like a mouthful of rancid grease.

"Lots of cat owners say cats can be good friends, and a cat *can*, but it's nothing like a hedgehog. A cat is friendly in a hollow sort of way, like the way a prostitute is friendly."

I nodded in agreement, although I'd never been very friendly with a cat (or a prostitute[1]).

Jim went on. "And there's no guarantee it'd be a cat at all, there's no way to tell; I could just as easily develop an attachment to a potato. I'd probably even be happy, being friends with a potato. Can you imagine it: me sitting with a potato in my lap, stroking it, talking to it, asking it about the news?"

I could imagine it, but it didn't seem as funny as you might think. I didn't know what to say, and he didn't seem to have anything more to say, so we sat in silence. His sadness had leaked out of him through his tears and his words, and after a few more minutes I felt ok to leave him on his own.

"Jim," I wished I had said to him, once I was gone, *"I'm not going to pretend I know how you feel, because I haven't lost a good friend like you have. What I've lost instead is my purpose in life. I've lost all my goals; almost everything I know about myself has changed, and now I've got to start over, just like you. We can help each other; I can try to be a friend, and you can try to help me with a purpose. We can move on together."* I hadn't said it, though. I knew I was useless to him.

In the central room, Stanley and Dave were laughing and talking as they ate their lunch, unaware of the pain they had caused Jim, who sat silently only a few doors away. They hadn't meant to hurt him, but their callous,

---

Not that I've been mean to a prostitute (or a cat).

selfish behavior had done it anyway. My hands tightened and I discovered that I was still holding Jim's shoelaces, but they seemed better with me than him, so I just shoved them in my pocket. I started towards Stanley and Dave to say something about Jim, but I stopped and thought better of it; they must have had their own problems since they were in that place along with the rest of us; joking was just their way of dealing with whatever losses they had suffered. I asked one of the nurses to let Penelope know that I'd like to talk to her if she had time that day, and then I headed back to my room.

Back in my room, I looked through my possessions. Everything I'd had with me when I'd been arrested was there. There was my bag, which I went through. I took out some papers and diagrams I'd drawn, things I'd written as I thought I was tracking down the men who were behind the man in the heavy coat, behind Ron at the post office and Ron at Jack's Grocery Mart. I saw things I couldn't even remember writing. I had written 'Mom' above that shadowy group of men. At least I had circled her name with a dotted line, indicating uncertainty; in the greatest depths of my paranoia I hadn't even been sure who to be paranoid of, but that I had suspected my own mother meant that I was erring on the side of caution and simply being paranoid of everyone. I sighed and tore the papers in half, then in half again, and again. When I had shredded them enough, I dropped them in the wastebasket. It wasn't a perfect method of concealment—I could have eaten them, after all[1]—but it'd take quite an enthusiastic puzzler to put the hundreds of paper pieces back together, and in any case I wasn't paranoid enough anymore to think that someone might want to piece together some torn up bits of paper with nothing on them but the insane musings of a reformed maniac.

Among other things in the bag, I found gloves and a ski mask, which I took out and dropped in the wastebasket on top of the shredded paper. I had been like a child, playing secret agent, writing down gibberish and hiding behind bushes, pretending I was spying on important and sinister men, ready with gloves and a mask to conceal my identity.

What would my mother say about me, after everything? What would she say *to* me? Would she even want to speak to me again? In the middle of my feeling ridiculous about myself, there was a knock at the door.

"It's unlocked, because I'm not crazy anymore," I said to the door, and Penelope entered.

"How are you doing, Oscar? I heard that you've been around today, sitting and talking with some of the other guys. That sounds like good progress to me," she

---

[1] Paper isn't as bad as you might think. Each publisher has their own flavor because of where they source their wood pulp from, and each book from that publisher will have even further flavors which are subtle but still very distinct, based on the ink content, the vintage of the book, etc. Books are certainly an acquired taste (the hardbacks are especially difficult to swallow), but I think, as with all things, one can develop a taste for it. I encourage you to try it with this book once you have finished reading it, rather than putting it on the used book market. Unless you're reading this in ebook format.

said, smiling.

"It's a lot better than hiding under the tablecloth, nervously listening in," I agreed. "I feel almost like a different person because of how differently I react, how I perceive things. Instead of feeling threatened by people talking, I can join in and enjoy myself. I wanted to talk about how great things are, and to thank you for your help, but actually I'm kind of having some doubts. I feel like a fraud."

She raised her eyebrows questioningly, but didn't ask any questions. I took that as my cue to explain.

"I was out there, listening, talking, and almost making friends, right? But it feels like that isn't me. Jim was feeling down about his recovery, and I had no idea what to say to him. Who am I to help anyone with anything? I came back here and I found that." I pointed to gloves and mask I had thrown away on top of a pile of shredded paper. "That's the kind of thing I do, sneaking around in the shadows and pretending I'm making some kind of a difference. I haven't had any meaningful human contact for as long as I can remember, and trying to do it now makes me feel like a fake."

Saying that made me feel a powerful yearning for my family and my friends, for those times so far past that they now seemed to exist only in my memory. That feeling struck me suddenly, like a punch in the stomach; I almost felt sick, and paused to take a deep breath. "It's true that I don't feel paranoid anymore, and that is a big difference, but can I really have changed enough where I can share a genuine relationship with another person, where we can have mutual understanding?"

Penelope sat down next to me on the bed and looked thoughtful for a little while. I looked over to her and met her eyes, and she looked away quickly.

"Oscar," she said, turning back and looking into my eyes, "look at me, and listen. It *is* a big difference. All the years you were away from your family and your good friends weren't by your own choice, even though it might feel like you were choosing it. It's hard to believe anyone else can know what you're feeling, but *I* know. I felt the same things. Even after I was on Psylocybin, it was months before I was able to contact my family, partly out of the shame I knew I'd experience after facing them again, but also because I wondered even after that amount of time if I really had changed, or if perhaps I'd see them and just treat them with suspicion and coldness like I always had, when they'd never done anything to deserve it."

"When I finally did go to meet them, the whole family was there, and it was like a dam broke inside me. I nearly drowned in tears and happiness." I was looking into her eyes as she spoke, and tears shimmered at the rim of her eyelids. "My family wasn't judgmental or angry like I worried they'd be. They'd actually contacted the hospital while I was a patient here and found out about my condition, all the symptoms, how it made me behave, everything. When I got back they didn't treat me like a freak, they treated me like you'd treat anyone who was ill but got better. Your mind was broken in the same way as mine, Oscar, and nobody blames you for that. The way you treat everyone now is up to you, but the way you acted before Psylocybin wasn't your fault. It's really not your fault. It's not your fault."

Hot tears spilled down my cheeks when she finished. My family would be the same, they would understand my illness; thinking otherwise was just the weak parts of my mind manifesting their miserable power by making up excuses to avoid anything that might turn into an uncomfortable situation. Sometimes my whole mind seemed to be made of those weak parts due to a lifetime spent placating and soothing them, hiding from and avoiding actual life.

I was crying and couldn't get my vocal cords to work properly, but, as always, Penelope seemed to know how I felt anyway. She put her arms around me and pulled me close, holding me until I was at last finished shedding my tears. I moved away and drew in a deep, shaky breath.

"Thank you," I said, exhaling. "Thank you for everything. Thank you for coming here today to help me through this; I couldn't have done it on my own." She handed me a tissue to blow my nose; I thanked her for that too. "I wouldn't have taken Psylocybin if you hadn't convinced me to. And if you hadn't convinced me to, then I'd still be in the old room in the security wing feeling like everyone was against me. I could have spent my whole life that way, but instead I feel like you've saved my life, you've made me 'me' again."

"Before the help and care you gave me, I was too caught up in my own problems to be of any use to anyone, but you've given me back my ability to help others. I'm going to try to pass that on." I wasn't totally sure if I should say what I said next, but I did say it. "Jim tried to kill himself. I went into his room and barely caught him in time." I reached into my pocket and held up his shoelaces. "I probably shouldn't have even left his room afterwards, but he talked to me for a while about how much he missed Mr. Hodge, and after that he seemed too physically and mentally drained to even have the will for trying it again, so it seemed alright. Plus, I've got his shoelaces."

"Hang on," Penelope said. "I'll get one of the other nurses to check on him right now to be sure." She pressed the nurse call button on my wall, and after only a few seconds, another nurse came into the room. Penelope talked with her in low tones so I couldn't hear what they were saying. Before, I would've felt like they were talking about me or maybe even planning a way to pin Jim's suicide attempt on me, but my medicine helped me to stand patiently. Soon the other nurse was gone, and Penelope resumed our conversation.

"Thanks for telling me," she said. "Don't feel bad about leaving him on his own; it was good of you to listen to him when he was feeling at his worst, and often that's all anyone needs when they're going through such a dark time, they just need someone to listen and understand." That made me feel a little better. I didn't feel like I had understood Jim's feelings, but at least I had listened to them.

"He probably told you that he was supposed to go

home soon," she continued, "but he'll need to stay here for a little longer now." Some of my dismay must have shown on my face, because she smiled at me. "Don't worry, he won't be going back to the security wing. He'll stay here, he'll still be able to socialize and live normally. It's for his own safety that he'll need to stay longer, and probably not very long, maybe just a few more weeks. He's not the first patient I've seen with attachment personality disorder, and people with his condition always have some of the hardest times adjusting to normal life after having experienced the security of such a preternatural bond to someone—or something. We'll talk with him and work with him until he's ready to handle being outside again and dealing with normal flawed human relationships."

She moved closer to me on the bed. "I'd really like to talk about you, though," she said. "That's why I came here. Today is your last day in the hospital, and I think you're ready for it to be the last. Don't let the doubts you had about today worry you; it's normal for most people to have occasional struggles with self-confidence, and you're normal, so you're going to have those same struggles too. What's also normal is to pick up your bruised emotions after you've dropped them, and then hold them up high again. But if you feel like those feelings are too heavy to hold up on your own and you worry you might be crushed underneath them, don't forget you can come here and speak to Dr. Boggs. Or…" she looked down for a moment before continuing, "You could always call me, too. I know what it's like for you, and I think I could help. Maybe we could help each other, since you're not technically my patient anymore. We could, you know." She moved to pass her contact card to me, but clumsily dropped it into my lap and then promptly stood up. She smoothed out her skirt, curtly said, "Good luck, Mr. Well," and then left my room after stumbling over my shoes.

I picked up the card and looked at it. My fingertips stroked the raised texture of the name 'Penelope Hope' in curly script, and I saw that her phone number was also printed on the card. What had she meant, that we could help each other? I thought that maybe she was flirting with me, but it was very difficult for me to tell things like that. I hadn't had a lot of experience with flirting, and my own attempts at it usually left me embarrassed and fleeing the room with a red face and a stuttered goodbye excuse, probably after stumbling over something. My girlfriends had always been of the type who were very forward themselves to make up for my lack of skill at courtship; someone's hand in your pants leaves no room for doubt.[1] It seemed unlikely as I thought about it more; after all, she had given me her number in case I needed help with my mental condition, not just to chat or arrange a dinner date. "Hi, I'm having an attack of paranoia and I'm not able to leave the bathroom because of it," isn't the best of ways to start a conversation with a girl. I reminded

---

[1] My attempts to carry on what I thought was a relationship with a Transportation Security Administration officer after an airport security screening were, however, met with a series of rebuffs and a rather rude restraining order. I guess every rule has an exception.

myself again that she was a professional, but as I went to sleep that night, I allowed myself to hope, for Penelope Hope.

The next day, after taking my morning dose of Psylocybin, I packed my things into two bags and made ready to leave the Maple Ridge part of my life behind. The only person besides Penelope I knew well enough to want to say goodbye to was Jim, so I went to find him instead. Everything was still the same in his room, except his shoes had been exchanged for the slip-on kind with no laces.

"Well, Jim, this is it for me," I said to him. "I'm leaving in a few hours, so I've just come to say goodbye."

"Good luck on the outside, Oscar," he said, looking down at his shoes for a moment. "I've got to stay a few more weeks; I guess they found out about what happened yesterday." There was no edge to his voice or accusation in his eyes as he said it. He knew, but he wasn't angry, and that was a relief to me. "Thank you. For listening yesterday, I mean. And thank you for telling them; otherwise I probably wouldn't be here right now. I do feel a little better today, and… that's something," he said, lifting the sadness from his face to reveal a small smile.

"I'll still be out pretty soon, they tell me; just a week or two maybe, that's not so long. Why don't you come around to my brother's place when I'm out? You know," he said, "my brother is the only one who ever really believed me about Mr. Hodge. Not that he has a mental disorder himself, because he hasn't; he just always believes me and trusts me. If I said it, he'd just say, 'Alright, Jim,' and that was that. Anyway, come by sometime when I'm out. It'd be good for us to be able to talk to each other, to talk to someone with shared experiences. Maybe we could help each other." He gave me his address and I wrote it down on a piece of paper which I put in my pocket. Maybe we could help each other. Maybe I wasn't as useless as I thought. When I got home, though, the paper with his address went into a drawer in the kitchen, along with the shoelaces I had taken from him the day before. The usual detritus of everyday life accumulated in the drawer after I'd been back at home for a few days, and the paper got pushed further back in the drawer. I'm getting a little ahead of myself, though; we'll come back later to that drawer and the note in it.

They escorted me out of Maple Ridge later that morning in a van—probably the same van that had brought me there months before. I sat sideways in my seat and looked out the rear windows as Maple Ridge Psychiatric Hospital shrank in the distance. Within seconds, the forest of maples had closed in around it, and all that was visible of the hospital was the road leading up to it.

The van reached my house, and the orderly who had ridden along in the van courteously carried my bag to the door for me. I thanked him for his help, and he handed me the bag. He said, "Goodbye, Mr. Well," and then I was alone with the sounds of the van fading in the distance.

Chapter 11

I opened the door and went inside my house. Everything was nearly the same as it had been before, which was a little disconcerting. I don't know what I had expected I might find. Homeless men no longer being actually homeless on account of taking up residence in my home? Goblins scuttling across the floor, maybe? Cobwebs, for sure. There was none of that, though. It was just my house. I flipped the light switch, and the lights came on. The hospital and my insurance company must have arranged to take care of all the bills in my absence. A huge stack of mail, several months' worth, was on the table. The floor was dusty, and, ah—there were faint shoe prints in the dust. That wasn't anything to worry about, though. Obviously, the insurance company must have had someone come around to check on the house, move the mail, chase away any house-squatting goblins, that kind of thing, while I was away. It was about time I got such good service. I had been was starting to think that insurance was a scam after years of paying a large premium every month for various types of insurance and yet never having had a single burglary or kidnapping or dismemberment happen to me, but at last my insurance was actually useful.

I went down the hallway, and saw that the bathroom door was open. The doorway to my bedroom—where I had kept the pictures and other information on the wall about the mysterious group of men I'd thought I was closing in on—was also open, and the dusty shoe prints went right in through the open doorway. Of course, they must have needed to check every room, because sometimes people left a pet alone in their office if they were suddenly taken to prison or the hospital, and that pet would be scrabbling anxiously at the door waiting to be let out because it didn't want to poop on the floor and upset the master. I didn't have any pets, but you can never be too careful, that's what my insurance agent always said. Besides, the pet insurance was only a few dollars a month and the current offer wouldn't last long, so I would have been a fool not to take advantage of it. Now who's the fool?

On the floor in my bedroom, the footprints led directly to the main wall, where all the photos, drawings, and notes had been torn down. That made sense too; the hospital had sent word to my insurance company about things that might trigger my paranoia, and they had taken care of it to ready the house for my return. The papers had been on the wall so long that the places where some of them had been were surrounded by rectangles of dust, and the wall behind was bright and pristine, shining through like the ghost of the paper which had hung there.

Some bits of paper—corners, mostly—still clung to the glue or tape which had held them, unwilling to go where the rest had gone. There were pieces of sentences you could still see on those abandoned papers; a lone noun here, an adverb lying forlornly there with no verb left to modify. There was a circle drawn on the wall in red marker, like it had been around something important, but I couldn't remember what.

I had covered that wall with papers and photos, but I couldn't imagine myself doing it. The Psylocybin in my body was causing my brain to function properly for the first time, and I was no longer capable of producing the feelings or entertaining the paranoid thoughts required to put so much effort into making those senseless connections between people and events and recording it all here in my bedroom office. When I remembered it, it was like remembering a movie with an unrealistic character who had papered the wall with suspicion. I would give that movie three stars. Four, at the most. Out of ten.

There was no way to piece together the small bits of information still on the wall, but instead of loss, I felt relief. I had worked hard to create the wall, but there was nothing on it for me now, and everything could be new, everything could be the way it was supposed to be. I hammered a nail into the wall and hung up a picture of my family which had been lying face-down on the floor.

I sorted through the huge stack of mail on the table—some of which had been opened (by the insurance company, to get information necessary to pay bills). Next, I made out a list of family and friends I wanted to talk to, with Winslow at the top.

"Hello?" he answered, on the first ring. I hadn't planned what to say, and there were so many things I wanted to say that they couldn't get past each other and all got caught in my throat. It was good to hear his voice again. "Hello, who is this?" he asked, and then he hung up on me. I stood, still holding the phone against my head; this wasn't exactly how I'd thought it might go. After a few moments, I called back. It was eight or nine rings that time, but he did answer at last. "I don't know who you are, but I've already called the cops," he said, in a shaky voice.

"Winslow, it's me," I said.

Silence. Breathing. "Oscar? Oscar, is that you?"

"It's me," I said, because although I don't enjoy repeating myself it is important for people to know who you are.

"How?" he asked. "They said it'd be a year before you came back."

"I've actually been better for a few weeks, but I only got to come back home today; they wanted to keep me for that extra time just to be sure."

"That's great, but… is it really… you?" He sounded unsure if it was ok to ask.

"It's really me. I'm taking Psylocybin, except I'm *actually* taking it this time. I haven't had an actual paranoid thought since last month."

"That reminds me," he said, 'I haven't actually called the cops. I thought someone had broken in and was using your phone. I just wanted to scare away whoever it was." A pause, long enough for me to pull the phone away from my ear and look at it to see if the call was dropped, but I put it back to my ear just in time to hear Winslow saying, "How do you feel, then? I mean, you said you haven't had a paranoid thought in a while, but, uh, *really*? It's hard to believe, because the last time I saw you, you thought I was basically working with Satan to kill you."

"That's a little bit of an exaggeration—more like working with Stan." I felt like I deserved that anyway, or at least I had expected it. "Winslow," I said, "It's important for me that you understand it wasn't really *me* thinking that about you. I have a medical condition that makes my brain work differently, and it's only my new medicine that guides my neurons down the right path. There's a lot involved, and I'll explain all the details to you at lunch or something. The important thing is that I don't feel that way anymore. I know you were just helping me, and it must have been incredibly difficult because I didn't even appreciate your help at the time, and actually the more you helped the more I suspected you."

"I want you to know, now," I continued. "I do appreciate it. Without your help, I know I'd still be in prison right now. I wouldn't even know that I had a mental problem that needed treatment, and I'd just think it was all a conspiracy against me—a conspiracy that you were in on. But you let the guard know, and he let his boss know, and he let the Maple Ridge people know, and now I can actually enjoy a normal life, all thanks to you." My chest was tight with emotion as I spoke, and my eyes burned. "Every day I've been thinking about what to say to you, about how much I owe you, but I still don't know what to say, I can't explain it. I owe you everything, Winslow. You're my friend, and you brought me back," I finished, as my tears overflowed my eyes.

"Thank you," he whispered, through his own tears. "Thank you. That makes me feel better than anything else you could have said. I've worried that maybe you still felt the same as you did when you left, that perhaps you'd grown to hate me or even to think of me as your enemy. I've been your friend all along, Oscar, and all I wanted was for you to know that and to have you as my friend again, too."

Afterwards, I sat down against the wall, holding the phone and smiling between two streaks of tears. I had braced myself against him being angry, hurt, and defensive; I was prepared for anything other than him being kind and understanding. But he was willing to let my bizarre paranoid behavior go, because he knew it hadn't really been me doing it, and to accept me as his friend. Penelope was right about how understanding people could be. I was lucky to have a friend like him, and I hoped it would go as well when I spoke to everyone else.

Chapter 12

I had quit my last job years before because I suspected several of my co-workers were plotting to put a tracking chip in me while I was napping on break, but I still had substantial savings, because I had been paranoid about buying any new products and so most of my lifetime earnings sat in the bank collecting interest. Nearly everything in my house had been there for ten years or more. If something broke, I repaired it myself, and if I couldn't repair it then I'd do my best to find something to replace it from a charity store or antique store, because most new products have radio frequency ID chips installed in them—but you probably already knew that.

My savings wouldn't last forever though, especially now that I wasn't paranoid and would be able to buy things like a new toaster even knowing it had an RFID chip in it. Perhaps I'd even get one of the hi-tech ones that allows for precision selection between perfectly delicate shades of toasting, each shade more delicately toasty than the last. And since my savings wouldn't be lasting forever, I'd need to get a job. That thought fluttered into my mind, light and airy like a butterfly[1], and it hit me

[1] A misleading name for an insect which is neither part butter nor part fly, and certainly not any kind of flying butter as the name might suggest. When I was young, I used to enjoy eating raw butter, and you can imagine my great disappointment the first time I put a butterfly in my mouth. I say 'the first time', because I thought maybe that one had just gone off a bit, so I tried again. And again. Actually after a while I sort of developed a taste for them to the point where I began to be disappointed that *butter* didn't taste more

again how different my thought process had become after just a few weeks of Psylocybin. Months ago, if any part of my mind had suggested getting a new job, my whole existence would have been filled with a nameless dread[1] and I would have imagined a million fearful reasons for huddling in a corner with the lights out instead.

The next day I took my Psylocybin and fetched a newspaper, then spent all morning poring over the want ads, glorying in each new job I read about, jobs that I wouldn't feel terrified about having, that I'd be able to go to each weekday, jobs sitting at desks where I could have conversations with co-workers about things like Last Night's Big Game, jobs standing at counters serving customers and not worrying that the money they were handing me was being handed by a master assassin at just such an angle so as to cause paper cuts[2], jobs at zoos, jobs as salesmen, jobs doing plenty of things that I could—and maybe would—do.

Of all the ads on the page, one job ad in particular stood out. They could have printed it just for me:

---

like *butterflies*, and I don't think it's boasting to say that I'm largely responsible for keeping the United State's population of butterflies down to manageable levels. Without my help they would surely consume us all.

[1] Although, were it to have had a name it would have been a name like Butch or Biff. Maybe Billy Bob, but probably not because that can also be a friendly kind of name in addition to being the name of a backwoods serial killer.

[2] Which might not seem like much to worry about, but a paper cut not properly treated can lead to infection which can lead to illness which can lead to death. I don't think it ever has (the medical literature on the subject of death by paper cut is spotty at best), but it could. And even if it doesn't, paper cuts still hurt a lot.

Need motivated self-starter for stay-at-home job
Technical writer, need previous training/exp
Be your own boss, work your own hours
Med/dental after 60 days - 2 wk pd vction/yr

I'd taken one course of technical writing in high school, which probably wasn't as much training or experience as they wanted (more than I had as a zookeeper, though), but I did pretty well in that course and I could be convincing enough to get my foot or hand or some other body part in the door far enough that they couldn't close it, and then I'd have them. The thing that most drew my eye to the ad was that you could work from home and set your own hours. It wasn't the most socially forward of jobs, but it would be a good first step, and after all, there was no need to test myself in every paranoia-inducing situation just yet, because I'd been discharged from a mental hospital less than twenty-four hours before. I figured I'd probably be interacting with a boss and probably a few co-workers over the phone, through e-mails and instant messaging, which was a good way to just dip my toe into the social waters without getting soaked or drowned or eaten by a shark[1].

---

[1] Not an actual shark, it's just a metaphor. The Psylocybin had made it so that I wasn't paranoid that a shark might eat me (which is a feeling I used to get even while swimming in an enclosed public swimming pool, and also, when I was younger, a feeling I used to get while in the bathtub), and I knew that it was extremely unlikely for anyone to be eaten by a shark, or even to be bitten by one. In fact, you're much more likely to be struck by lightning than to be bitten by a shark, but people generally seem more afraid of sharks than of lightning. People even use lightning strikes as an example of how unlikely you are to win the lottery ("You're more likely to be struck by lightning than win the lottery, stop wasting your money on those tickets and

I called for more information and they said they had an interview slot open in an hour because they'd just had a cancellation. I leapt into action, into my car, and across town to Global Partners & Associates. They were located in a rentable storage unit (the kind with the roll-up door), and while I'm pretty sure it isn't legal to run a business out of a storage unit, I'm not a lawyer, so I wasn't going to question their business methods. Also, "they" is a generous term, because it was just one filing cabinet which was behind a guy who was behind a desk. I guess everyone has to start somewhere, and perhaps this guy was like Jim (except at least Mr. Hodge had a pulse) and considered the filing cabinet and desk to be his associates. So as not to offend him, I started off by saying "Hello, gentlemen," and nodding around the room. He opened the file cabinet and got a drink for himself and me from it, and the interview then opened with the usual questions.

"How many rooms are in your house, Mr. Well? Which room would you work in, were you to receive this position?" This, to know if I'd be distracted, say, by working in the living room near my fish tank. Or, if they gave me any expensive equipment to use at home, would I take it into the bath with me and possibly drop it in

---

come back to bed, it's 3 in the morning, you'll wake up the baby, you're not wearing any pants, etc.!"), and it's true—almost 25,000 people a year are struck by lightning, and several thousand of those strikes are fatal. However, you never hear that you're *more* likely to win the lottery than you are to be eaten by a shark, because thousands of people a year win various lotteries and only around 20 people are killed by sharks, which makes you feel pretty good about life when you think about it—you're more likely to be fabulously/filthy rich than to be mercilessly savaged to death by an emotionless sea monster, which isn't a bad way for the universe to have organized things.

while scrubbing my toes.

"Do you have any moles, birth marks, or other distinguishing features?" In case of an industrial accident, if my face were mutilated they'd still be able to identify me.

"Are you worried that if you take this position we'll read your emails, know your whereabouts, and generally monitor your every move, even knowing your heart rate while you're asleep and how many times each day you urinate?" That was just weeding out the crazies; I knew that all successful companies did the same sort of micromanagement of your biological functions[1], so of course I wasn't worried, and I told him so.

"Alright, everything's fine with him," he said, to nobody; I even looked behind me to be sure, which confirmed my suspicion that his associates (and I write this while doing air quotes with my fingers) were the desk and filing cabinet. I didn't want to screw up the interview though, so I said nothing and kept a smile in front of my face; I could always bring it up later, once they had hired me and employee protection laws covered me.

"You're hired, Oscar," he said, "I think you're just perfect for the position we have in mind." He took a

---

[1] I read in the New York Times that years ago Microsoft allowed employees one bathroom break per eight hours. If you needed to go more often than that, you had to take a vacation day. They had an armed guard posted at each urinal and stall to enforce it. They had to stop the practice after certain powerful companies in the urinal cake market accused them of holding a monopoly over urine and the International Court of Justice ruled against them and threatened to break the company up into several smaller software, hardware, and bathroom companies if they didn't change their business practices. That's what I read, anyway.

picture of me, took my fingerprints, had me look into a machine to scan my retinas, took a blood sample, and took a few strands of my hair as well, "for security reasons." It was a hassle, but of course I wanted to be secure.

He opened a different drawer of the file cabinet and took out a laptop computer, a phone, and a set of business cards that already had my name on them. I wondered if the file cabinet actually had any files in it at all, but I supposed there was no rule against using a file cabinet for general storage.

When I left, he rolled the door up. I looked down at the business cards. I had a job.

Chapter 13

I set the laptop up on the desk in my spare room, which was now going to be my office. I put the business cards on display in a business card holder next to the laptop. The phone I kept in my pocket; it was important for GP&A to reach me at any time, because he'd said "they" would contact me with details about what I needed to do. I used the laptop to search for the company on the internet, but I came up with nothing, not even a 'coming soon' banner; the company was either too new or too small to have any sort of web[1] presence. I checked my business card to be sure; there was no web address there. I wanted to be able to tell people, "I work for Global Partners & Associates," and when they said they hadn't heard of them, I'd say, "Oh, you haven't? Well, they're pretty global. There are a *lot* of associates. Why don't you check out their website?" They'd go to the website and be blown away that I was an associate to such prestigious global partners. There needed to be a website for that to happen, though. I decided that while I was waiting for one of the partners from GP&A to call me and let me know what my job was actually supposed to be, I'd use my free time to create a website for us.

I registered globalpartnersandassociates.com, which I know is a long and boring web address that most internet

---

[1] I hate saying 'web,' but I guess it's better than 'net,' so I don't complain too much.

users would only get halfway through typing before giving up and looking at pictures of cats instead, but gpa.com was already taken, and I wasn't going to settle for a .net or .biz address like a homeless alcoholic might have to. I spent a while looking for a good stock image of a few important-looking people standing around in business suits looking at the camera; when I found the right picture I put 'Global Partners & Associates' on it in a serious font, and put that picture on the front page of the website.

After lunch—which, thanks to my medication, I did not eat while hiding under a blanket—I got back to work on the website. I created a page for partners and a page for associates. I dithered over whether I should make myself a partner or an associate—was I as good at my job or as important to the company as a file cabinet was? My business cards settled it; I looked to them for guidance and saw *Junior Associate* under my name. It wasn't the best title but it did leave room to grow; in time I could move up to Associate, and then Senior Associate, and perhaps, at last, VP of Associates; once I was VP they'd probably put my name in the running for Global Partner. That wasn't all happening yet, so I used the webcam to get a picture of myself for the Associates page, and listed myself as a Junior Associate, with a biography of a few paragraphs which left out my short stay in a mental hospital but mentioned my collection of hats, so people didn't think I was all business all the time.

Before Psylocybin, I would have never put information like that on the internet—what if a hat admirer who was searching the internet for new information about hats saw my biography, decided that he wanted the hats for himself, cross-referenced my picture to something[1] to find out my address, waited until I was at work, smashed my window or my door, hid in my closet, and rubbed his body all over my hats? With the aid of Psylocybin, I realized that it was an extremely unlikely thing to happen, so after I wrote and published my biography to the internet I just did the sensible thing and taped a hair over my hat closet door so that if I ever did happen to go for opening the door and saw that the hair had been dislodged, I'd call the police; I wouldn't be caught unawares by the grunting, mostly-unclothed man in my closet, squatting down over an upturned, unwilling bowler hat with his genitals resting inside it against the soft, cool, velvet interior.

You might think that sort of person doesn't exist. Maybe you suspect my Psylocybin wasn't working anymore, that I was just being paranoid. And so maybe you'd say to me, "Nobody likes hats that much," but I've been an internet user since 1995 and I've seen things you wouldn't believe (so I won't list them here, because you wouldn't believe them and it would be a waste of my time and your time, and my time especially does not care to be wasted because I'm a Junior Associate in an important—a *global* – company; perhaps you've seen my biography on their website; you haven't? well here's my card, educate yourself); uninvited male house guests *in* hats being among the least of them. I was simply being practical.

Around quitting time—2PM, because I was my own

[1] I'm not clear exactly how that would be done, but I'm sure there are databases you can use.

boss and was setting my own hours—there came a knock at the door. I peeped through the peephole and was disappointed to see that it was a man in a suit. Someone not wearing a suit might be selling doughnuts for a church fundraiser, and that's always a good day. I saw that he had a large suitcase on wheels, though, and it seemed the right size for doughnuts, so I took a chance and opened the door.

"Good afternoon, sir," he said. "My name is Wallace, and I'm sorry to interrupt your work but I'm here to install the equipment."

"I didn't order any equipment, and I don't need any," I said. I was familiar with this roundabout pitch. They pretended you'd ordered something, or maybe that they got the wrong address, but since they're already out with their big heavy suitcase would you mind if they demonstrated their product to you so it wasn't a wasted day for them? "I don't want any, either." Then, I thought I'd been too quick in denying the unknown product, and said, hopefully, "Unless you have some doughnuts."

"Sorry, I'm not selling doughnuts. I'm not selling anything; Ron sent me." Wallace began to look doubtful. "You are Oscar Well, aren't you?" He waved my business card away as I handed it towards him, and said, "I'm with Global Partners & Associates. I guess Ron didn't tell you earlier, but this equipment is supposed to be installed in your office."

"Oh, my apologies," I said, and explained, "I usually get Mormons. Or vacuum cleaner salesmen." Ron from the storage unit hadn't told me anything about this—he hadn't even told me his name was Ron, although that didn't seem important—but it always impresses people when you can say 'see this big expensive thing? I got it from work because I'm so important,' so I said, "Come in, I'll show you where to put it."

Once we were in my office, he unlocked his case and took out several things that were all wires and buttons and circuit boards. He got a screwdriver and began putting them together, until it was what looked like a bulky, ugly surveillance camera along with a wireless transmitting unit. I asked him what it was, and he said it was a surveillance camera with a wireless transmitting unit. He attached it to my office wall with large, thick screws, and asked if I did my work at the desk with the laptop. I said yes, and he adjusted the camera angle to point directly at the laptop.

"Isn't this…" I started to say, but then stopped. I wasn't really sure. I asked, "Aren't I my own boss?"

"Yes, of course you are," he said.

"Well, who's watching me then? My boss isn't, because I'm my own boss. If I want to watch myself, I'll set up a mirror."

"That's really just a figure of speech. They said the same thing to me when they gave me this equipment installation job. 'Be your own boss, install what you like, *et cetera*.' But you know you're not literally your own boss, because you get a paycheck from someone else, right? You're your own boss in the sense that you set your own hours and you decide where you work." He saw me looking at the camera, and said, "Well, that is, you decide where you work as long as it's within the field of view of this camera. It's one hundred and eight degrees though, so you get plenty of room to move about."

"You don't need to be worried about it; the camera isn't there for any unscrupulous purposes. GP&A has given you valuable equipment," he said, tilting his head towards the laptop and maybe towards the business cards, "and they just want to be sure that nothing happens to it. If you think about it, it's really like having an extra home security system that is self-contained and wireless, so nobody can cut the power or the transmission line. And it's not as if the camera is in your bedroom, right? Although, that reminds me, I'm supposed to put up a unit each in the kitchen and living room." I felt dismay when he said that—more of those ugly things all over my house? "They take up a lot less space because they don't have their own transmitting unit, they communicate with this one and then it sends all the video back at the same time."

"That's good," I said, relieved, as he held up one of the little cameras for me to see. They were small enough to fit in the palm of his hand and had a rounded, stylish design. "The smaller ones do look very nice. Are you sure you can't put one in my bedroom?"

My concerns about the cameras were taken care of, but I had other things I wanted to find out from him. "When I went for the interview, there was only Ron there, and the place looked so sparse with only that desk and filing cabinet that I thought he was the only person at GP&A. Now you're here; is there anyone else?"

"Oh yeah, there are others," he said. "There are lots of us; we're all over. That storage unit thing is just a local recruiting station for whenever headquarters needs someone taken care of around here."

I was satisfied with his answers, and I showed him out.

After, I walked through the house to check out my new cameras. The smaller units were actually quite cute. They had three curved legs which attached directly to the wall; that, along with the way their white bodies curved beneath the lens into a sort of smile made them look like happy little spiders watching over me[1]. I remembered what Wallace had said about it being like an extra security system and felt pleased; I could be grating carrots in the kitchen and if I accidentally slipped and grated my nose off before hitting my head on the edge of the counter and knocking myself unconscious, they'd alert the proper authorities who'd have about a 50/50 chance of saving me before I bled to death from my face. Everything seemed to be in order with my new job, even though I didn't yet know what my new job actually was, but I decided that rather than wait around for a call from Ron, I'd get on with reconciling things with my family and friends.

It had gone fine with Winslow, but next I had to talk with my parents. The days of shutting myself up in the clothes dryer when they came to knock on my door were over though, so I shut the door to the laundry room and put some furniture in front of it, cutting off my last refuge, and called my mom. She sounded happy to hear from me, and said she and my dad would love to come

---

[1] Some people would find that creepy, but spiders rarely cause any harm towards humans and they eat all sorts of truly harmful insects such as the flesh fly, which spends its working day walking around in rotting meat and its leisure time walking around on your food which can result in you getting leprosy or some other displeasing disease, as well as looking out for any chance to lay its maggot eggs inside any open wounds you may have. Spiders are really just free pest control, and you should welcome them into your home; at least they won't give you leprosy.

over for dinner that night.

Chapter 14

It felt good to be making food for my parents, being careful not to knock myself unconscious or grate any parts of my body off while getting the carrots ready[1]. I couldn't remember the last time I had made a meal for someone, because for years I hadn't trusted anyone to come farther into my house than the living room, not even Winslow. The doorbell rang just as I turned the stove burner on under the spaghetti sauce, and I experienced another new sensation. Not a burning sensation, as you might suggest (I know how you like to make jokes at my expense), but eagerness to open the door and welcome visitors into my home. I turned the burner down on low, said a silent thank you to Psylocybin for giving me my life back, and opened the door to greet my parents. Up until this point I haven't described my parents, because there was no need to, and there's still no need to; you know how I look, and both of my parents look more or less like me.

They came inside, and we sat down together in my living room. They stared at me, and I stared at them. It had been years since we talked at all, and even longer since I had been properly sociable towards them. But they were my parents, and they seemed to have no trouble talking to me, even with that long distance of time

---

[1] I don't want you to get the impression that I'm always grating parts of my body off. I'm not. It happened once, alright? Let's move past it.

between us. I could feel the love in their voices and in their eyes, like I had never caused them any trouble and never treated them badly. They had given me so much, and I had given so little back. Instead, I had taken more, and more, until when I was at last getting old enough to give back, I had fully given in to my overactive amygdala and had cut all connections to them, so they never got to enjoy the harvest of a pleasant adult child who should be their rightful reward after years of particularly heavy toil in the fields of parenthood. I looked away from them. My nose was burning. Was I to experience a different type of shame every time I spoke with an old friend or family member? I deserved the shame, even though I had been told I didn't by Penelope and others who understood my condition, but even so, I didn't know if I could stand the constant ups and downs of this shame and reconciliation within myself. I was lost in thought, but then my father spoke and brought me back.

"Oscar," he said, "your mother and I have talked a lot about you, and we both feel the same way." I looked meekly towards my father to give my attention to what he had to say. I would bear it, whatever it was. "I won't say it hasn't been hard. It has been hard, very hard. But we've spoken with your doctor at the Maple Ridge and we know it wasn't your fault. I can tell that you don't quite believe that. I've spoken to your nurse, Ms. Hope, and she tells me the same thing, that you're getting better, that you took the big step of realizing you were sick, but that even after what they've told you, you haven't been fully willing to accept that it wasn't truly *you* and you're not responsible for the things you did before you started taking your medication."

Penelope and Dr. Boggs had both told me the same thing, several times: none of it was my fault, because I was basically a new person after Psylocybin. But it definitely *felt* like me doing all those things. It wasn't just that I had done them, no; I would have been able to accept that and move past it. What really crouched behind my eyes and gnawed at my mind was that I had *wanted* to do those things. I stalked a man and killed him on his own property. I nearly beat another man to death, a man who was trying to help me. I hadn't wanted to hurt them so badly, but I had wanted to hurt them. Dr. Boggs showed me pictures of the orderly I had attacked, and I was shocked that I had caused so much damage, even in denial that I had beaten him so severely, but I still didn't regret it. Psylocybin made me feel sorry that I had killed a man, and sorry that I had sorely wounded another, but I still couldn't get rid of the feeling that it was what I had wanted at the time and that if it happened all over again I would still want it because it was the right thing to do.

I couldn't explain all that to my parents, though. Even though they were understanding about my mental condition, I wasn't sure if they knew about the violent things I had done, or what they would think if they knew I felt like I could still want to do the same things. Instead, I replied more simply. "It felt like me, Dad. I can't disassociate myself from the things I did. Even if I was under the influence of something else, it was still me that wouldn't call Mom back even when she left a crying voicemail; it was still me that broke into your house and rifled through everything in your office."

"That was you?"

"It was. I assumed you knew it was me." I felt a little

sheepish at having revealed it was me since they didn't already know.

"But—" my father began.

My mother burst into the conversation with, "There were possum tracks!"

"That's right," he said. "There were possum prints all over the floor, all over my papers."

"And there were possum teeth marks on the door jamb, Lindley," she said, using my father's first name. "The police said they had never seen anything like it."

"That was me," I said. "I was picking splinters out of my teeth for days."

"My peanuts were gone," my father said, mournfully. "That possum took my peanuts."

"Dad, there was no possum. I took your peanuts."

"The police said that a large trained possum with a taste for peanuts must have escaped from the circus or someone's private collection and smelled the peanuts from outside. Do you remember that, Maria?" They were looking at each other, having this possum conversation and not paying attention to the pertinent facts I was adding. She nodded that she did remember, and continued the possum investigation tale from where he left off.

"They weren't really clear on what happened after that," she said, "but it seemed to me that the possum must have picked the lock with his teeth, read through all our important papers out of simple marsupial curiosity, and absconded with the peanuts."

"Mom, Dad, listen to me," I said. "I was that possum."

They both turned to me. My mother had a worried look.

"Oscar," my father said, "you listen to *me*, son. You are not, and have never been, a possum. Maria, call the doctor so he can tell Oscar he was never a possum."

"Oh Lord, Mother," I said, taking the phone away from her as she started to dial.

"Maybe it's a side effect of his medication," she said to my father. "When I was taking Ambien, it sometimes made my toes tingle as I was falling asleep." Then, to me, "Do you feel any tingling, Oscar?"

"I'm not tingly. I know I've never been a possum. It was me that read your papers and took your peanuts, though."

"Did the possum let you in?" my mother asked, thinking about believing me.

"There was never any possum."

"But there *were* possum tracks, Oscar, so there was a possum," my father said. "Have you seen the crime scene photos? Possum tracks all over the place. I have copies at home if you want me to bring them."

"I need a drink. Does anyone else want anything?" I asked, as I headed for the kitchen.

"Look it up on Facebook, Oscar," my mother called after me. "They're in your father's possum album."

I came back with two glasses of cola on ice for myself and my mother, and a glass of water for my father because he doesn't like strong drinks. I threw back a large draught of mine, grimacing as the carbonated liquid burned my throat and focused my mind. "I wasn't a possum, but I was there," I said.

"Did you see the possum?"

"There was no possum, Mom," I said. "I wore possum-print shoes. I carved out the soles of a pair of my shoes so that each shoe had two little possum feet on the bottom. After gnawing on the door to throw everyone off the trail, I let myself in the house using my old key. I took small steps to simulate the walking pattern of a possum, and also pressed my shoes all over your papers after I read them. And then I took your peanuts. "

"And at the bottom of the can...?" my dad ventured, still clinging to the hope of a possum villain.

"M&M's," I answered. "I ate them."

My parents looked at each other. They burst into laughter. They threw their arms around each other. They hooted. They howled. I shifted in my seat, but they only slowed down a little.

"Aren't you angry?" I asked.

"No, Oscar," my father said, taking a break from his laughter to cough. "What's to be angry about? It's just..." and then he mimed opening a door and moving his hands in tiny steps as he looked around stealthily, which sent them both into delirium again.

I felt annoyed that they weren't taking it seriously, but I soon found I couldn't stay that way. It actually *was* pretty funny to think about. For years they had really believed that they were the first ever victims of a possum home invasion.

Their laughter eventually slackened and then slowed to a drip, and they both took off their glasses to wipe their eyes.

"We're not angry," my mother said. "It was years ago. I've felt sad and upset that you wouldn't answer the door or return my calls for so long, but that was before we knew why. Now, we're just glad to have you back." My father nodded agreement, and they both smiled at me. I returned their smile with my own. It was good to be back. It was good to feel like I was actually their son again. Their love and acceptance had washed over me and swept away my shame.

Later, we sat in the kitchen eating dinner. Possums were still their favorite topic of conversation.

"I don't know if the police would agree with our lack of anger," my mother said, between meatballs. "They actually put quite a lot of work into finding that possum, and they linked several burglaries in the city to it. They worked up a good sketch of the possum; you would have liked it. He was a big, muscled fellow." My father looked around the room as she spoke, and I felt pleased that he was taking note of the effort I had made to decorate the house; I had also put a picture of him and my mom on the kitchen wall. "One of the detectives had a theory that he was some new species of possum, mutated somehow, and they'd drawn him with thumbs. That's how they figured he opened the door and carried the can of peanuts off. Honestly, we were a bit skeptical to start with, but then I remembered that hamster—"

"Nibbles," my father offered.

"Right, Nibbles. I remembered that hamster you had when you were little and how he figured out how to let himself out of his cage, and he could do the little tricks and you almost had him juggling before he died. And possums have a larger brain and that prehensile tail—"

"And the bifurcated penis." My father was staring at the wall, but he was still listening.

"Bifurcated penis?" She asked.

"Possums have a bifurcated penis. Two-pronged. Shaped like a 'Y.'"

"Yes, but I don't think he'd have used that to break into a house, Lindley," she said. "They also live about twice as long as a hamster, so we figured if you could teach your hamster all that in only about a year, then maybe someone could teach a possum how to be a burglar since they'd have more time and more to work with."

"Oscar, what is *that*?" My father said, pointing at the wall with his fork. "I've been staring at it trying to figure out what it is since the entrée."

We followed his pointing to the camera on the wall. "I wondered that too," said my mother. "There's also one in the living room. Is it some kind of wall sculpture?"

"Oh, those are just my cameras. There's also one in my office."

"Your cameras?" my mother asked.

"What do you need cameras for?" my father asked. "Nobody has cameras watching the inside of their house. They look very recent, too, Maria. There's even sawdust still on the floor from the drilling."

"Oh, they're not mine," I explained dismissively, realizing they thought I had put the cameras up to keep an eye on them that night. "The company I work for installed them here earlier today. It's just to keep an eye on me and make sure I'm doing the work I'm supposed to, because I work from home."

"That's good to hear," my mother said. "What's your job?"

"I work at Global Partners & Associates," I said, sitting up straight.

"Global Who & What?" my father asked. "I've never heard of them."

"Most people haven't," I said. "They're not a public-facing company. They're all over, though, globally, and into a lot of things. Here's my card." I slid my card across the table. My father picked it up.

As they examined the card, I continued. "I'm just a junior associate right now, but there's plenty of room for advancement. I think within a few years I could be a partner."

"What kind of work do you do for them, as a junior associate?"

I considered making up something about imports and exports. Acquisitions, maybe. Hedge funds. I decided just to be honest.

"They haven't actually told me yet exactly what I'll be doing," I said. "I was only hired this morning. They've given me a laptop, though, and installed the cameras, which shows they're invested in me."

"They haven't told you?" my mother asked, while feeling the raised texture of my name on my card. "How do you know you can do it?"

"Well, the job ad was for a technical writer, and I had that technical writing class in high school."

My father: "You didn't finish it, though."

"Yes, but I feel pretty sure if I had finished it, I would've got good grades."

"Do you really feel alright about these cameras, Oscar?"

"Of course I do, mom. It's like a free security system, if you think about it. Not that I need one, or even want one. But if something happened, like if you choked on that meatball, they'd see it and an ambulance would be on the way. It does make you feel secure."

"It makes *me* a little uncomfortable, though." She frowned at the meatball. "Are they really watching right now? You're not even working."

"Well, I set my own hours since I work from home. So I figure they're always watching, because the hours I set could be any time. I might wake up at two in the morning and decide to do some work; they need to be ready."

"I don't like it either," my father said. "They'll be watching you all the time. They'll know when you leave the house, when you go to sleep. I'll give you the benefit of the doubt and assume there isn't one in the bathroom, but they'll know when you're in there anyway because you won't be in the other rooms."

"And you don't know who's watching either," my mother added. "It could be anyone."

"Be reasonable, mother. It couldn't be *anyone*. It couldn't be you, for example. It couldn't be a blind person."

"Now you're being childish, just like when you were a child."

"I'm not," I said. "I've been hired by a reputable, global company with high ethical standards, and I trust them to keep an eye on me."

"They don't trust you, though," my father said, pointing to the camera.

"And why should they?" I asked. "I've only worked for them a few hours, and I have their expensive equipment here. The cameras alone must be worth thousands of dollars. What if you two tried to steal them?"

"So the cameras need to be here in case someone tries to steal the cameras? Wouldn't they just be safer somewhere else?"

"That's not the point," I said. "*I* don't feel worried, and they're in my house."

"It just doesn't seem like you, Oscar."

"That's only because the me you're used to is constantly paranoid; it's not like me because I'm not the same as I have been for years. Now you guys are the paranoid ones. My medication has made me realize that I shouldn't be concerned about these cameras any more than I should be concerned about either of you. And I'm not concerned about you, in case you were wondering."

My father put down his fork and put up his hands. "You win," he said. Then, turning to my mother, "He's right. Before, he'd have had a camera outside to see who was there and wouldn't have let us in because he was suspicious we were government spies. At least this way we're inside, we're having a conversation with our son, and we're enjoying a nice dinner that we didn't have to cook. This is certainly a life I could get used to."

"That's true," my mother said. "You're right. All I'm saying though, Oscar, is that it's ok to have a little caution, it doesn't have to turn into paranoia."

"I know, mom. I'm still cautious about some things. I sleep with my mouth closed so spiders don't crawl in, just like you taught me. I don't cross the street without looking both ways. Psylocybin hasn't made me a bumbling idiot ready to have my head smashed by the first power tool I come in contact with; it's just made it so that I can live my life without being in a constant state of worry and fear. I'm able to sit here under the watchful eye of this camera and not feel bothered at all."

I paused for a moment and then put my hands out to

the side, palms upturned, to demonstrate that I could sit still in front of a camera without running for cover.

"If you think about it rationally, there's nothing the camera can do to you. I have nothing to hide. So what could I have to fear? It doesn't actually matter if someone is watching me right now; I'm not doing anything wrong, so all they're going to see is a man enjoying dinner with his parents."

"And parents enjoying dinner with their son," my mother added. "To a happy family," she said, raising her glass.

"To a happy family," my father said, raising his glass as well. "Don't clink them, please. You know how I don't like loud noises."

That night, I laid in bed reflecting on the day gone by. My parents still didn't understand how I truly felt, but that was ok. And it was ok that I didn't feel like a different person from the one who had done all those paranoid—and sometimes violent—things. Even though I was different now, it *was* still me who had done them, but I didn't have to be bothered by that. My bedroom door was partly open, and I noticed that the living room camera could see me lying in bed. Because my mother would have wanted it, I got up and closed the door.

Chapter 15

I took my Psylocybin. I made myself breakfast. I went to work, propped up my feet, and ate bacon, eggs, and grits. I gave the camera a thumbs-up. So far, this was the best job I had ever had. I pulled the laptop onto my lap and spent some more time on the website, adding information about how committed GP&A was to employee safety through surveillance. Since I knew Ron's name now, I added him to the partners' page, and I added Wallace to the associates' page. Soon, it was going to be a pretty respectable website.

I looked in the fridge. No juice. I decided to take a break from work and go to Jack's Grocery Mart to see how they were situated for juice, because I had only one empty carton to my name. Maybe they'd have my old brand of juice back, since I'd been away so long, and if they didn't maybe I'd give a new brand a taste. It wasn't very far away, and since I was enjoying my life more now than I ever had been, and I wanted to enjoy it even more and for much longer, I didn't take my car, because it's healthier to walk.

By the time I was halfway, though, I regretted that choice. Walking may be healthier, but it doesn't have quad-directional air conditioning or lumbar support. I took what I thought would be an easy shortcut off the main street and also regretted that; after a few turns, I was lost. There was no moss on the telephone poles and no spiders building webs, so I couldn't know north or south. I deduced that towards the sun was east, because it hadn't yet risen to its zenith. That wasn't actually any help, because I didn't know which compass direction Jack's Grocery Mart was in anyway. Sections of this part of town had been abandoned, renovated, and abandoned again. I followed a rusted, bent sign which said 'Main Street,' but it only led me down an alley which was newly bricked up at the end, and I had to come out again. The other side probably held a new housing development and the developers didn't want their residents having an unsightly view; their unspoiled view was quite inconvenient for me. On the bricks, there was graffiti of a large red fist ringed in gold. Who would go to the effort of spraying a thing like that on a wall?

Zenithal or not, the sun was roasting me; I wiped my forehead and my hand came away slick with sweat. I sat down in the shade to cool off, and out of the corner of my eye, I saw movement. I looked towards it, and my heart leapt for the safety of my throat. Down the street, a dark shape had just dropped out of sight behind a car. Someone was watching me.

I felt faint, and my legs threatened to abandon their support of me as I stood up. Behind me, I heard a sound and I quickly turned, losing my balance and stumbling against the wall. A cat froze in mid-stride and looked towards me; it must have caused the sound, probably rooting through old cans. Once it saw that I was just a human, it went back to its business. I pressed my back against the wall and felt the firm roughness of the brick with both hands. I took comfort from having the solid wall covering my back so I only had to worry about what was in front of me, and I was able to calm down a little and think about my situation. Someone was definitely following me, and it didn't seem like any kind of paranoid delusion; this was real, one of the first real things that had ever happened to me.

I was sweating and I was nervous, but otherwise I was in a fine mental and physical state. I decided that I would flank them and confront them; I would make them tell me why they were following me and what they wanted from me. Could it be Ron from the old days, from before Maple Ridge? I hadn't thought about him for weeks, but now he filled my mind.

I dropped down onto my hands and knees behind a trash can. From there, I rolled behind a car, and then to another car. I peeked up over the car's door and through the window to look across the street, and I immediately dropped back down; he had been looking directly at me, waiting for me to show myself. He knew what I was doing. I could be quicker than him, though. I could outsmart him. My hand was resting on a stick which had been lying in the road, and I closed my fingers around it. The rough texture of it meant that I could grip it firmly, even with my sweaty palms. It felt nearly rotten in my hand, but it looked thick and solid. It would be enough.

I held my breath and waited for my chance. The sound of dogs barking in a fight somewhere nearby gave me the opportunity, and I rushed across the road, using their noise to cover my own. Now I was on the other side of the road, and we were both on opposite sides of the same car. I had kept a watch on the car as I crossed the road, and I knew he hadn't seen me because he hadn't looked up from behind the car. Even I hadn't heard my own footsteps as I crossed the street like a daylight ninja, so he couldn't have either. I had the advantage, now. I knew where he was, but he didn't know the same about me.

I waited for a few moments to steady my breath, and then I crouched up into a ready position. In one movement, I came around the back of the car and raised my weapon, ready to strike him. He wasn't there. My adrenaline had surged, and I stood there shaking, drenched in sweat. How had he gotten away? Then, even worse, I realized he had never been there at all. I'd had a brief attack of paranoia, even under the influence of Psylocybin. This was serious. I'd have to talk to Dr. Boggs about it after I had found my way out of there and to Jack's, because I still had the juice to think about.

Then I felt the barrel of a gun pressing into my spine.

The sun was still burning hot, but my sweat turned cold. I had not been wrong. My skin seemed to shrink in on me and I felt dried up inside. My ears filled up with the sound of my breathing. My stick clattered onto the ground.

"Put your hands up, mister," he said. His voice was deep and rough, like a man talking through thick cloth, and it made my stomach tremble. The front of my pants became moist and warm, and it wasn't because they were self-warming, self-moistening, comfort pants. My hands rose up on unsteady arms, but then the gun was pulled away and I heard a child's laughter behind me. I looked over my shoulder, and saw that there was only a small boy standing there. He was holding a stick in one hand and a thick cloth in the other.

I also laughed. It was either that or explain to a small child that I had thought he was actually trying to kill me while he was playing an imaginary game.

"Pew, pew, pew," he said, pointing his laser-gun stick at my stomach. I had been routed by a seven year old—or so he thought, except he probably didn't think words like 'routed' yet. The game was still on, and I knew what I had to do. I clutched my hands to my stomach to cover up the open wounds and try to keep my most vital organs from tumbling out into the unforgiving atmosphere. The car came up behind me as I stumbled backwards, and I slid down against it, down to the ground, leaving a bloody trail behind me on the body of the car. He still kept his gun pointed at me. My legs splayed out in front of me and my head slumped forward; I was losing blood fast, and the energy for holding my head up was needed elsewhere. I had to be quick, and I knew I would only get one chance against this villain. The pain was immense, but still I waited. At last, he lowered his gun. He had defeated me, and he knew it. When he was well and truly convinced, I seized my chance and lunged for my own gun which I had dropped to the floor. I took it in my hands and twisted my body towards my enemy, ready to give him a taste of his own laser-flavored medicine. He was ready for me, though. Before I turned back he had his gun already pointed at me and I was looking directly up its barrel. He had never really dropped his guard. My hands opened weakly to let the gun fall to the floor; I knew there was no use in trying anymore.

I had been beaten by a superior opponent, but still I didn't want to die. I tried reasoning with him, even though I could see the righteous madness in his eyes. "Killing me won't bring her back," I whispered.

"Pew—" was the last thing I heard, before I heard,

"Michael, come in for lunch," when his mother called him.

"See ya," I said, waving to him with a grin. "You'd better go." He returned my smile with his own before running towards the sound of her voice.

"Aw mom, I was having fun," he complained to his mother in the distance, and I trained my sights on the back of his head. But he had been such a worthy opponent that I couldn't pull the trigger and end his young life.

He had left his cloth, and I used it to wipe the sweat from my face. The cloth came away soaked. I allowed myself a laugh at the situation and myself, at how paranoid I had been over a small boy playing on the street outside his house. It had ended up alright though, and I'd actually had an enjoyable time with the game.

By the time I stood up, the adrenaline had mostly worked its way out of my bloodstream, and my legs were steady, or at least as steady as you're ever going to get with normal human bipedal locomotion[1].

I worried that maybe the Psylocybin wasn't working, or even that I was becoming resistant to it and I would fall back into constant, total paranoia. I worried that my worrying about the Psylocybin was itself a form of paranoia. Eventually, though, I passed a man on the street and asked him for directions to Jack's Grocery Mart, and I followed them without worrying that I was being led into a trap and having to follow a more

---

[1] Three legs would be much better for us any way you look at it, and I think the fact that we only have two legs is a black mark against creationists *and* evolutionists.

circuitous route, which is what I would have done before Psylocybin, so it seemed like it was still working. I also hadn't had any headaches when I was paranoid about the boy; Psylocybin had completely stopped those. I could call Dr. Boggs to find out, but he was a doctor and he was probably very busy. I had Penelope's number. Maybe she would be able to explain what had happened to me.

Chapter 16

I put my orange juice in the fridge for later and called Penelope. She wasn't off work yet, but said she'd love to talk to me later, and gave me directions to her house so we could talk in person.

It was just a professional visit, but I still spent some time checking out my appearance in the mirror before I left, and I was happy to see that I looked even better after a few days out on my own. Even the lines in my forehead from long years of worry had faded some now that my face was constantly relaxed. The sweat and urine soaked clothes from the incident in the street were a problem, but a quick shower and change took care of that.

I knocked on her door, and waited nervously. Not in the abnormally nervous way I had been before, but just in the regular sort of nervous way when you like someone. It might seem futile, since several times she had seen me weeping openly about things which existed only in my mind, but I still hoped to make a good first impression. This was the first time we had seen each other outside of the hospital and outside of the nurse-patient relationship, and I was anxious for it not to be awkward.

She opened the door.

"Hi," we both said, at the same time.

"Sorry," we said, again at the same time. I decided not to say anything further, and mentally berated myself for not stopping after the first word to let her say something. Now I'd made it awkward.

She looked down and took my hand. "Come on in," she said, and led me inside.

I sat down at her request, and she sat next to me.

"I'm just going to say it," she said. She spoke quickly, but I still had time to worry about what it was that she might say. "I'm sorry I made it awkward for you. This is the first time you've seen me outside of the hospital, and I wanted to make a good impression as a hostess. I want you to see me differently; as Penelope, not Nurse Penelope."

"It's alright," I said, and laughed. "Actually, I thought I'd made it awkward for you."

"Really?" she asked. "You seemed very calm and cool, standing there silently. I thought you must be thinking I was an idiot and wondering whether you should turn around and go back home, and I was thinking the same, about being an idiot."

"Well, I guess we're a pair of idiots, then. I was actually taking that time to shout at myself inside for spoiling our greeting."

"I don't think it was spoiled at all," she said, softly. "I'm happy you're here."

Something about the way she was looking at me as she said that made my heart speed up. "I'm happy too," I said. "About us," and then, quickly: "I mean about me, and about you, and we're here, right?"

"We are," she said, leaning towards me. I had read that a very effective way to show someone you like them is to mimic their actions during conversation, so I leaned towards her as well. And when her lips parted, so did mine. It worked, and I think she realized I liked her from my expert copying of her actions, because then she was kissing me, which is an even better signal that someone likes you. She put her arms around me as we kissed, pressing her soft lips and her soft body against me.

"You understand me, don't you, Oscar?" she asked, pulling back a few inches. "I want you to understand me. I've wanted someone who understands me."

"I do understand you," I said. Did I? It didn't seem like the time for uncertain answers. Maybe I understood her.

"Then you'll understand if I want to frisk you for any kind of weapons or listening devices or vials of infectious diseases."

"I…" I wasn't sure. "Sure," I said.

She had me stand up and moved her hands over my body, checking for contraband. Everything seemed to be to her satisfaction, because then we were kissing again. After an indeterminate amount of enjoyable time, I stopped to speak. I wanted to make things clear.

"Penelope, I like you," I said, and then pressed my lips to hers again.

"I like you too," she said, breaking contact for a moment. "I hope you don't think I was too forward."

"You only seemed about the same amount forward as me," I said. "I think we were both leaning at the same angle."

She laughed, and asked if I would like something to drink. I said I wouldn't mind something, and so she went to get food for us. I spent the time looking at a houseplant next to the couch, which had particularly long, fuzzy leaves.

"I know you came here for professional reasons," she said, setting two glasses of wine on a low table in front of the couch. "It probably almost seems like I convinced you to take Psylocybin back at the hospital just so I could take advantage of you and your new trusting nature."

"Again, I felt the same way. Don't get me wrong, I called you for a legitimate reason, but I was hoping there'd be something more. Not that whatever more there might be wouldn't be legitimate, just that it might not be so professional. Not that it would be amateur. And I don't mean to imply that you're a professional at this — "

"I get it, Oscar," she said. "Why don't we talk about what you called about? What happened?"

I told her about my experience earlier in the day when I was lost, how I had seen the movement and felt so paranoid and nearly hit a small boy with a stick. I left out the part where I had peed my pants, because it didn't seem integral to the story.

"It sounds like you just had a standard mild panic attack," she said, when I had finished. "It's nothing to worry about."

"Isn't a panic attack bad?" I asked.

"It's not exactly good," she said, "but it's a normal thing. Your excessive sweating probably lessened the effect of Psylocybin, which I've seen happen before, and that might have made it a bit worse."

"Every time you feel worried, scared, or even paranoid, it doesn't mean that your condition is coming back. Regular people get those kinds of feelings all the time. For example, I left work late today and it was already getting dark. I was alone in the parking lot, and my car was one of the only cars there." She had been looking down as she spoke, and now she looked up at me, slowly lifting her eyelids. "I felt a little scared, and I wished someone was there with me, someone who could understand that paranoid feeling. Sometimes when I get in my car, I check in the back seat, even though I've had the doors locked. The chances of being attacked in a parking lot are small, but it doesn't make you a paranoid delusional to feel a bit worried that something might happen; in fact, it makes you normal."

"I didn't feel normal, getting ready to beat a small child with a stick," I said.

She dismissed what I said with a wave of her hand. "You weren't ready to beat a small child with a stick. You thought you were being stalked, possibly by someone violent, certainly by an adult. When you saw that it was actually a child, you weren't paranoid anymore and you didn't feel threatened."

"You're right," I said, leaning back into the couch. "Other than that, I haven't felt paranoid at all since I've been back at home. It's funny, because I had dinner with my parents last night—which went really well, by the way—and they were the ones who seemed paranoid."

"I've had that sometimes with my family and friends too," she said, nodding. "Last year, when birds with the flu was our biggest national concern, my mom tried for weeks to get me to wear one of those surgical masks every time I went outside."

"Yeah, that's how it was with my parents," I said. "I've just got a new job and they've installed a few cameras in my house—"

Penelope sat up straight. "Cameras?" she asked. "Did you say cameras?"

"Yeah, it's just a few cameras for work, so they can keep an eye on what I'm up to."

She got up from the couch and locked the doors. Her

front door had an elaborate series of locks and bolts on it; she locked and bolted each one. That was how my door had been before I had ended up in prison and Maple Ridge. The insurance company must have removed nearly all the locks on the door before I came back, because there was only the regular lock and the deadbolt left. Penelope's door looked like mine before I was taking Psylocybin.

"What company did you say you were working for?" she asked, as she curtained the windows in the room.

"I didn't say, but it's Global Partners & Associates. Here's my card," I said, holding it out, meaning to impress her. She took a step back as if the business card was a live tarantula. I hadn't counted on that, and now I didn't know how to lead into a description of how I was an associate to all those global partners. I noticed that her hands were shaking.

"Penelope, what's the matter? What's going on?"

She fixed me with a long stare. I felt uncomfortable, and lowered my eyes. When I looked back, she seemed to have relaxed, and her hands were no longer shaking. The curtains remained shut, though, and the door remained securely locked.

"It's nothing," she said, and let out a deep breath. "It's just... I get this way sometimes. I told you how sometimes everyone gets an irrational fear of things. Well, sometimes you get that irrational fear and it stays with you for your whole life. I knew a guy who would fall to the floor, weeping, and clutch his knees to his chest if a bee came within twenty yards. I guess I'm like that, but with cameras."

"You're afraid of *cameras*?" I asked, raising my

eyebrows. Her explanation didn't really fit.

"Don't make light of it, please. From what you experienced earlier today, you know the Psylocybin isn't always one-hundred percent effective, and some things make it less effective, like sweating, or a raised heart rate like mine has been tonight because of you. It's nothing to worry about, anyway; it will pass."

"I don't understand, though. There aren't any cameras here. They're back in my house. What's to be afraid of?"

"Out three days and already they've got cameras in your house," she said, halfway to herself. "How did you get that job so fast? Was there even time for an interview?"

"I saw the job in the paper—".

"In the paper! Who even reads the paper anymore?"

Penelope lifted the corner of a curtain and peeped out the window. She looked at me expectantly and said, "Go on, then."

"Well, um, I went to the company's location, in a storage building—"

"You had a job interview in a storage building, and that didn't seem weird to you?"

"It's a small company," I said, feeling defensive about my new employer because I had invested so much into them already, "they can't afford large facilities."

"But didn't you feel worried that... nevermind, of course you didn't." She paced behind the couch.

"I can probably get you an interview too, if you want," I offered. Maybe she felt envious of me and my great job where I got to eat a bacon sandwich anytime I wanted.

She stopped pacing. "I don't think you understand, Oscar," she said. Her face was sad. I resolved to set up an interview appointment for her. "I can't make you understand, either, not right now. I think you'd better just go for now. You can use my secret entrance, in the back."

"You have a secret entrance?"

"Actually, I guess it's better to use the front door. Everything is fine, right?"

"But why do you have a secret entrance?"

"For entering secretly," she said, pushing me gently towards the door. "It's... you know, sometimes you just need to avoid someone. But you don't need to avoid anyone, so it would be suspicious if you used it."

She unlocked several things and opened the door for me. I went out onto the first step.

"Oscar?"

I turned around; she pulled me close and kissed me.

"Remember: everything is fine, right?" She said.

"Everything is fine," I repeated, although it didn't seem actually true.

"I'll call you," she said, and closed the door. As it shut, her face lit up with light reflected from the door's window and I saw a tear sliding down her cheek. I heard the locks and latches being fastened again on the other side of the door.

What had I said that made her so worried? She was behaving like I had, before she helped me, before Psylocybin. I realized how tremendous that thought was as soon as it entered my mind. Maybe she *wasn't* on Psylocybin. Maybe it wasn't working. If it stopped being effective gradually, you wouldn't even know; you'd just feel paranoid again, but you wouldn't realize anything had changed. Maybe her body had become resistant to some of the effects and she needed a stronger dose. If it was true, though, she'd never listen to me about it. Once it stopped working you'd probably become paranoid about taking it at all, so you'd completely come off it. That explained the locks, the pacing, the frisking, the fear of cameras, and everything else.

What could I do, though? If it was true, she wouldn't listen to me. Maybe she would listen to someone else, though; maybe she would listen to Dr. Boggs. He was her boss, a respected medical professional, and had been her friend for years. He'd helped her through her own crisis of paranoia just like she had helped me, and I knew she would trust him. When I got home, I picked up the phone and dialed.

"Good evening, you've reached Maple Ridge Psychiatric Hospital, where we stop dreams from coming to life. How may I direct your call?"

"I'd like to speak to Dr. Boggs, please," I said to the receptionist.

"I'm afraid he's already gone home for the day," she replied. "I can put you through to his voicemail if you like, though."

"Alright, put me through, please. Thanks." It wasn't especially urgent; Penelope had probably been resistant to Psylocybin for a few days already, so waiting one more night wasn't going to cause anything terrible to happen.

There was a click as the receptionist transferred the call, then ringing for a few seconds, and then another click.

"Dr. Boggs," a voice on the other end stated. I waited for a moment, but there was no beep; it wasn't his voicemail. "Hello?" he said, after I didn't say anything.

"Dr. Boggs, hi," I said. "I was expecting your

voicemail. The receptionist said you had gone for the day. This is Oscar Well."

"Oscar, I'm glad to hear from you. Has something gone wrong with your medication? Have you had a paranoid relapse?"

"No, everything's fine with me," I said. "The Psylocybin is incredible and I've never felt better. I've started to rebuild my relationships with my friends and family, and I've even got a job already."

"That's quite refreshing to hear," Dr. Boggs said. "Patients don't usually call me unless there's a problem." His chair creaked as he leaned back in it. "What can I do for you, then?"

"Don't feel too refreshed, Doctor. There is a problem; it's just not with me. It's Penelope."

"Nurse Penelope?" His chair creaked again as he leaned forwards. "What's the matter, then?"

"I was at her house earlier for a professional consultation about a paranoid experience I'd had—it turned out to be nothing—and I noticed a few strange things. First, she had tons of locks and bolts on her door even though she lives in a nice neighborhood." I considered whether I should say anything about the secret entrance. I decided not to; it wouldn't be very secret if I did. "I mentioned the cameras my employer has installed in my house—"

"Ah yes, the cameras," he said. "Go on, Oscar."

"Right, well; I mentioned the cameras, and she began to behave very unusually. She locked everything up and shut the curtains. She paced as she talked, and did a lot of hand wringing."

Had she wrung her hands? I couldn't remember

exactly, but it made my story more credible.

"She made me leave soon after. I know she's on Psylocybin too, and I feel like maybe it isn't working properly for her, because the way she was acting made her seem like someone with at least mild case of paranoia."

Dr. Boggs' chair made a long, slow creak, and then he spoke. "That's very interesting, Oscar. Very interesting. I'll speak to her tomorrow when she comes in, I'm sure I can find the underlying cause of it. And thank you for calling, Oscar. I'm sure you know what the paranoia you both suffered from can be like. Someone under the influence of an overactive amygdala would never ask someone for help, because they think everyone *else* is the problem. Without you calling, I likely never would have known about this at all."

I poured myself a glass of orange juice and breathed a sigh of satisfaction. Dr. Boggs would speak to Penelope, she would get a stronger dose of Psylocybin if she needed it, and then perhaps more kissing would be forthcoming. He'd said without me calling he wouldn't have known about it; that meant I was useful, and I had done a good deed. Penelope would probably also feel pleased when she found out.

Chapter 17

I woke up. I checked my messages. There was still nothing from GP&A about what my work duties would be. It wasn't too early in the morning, so I called Penelope. She didn't answer, and I got her voicemail. By the time she got the message Dr. Boggs would already have talked with her and got the Psylocybin issue sorted out, so I risked mentioning the cameras again and apologized for mentioning them the night before and upsetting her. I ended the message by saying I'd like to see her again and asking her to call me.

I took my Psylocybin. Feeling the two little pills go down my throat was a pleasant experience every time; my mind calmed down even before the regulating chemicals entered my bloodstream. Every morning and night as I took them, I was reminded that my life was now forever changed. No longer was I haunted by the poltergeist of paranoia. I was already starting to have normal social relationships—possibly including a girlfriend. I'd held a steady job for three days, and I'd only nearly beaten a child in the street with a stick one time. It was like being a regular person.

Since I didn't have any work to do, I called Winslow to see if he wanted to come over. He did. I read the letters to the editor section of the newspaper while I waited for him to arrive. Yennifer Stroumph had written in to complain about the new traffic cameras which had been installed on the main street, saying she wanted to be able to drive to work without being watched, and besides that, who was to say that the cameras wouldn't be used for something else, like license plate tracking. Someone else had written to say that it was a great idea to reduce traffic accidents and catch criminals, that rumors about license plate tracking were nothing but alarmist claptrap, and if you didn't want to be watched you were welcome to stay in the privacy of your own home where there were no cameras. That was the sensible view; if Ms. Stroumph had nothing to hide then she had nothing to fear, as I knew more than most because of the camera in my kitchen, which watched me while I read.

The doorbell rang. Winslow and I sat in the living room and talked; he was happy to hear I was getting on well with my family, and I was happy to tell him that only hours before I had been lips-to-lips with Penelope. It may have sounded like bragging, and that's because it was. I didn't feel too bad about it though, because I felt I had reason to brag since only weeks before I was weeping in the corner of a room in a mental hospital's security wing, barely able to feed myself or pee outside my pants ("barely" is actually an overstatement of my abilities at the time), and now I was in the middle of what could be the start of a happy relationship with a beautiful woman, and she was only a little mentally unstable. I also left out the fact that she had pushed me out of her house and locked the door on me afterwards; such details often spoil a good story.

As seemed to happen with everyone in my house, Winslow became curious about the camera in my living room.

"So you're telling me right now we're being watched?"

he asked, when I explained.

"It's hard to say, exactly. There are three cameras in my home," Winslow's eyebrows went up when I said that, "and probably other GP&A employees who work from home also have cameras in their houses, and I don't know if all the cameras are being watched all the time. At any time, they *could* be watching, though, which keeps me on my best behavior regarding work."

"You aren't actually doing any work, though," he pointed out. "They also haven't told you what you're doing. It's like you're being watched just for the sake of the watching. It makes me feel nervous. I can't believe it doesn't make *you* feel nervous, Oscar. A few months ago, you'd stand to the side at the ATM so the camera there couldn't see you, now you have cameras all over the place in your home."

"They're not all over the place," I said. "I have five rooms, and the cameras are only in three of them. If it would make you feel better, we can go into the bathroom and talk."

"It's not about what room we're in," he said, standing in the shower. "It's the principle. You're being watched in your own home, by you-don't-know-who."

"You don't know who either," I said. "What if it's someone nice?"

"It's probably not anyone nice. My grandmother isn't watching you from across town while she bakes cookies. Look, Oscar, I'm really very happy that you aren't paranoid anymore. Its fantastic being able to have a conversation and a glass of wine with you where you don't accuse me of poisoning your glass, but I also think you're taking it too far. Some caution can be good."

I needed to camouflage the cameras in some way, and then I wouldn't have to deal with everyone asking me questions about them for the rest of my life. Maybe I could sew one of them inside a teddy bear and have the lens looking out through one of his eyes.

"You should look into GP&A," Winslow said. "What do you really know about them? You should find out who runs the company, maybe it's someone who has something against you."

"Who would possibly have anything against me?" I asked. "I've never hurt anyone."

"Never? How about the man you stalked and killed, the man in the cat's-paw-print pajamas, remember? The thing that started all of this?"

"Don't talk to me about that." I stood up from the toilet. "I didn't do it."

"What do you mean, you didn't do it? You went to jail because of it."

"It wasn't me, though, I'm different now."

"But it still happened. Even if you're different now, nobody else will know that. As far as they're concerned, you're a murderer."

"I don't want to talk about this, Winslow," I said.

Then I think he said, "You can't just ignore me," but it was hard to hear for sure over the sound of the hair dryer and sink taps that I had turned on.

The inner corners of his eyebrows turned slightly inwards and upwards in a sad expression, and it was more than I could take. I sighed and turned off the noisy things.

"Please don't shut me out again," he said, quietly.

"I'm sorry, Winslow. It's just very hard for me to talk

about."

"You can tell me," he said, with his eyebrows now being flat and raised upwards across their length, inviting me to talk. Winslow's eyebrows had an incredible talent for convincing me.

"I know I killed that man," I said. "Everyone says I've changed, but what hasn't changed is the feeling that I *wanted* to kill him. I think if it happened all over again that I would kill him again. It's not just that man's associates who think I'm a murderer."

I paused, and took a breath. I felt very tired.

"I feel like a murderer myself."

"Oscar… I didn't realize. You acted like you hadn't given it another thought. I'm sorry I brought it up."

"I've thought about it a lot, Winslow. I feel tired now. We can talk about it another day."

He left, after I assured him that I would be fine. I was going to be fine, but I did feel so tired. Admitting out loud that I truly felt as if I had killed that man and meant to do it had taken a lot of energy from me. How could I ever feel ok about it? And what must his family think of me? They probably wouldn't even know that I had been released from prison.

I had to talk to them, to tell them about my mental condition and that I had received treatment for it, that I was no longer a danger to just any man leaving his house for work in the morning. I would also apologize for what I had done. I didn't know if it could actually help them, but was the right thing to do. I didn't feel suspicious of them as Winslow did, but I knew I should talk to them.

Never put off until tomorrow what you can do today, I

always say[1], so I got dressed in some going-out clothes and went directly to the house of the man who I had last seen in the gray pinstripe suit, stained red.

The house looked the same as when I had been there last, which is what you would expect, but somehow it was unexpected, and I was surprised. I knocked on the door, but there was no response. I tried to look in through the windows in the front of the house, but the curtains were drawn. The front step of the house was dirty from months of rain splashing on the ground near it, and there were no footprints in the dirt, as if nobody had opened the door since that long-ago morning.

I walked around to the side of the house where I had hidden behind a bush months before. The curtains there weren't closed properly; one corner was caught on a window ornament. I looked through and saw that the pans he had used while cooking dinner on that decisive night were still on the counter, apparently untouched. A spotlight-style bulb over the food preparation area was still burning. There was a layer of dust over everything, like nobody had been in the house for months. Why hadn't his family come to sort through is belongings? *Something* should have happened. The electric company should have cut off the lights after months of unpaid bills—who was paying them? It wasn't like my house where the insurance company took care of everything while I was in the hospital; here, the resident wasn't

---

[1] For the sake of accuracy let me say that I believe it may actually have been Benjamin Franklin who always said that particular thing, but I find that he and I are so similar in other ways it's often superfluous to draw any kind of distinction between us.

coming back, and there was no need to keep the house in a similar and livable state for months.

I drove around for a while, not sure what to do. I had come to speak to his family, but his family wasn't there, and didn't appear to have been there at all. Closure was an important thing for me, or for them, I felt sure of it. I had seen it in movies.

Cruising slowly in town, I drove past the Office of the County Clerk. This was the real test. For too long, I had avoided that building because I was avoiding the man inside. Well, I was a citizen of the county just like any other, and I decided to avail myself of my rights to public information.

Inside the office, there was a counter with a single window, and behind it stood the county clerk. Behind him stood stacks and file cabinets and shelves as far as the eye could see, which usually isn't very far when you're indoors. In this case it was only to the end wall of the building, about thirty feet away.

The county clerk was a heavyset man with taut suspenders that held up his stomach by way of holding up his pants. His stomach balanced delicately on his waistband and strained against his shirt, yearning for release. Behind his large, round glasses, his eyes looked at me like you would look at a sausage.

"Can ah help you, sir?" he asked, with a drawl you could spread on toast.

"I'm—" My voice came out in a squeak. I clenched my hands behind my back and dug my nails into my palms. I was not afraid of him, because there was no reason to be afraid. I cleared my throat and started again. "I'm looking for any relations of a man who was killed a few months ago."

"I can indeed help you then," he said. He licked his lips. That was okay. Sometimes people do that, not for any particular reason. "What was the name of the late gentleman?"

I hadn't really thought this through. I didn't even know the name of the man I had killed.

"Sir? His name? Or do you know what his address was?"

I did know the address, and I told him what it was. The gentle giant of the office lumbered off to locate property records. I waited for what I truly believe was three days, but there was no way to tell for sure because the drab interior walls held no clock, so it could have just as easily been three minutes.

When he returned, he slid a document through a slot at the bottom of the glass barrier over the counter.

"Mr. Ronald Smythson." He tapped the name on the property tax form.

He lifted up a dog-eared phone book and dropped it onto the counter with a thud. "Now, sir, I know this book by heart, but I'll go through it for your benefit. Let me warn you, though: you're going to be disappointed." He lifted the book ceremoniously into the air and felt along the ridges of the paper with his fingers. Without looking, he opened it directly to the 'S' pages and sat it back down on the counter. Then, without any sort of warning, he put his hands palm-down on both sides of the phone book and thrust himself forward, tilting his head and opening his eyes wide, while raising his eyebrows in a challenging manner.

I took a step backwards, ready to defend myself or

launch backwards through the door, but then I realized that as a county clerk you don't get much chance to demonstrate your skills. He was simply showing off. I knew what he wanted. I brought my hands together several times, clapping. "Very impressive," I said. "I don't think I could do that."

"You couldn't," he said, making a definitive statement as he leaned back and lowered himself flat onto his feet again. He had begun to perspire, and several drops had fallen on the phone book. He slid his finger down the pages and I followed the movement as he smeared his sweat on the paper. He went through several dozen Smunsons, and just when he was getting to the point where you thought there might be a Smythson, it turned into Smyles. There were no Smythsons.

"Maybe they're unlisted," I said.

"Sir," the clerk lifted the waistband of his trousers up as if girding himself for combat, "this," he held his hand above the book and then tapped all of his fingers downwards onto it, "is the county phone book. Nothing is unlisted for us." He paused for a moment, and then said, with some finality, "Nothing."

To demonstrate, he held the phone book in front of his face, this time by its spine. "Deedle deedle dee," he said, tickling through the pages with his surprisingly nimble fingers. He looked at me from behind the phone book and opened his eyes wide with that challenging look again, while his lips pressed tightly together in concentration. He raised the phone book high in the air, flipped it over, and slammed it down to the counter. The page was open to 'W'. I followed his finger again, and it led me directly to 'Well, Oscar'.

"You're an unlisted number, Oscar."

"Alright," I said, rather wishing to leave, "I get your point. If they're not in that book, they don't exist."

"Exactly," he replied. Then, after some consideration, "Or they don't have phones. That could also be the case."

"Can I take that paper with me?" I asked, indicating the property tax form.

"You can't," he said. "County property."

"Thank you for your help, then." I turned to leave. It hadn't been so bad, dealing with the county clerk. I laughed through my nose at how ridiculous I had been, avoiding that place for years.

"You *can* make a copy of it though," he said, "at the copy machine there."

I closed the form under the lid of the copier and pressed the green diamond button that is the universal sign for 'copy'. Nothing happened.

"It needs ten cents," the clerk said. "On the wall," he said, pointing to the coin slot next to the copy machine.

"Ten cents," I said to myself, and searched through my pockets for a dime. Who carries a dime? "Can I borrow ten cents?" I asked, and turned to the clerk. Before I turned around he was already holding his hand out, palm up, with a shiny dime in it, and I suspected he had been that way even before I asked. He thrust his hand through the slot in the glass partition. I moved my hand to take the dime, and he closed his hand gently around mine. I tried to pull away, but his grip was stronger than you'd expect the grip of a county clerk to be.

"You have very soft hands," he said. I managed to step back a little, which pulled him forward, but I couldn't work my hand loose without letting go of the dime, and I needed that copy.

I stepped back further, and his face was now pressed against the inside of the glass so that it fogged with his breath when he said, "Y'all gonna have to work to earn that dime."

He braced himself against the counter with his other arm and slowly pulled me back towards him, making my shoes squeak on the tiled floor. The veins on his hairy forearms stood out against the bulging muscles. Just at the level of the counter, he bulged in another way. His fingers stroked my wrist as he pulled me in. Now my hand was through the slot in the glass, and he began to breathe heavily. I unclenched my fist, and since my hand was slick with sweat because of the Psylocybin, it slipped easily from his grip. As my hand slid free, I snagged the coin using my fingertips. It fell onto the counter directly under the archway of the slot in the glass and our eyes fell on top of it. I snatched it up before he could move. Both of us were breathing heavily, me from the effort, and he from... something else.

He wiped his sweaty brow and looked at me through the thick glass. Somehow, the way he watched me as I put the coin in the slot made me feel used. I pushed the copy button several times, eager to leave. He wiped his brow and stared at me. My copy came out; I grabbed the warm paper, dropped the original onto the counter, and backed out of the office, still watching him as he panted behind the glass.

I drove away, checking my rear view mirror as I went. I halfway expected the county clerk to burst through the door in a shower of splinters and give chase. After several miles of driving and not being chased, I was able to relax and think. I looked at the copied paper in the passenger seat, where it sat upright and buckled in. "He had no family in the tri-county area, and he apparently had no friends either," I said aloud. "Yet his former house is being maintained. What does it mean?" I asked the paper. Mr. Ronald Smythson stared back at me.

To start, it meant that some weight had been lifted off my heart. If he had no family or friends, my mostly unintentional killing of him didn't really affect anyone. Except him, of course; it had affected him in a quite severe manner. It was also sad, that a man was dead and nobody really cared, except me, the one who killed him. I hadn't given any credit to Winslow's theory about Mr. Ronald Smythson's grieving relatives setting up GP&A as a shell company solely to watch me, but since there were no grieving relatives, or any relatives at all, I'd be able to put Winslow's mind at ease about it. According to the county clerk, it meant that Ronald Smythson did not exist, and never had. Beyond that, I didn't know what it meant. How I had killed a man who didn't exist was certainly perplexing.

I drove under several traffic lights as I went, and I saw that they'd recently had cameras fitted on top of them. The cameras watched me as I drove under. They watched all the cars. It was good that someone was keeping the traffic under control.

By the time I got home, it was late in the day. I called Penelope. Maybe she could make sense out of it or give me some idea of what to do next. I only got her voicemail, though, and she still hadn't returned my earlier message. She must have been home by then, so I thought perhaps the night before had been more upsetting for her than I had realized. Dr. Boggs must have talked with her at work as well, so she probably had a lot to think about. I decided to give her more time before I called again, and didn't leave another message.

Chapter 18

I took my Psylocybin. My wrist hurt from the county clerk encounter the day before, so I took some ibuprofen as well. Normally I would have a shower in the morning, but I'd had one the night before because I felt dirty when I got home. Since I didn't have a shower, I left the bathroom more quickly than usual, and as I walked out I happened to look at the camera on the wall and I saw that it was moving. I felt sure that it had been pointed directly at the wall of the bathroom. When I looked at it, it stopped moving. I walked into the bathroom and out again several times, but the camera didn't move any more. I would have to let GP&A know that they needed to fix my cameras in place because of their tendency to wander.

On the front page of the paper, there was an article about the new traffic cameras in town. In the space of only a week, traffic accidents at red lights went down by 95%. The license plate tracking software installed in the cameras had also been very effective, and the police had apprehended several wanted criminals. Prominent among those caught by the cameras was Yennifer Stroumph. So she had only complained about them in the paper because she was trying to hide her own misdeeds. It was very bold of her to complain so openly; surely she must have known it would only draw attention to her. In any case, according to the paper she was beginning a long custodial sentence. I felt safer already.

I spent most of the day playing social internet games on my company laptop. Winslow had remained forever unwilling to accept my invites to Puppy Planet so I could earn more puppy points to do more puppy playing, but I sent another invite anyway.

Penelope still hadn't returned my calls by dinnertime, so I called her again. There was no answer. I didn't leave a voicemail, because I didn't want to make her think I was weird by constantly leaving messages for her. Instead, I decided to drive over to her house late at night and uninvited. There was a craft store close to her house, and if she asked why I'd come I could say something about already being in the neighborhood buying embroidery supplies. I also put a pillow in the car so I could point and say, 'look, there is the pillow I will be embroidering.'

To bolster my embroidery story, I stopped at the craft store and picked up some actual embroidery supplies. There was a surprising selection of embroidery mesh, but I did eventually choose a few good models. Thus equipped, I continued on to Penelope's house.

There was a light on in her living room. I knocked on the door, but there was no answer.

"Penelope? It's me, Oscar," I called through the keyhole. "I brought you some meatloaf." I had not brought any meatloaf, but it seemed like a suitable lure, and one which I could explain away by saying, 'actually, I meant embroidery materials.' She still didn't answer. I walked around the house to see if there was another door to knock on or perhaps a window to look in. The curtains were closed, and I couldn't see anything through them. There was a dark shadow on one of the living room curtains and the curtain was pressed against the window, as if something heavy had fallen against it. I stopped walking when I saw that. The shadow was shaped like a human head. The glass was cracked where it touched. It was Penelope. She must have tripped and fallen, striking her head on the glass. That was why she hadn't returned my calls; she had been laying there all of yesterday. In fact, she could have hit her head immediately after she locked the door the night I was there; she could have been lying there all of that night as well. I could have kicked myself for not coming over sooner[1]. I reached up and knocked hard on the window near her head.

"Penelope," I shouted. "Penelope!" There was no answer; she was definitely unconscious – or worse, but I put that thought out of my head immediately.

I tried the knob on the front door, but it was definitely locked. I jiggled the door, but all the locks made it very secure and it didn't move at all.

I moved down the stairs and then charged up them at the door, slamming my shoulder into it, but the door was not persuaded. It was very obtuse. You have never seen such a stubborn door, I wager. I stepped back down and rubbed my shoulder while I considered my possible options. The window was cracked from the inside, which meant it was weak and probably easy to break with enough force. Her house was raised up though, on a high foundation, and there was no way for me to get on an even level with the window to kick it in. There was a chimney, but even though I thought I could probably leap

---

[1] But I could not have, because my legs were not formed at the proper angle for kicking myself. This is one of the great tragedies of the human condition.

onto the roof if I climbed one of the nearby trees, I wasn't going to risk getting stuck in the chimney out here at night.

Then I remembered the secret entrance she had mentioned. Where was it, though? I circled the house. I tapped every suspicious stone I could see. I kicked the walls. I squeezed a worm that seemed out of place. I pulled away the ivy that was crawling up the house, but there were only blank bricks behind it. I picked up a rock and threw it at the cracked window. The rock only bounced off, leaving a tiny chip in the glass.

At last, I sat down in a lawn chair and leaned back in it. I massaged my shoulder. I had to think. I leaned back, and looked up into the sky. The dark night clouds briefly moved from in front of the moon and I saw the chimney in silhouette against the bright lunar light. The chimney was located on the roof directly above the far wall of the living room. But I had been in there only a few days before, and there was no fireplace in the living room. That could only mean that the chimney was the secret entrance.

I clambered up into a nearby tree. An owl turned its scornful eyes towards me, but I had no time to stop for a discussion of my worth. I leapt out of the tree. The roof was steep and I found very little purchase on the roofing shingles, which caused me to slip and slide back towards the edge, but I was able to lie down and spread my body out to create enough friction to stop myself falling to the ground. I crawled up the roof towards the chimney in that fashion, wriggling my body and scrabbling for any slight handholds that made themselves available.

At last, I reached the chimney. I wrapped my arms

around it, shuffling them upwards gradually until I was standing against the chimney. The wind of a gathering storm whipped against my body, and I held on tightly to the life-saving bricks. Lightning shot to the earth far away from me, and the air rumbled a thundering response.

The builders had sealed the chimney with a screened vent to allow smoke out but to prevent any squirrels or men from getting in accidentally. Several warning decals were on the vent, including one showing a man climbing into the chimney, circled in red and crossed through. I hadn't made it this far by letting warning labels rule my life, though, and so I dug my fingers into the vent and ripped it out, then flung it to the ground below.

I hoisted myself up delicately and turned around, putting one leg into the chimney as if I was going down a ladder. For a moment, I looked very much like the man on the warning sign. The wind gusted, which made me lose my balance, and I fell backwards. I was wedged in the chimney, with one leg down and one leg up. I was able to rock myself free, and I lifted up again, allowing me to put the other leg down the chimney. I then began to inch my way downwards, bracing myself against the walls of the chimney with my arms and legs. Down in the chimney, I saw nothing but blackness. The shrinking rectangle of light at the top of the chimney looked down on me from above.

The chimney narrowed as it went down, and once I had made it what I thought was about halfway, I suddenly realized that I could move no further. I was stuck. This was the worst secret entrance ever.

I scratched at the walls like an ineffective Victorian chimney sweep, trying to widen the chimney. Plenty of caked-on soot flaked away, but I still couldn't move further down. I heard a light tapping above me, and I looked up just in time to get the first raindrops of the night directly in my eyes. Then the sky poured down, and the chimney acted as a funnel to direct more than my fair share of rain onto me.

I sat for a while, hanging soggily inside the chimney. I didn't know what to do. I could go back up, but then I wouldn't be able to get inside and help Penelope. She needed my help. That thought gave me energy, and I strained all my muscles and kicked my legs against the inside of the chimney. After several kicks, my shoe went into the chimney wall. The house was old and some of the bricks must have been loose; the rain must have loosened the aging mortar and I had loosened them further with my flailing. I worked my foot farther in against the brick until it moved free, and I heard the brick thud onto the floor in whatever room I was next to. I used my feet to feel the other bricks around the newly empty space, and several of those felt loose as well. With more kicking, I was able to dislodge them until I had a respectable hole. Knocking out those few bricks had taken several minutes; it was a laborious process, and I hoped I wouldn't have to dismantle the whole chimney from the inside in order to get down to Penelope. If I had to, though, I would.

I rested both of my feet in the hole. If I'd had the time to appreciate it, I would have enjoyed the comfortable perch I had created. I didn't have the time, though, and I pressed down with all the strength of my legs, pushing my back solidly against the wall. The wall gave way and crumbled behind me, and I launched backwards out of the chimney and onto the floor, trailing a cloud of soot behind me and spreading it out in a large puff when I landed.

I was unhurt. I had been farther down than I thought, nearly at the floor already, so I only fell two or three feet. Standing up, I saw myself in the mirror by the light of the moon through the window. I was soaked and my clothes were dyed black, but the rain had mostly washed my head and face free of soot.

When I looked around, I saw that I was in Penelope's bedroom. Moreover, there was a fireplace below the chimney in there. Which meant that the chimney actually wasn't a secret entrance; I had smashed my way in through a perfectly normal chimney. No matter; I was in. I walked towards her bedroom door, and then stopped. I looked down and saw that I was leaving dark tracks with my shoes. I took them off, because when I roused her from unconsciousness I didn't want to have to explain all of the carpet in her house being ruined by someone who wore shoes suspiciously like mine.

I opened the door and went into the living room. It looked like the scene of a violent struggle. The coffee table was smashed. Books had been knocked off their shelves and strewn about. The drinks we'd had the night I was there had been knocked over and spilled on the floor. Near the drinks there was a dark stain of what appeared to be blood. There was blood on the front door knob. I had not expected to see those things. I did not see the only thing I had expected to see, which was Penelope sat against the wall with her head against the window. Instead, there was her houseplant with the particularly long, fuzzy leaves, which had fallen over against the window and cracked it at the point of impact, looking very much like a woman's head from the outside. I checked the bathroom and the kitchen. Penelope was not in the house at all.

All of this meant that Penelope needed my help even more. She had been kidnapped, and the blood meant that she was wounded, too. I picked up the phone to call for help, but there was no dial tone; the kidnapper had cut the line.

I went back to the bedroom and prepared to go up the chimney. Then I felt curious, and I went to check the door. The extra latches and locks on it were all unfastened, and only the single flimsy lock built into the knob secured it. That one could be locked from the inside before you went out, which meant Penelope had unlocked the door for the kidnapper to come in, but why? Who? There was no time to sit and ponder, though, she needed help. I went out the front door myself, and locked it.

Back at home, I called the police. The woman on the line took my name and address, and Penelope's address. She said that an officer would first visit Penelope's house, and then someone would come speak to me as well.

I waited impotently, sitting on the couch. For the first time, I felt the limitations Psylocybin had imposed on me. Months before, I would have felt suspicious of twenty people by this time in the day, and I would have immediately suspected someone—anyone—of being Penelope's kidnapper. Now, with my amygdala under control, I didn't have even the slightest funny feeling about so much as a meter reader. In the past, perhaps my suspicions would have been wrong, but I wouldn't have felt so helpless. I would have rushed out of the house and pursued every lead until Penelope was safe and I was satisfied. Now, there was nothing. Penelope was gone. I didn't know who had done it, and without my paranoia I was powerless. I was a normal person, now, and I had to rely on the police and others in authority to help me and to find her.

After I had waited for several hours and had re-arranged my furniture to allow myself some feeling of control over my life, I started on my embroidery with the things I had bought as a cover story when I went to Penelope's house. Then, someone knocked on the door. I answered it to find a man in a suit. Water dripped off the brim of his hat. I recognized him as being one of the several men who had questioned me when I was in jail. I remembered that his last name was Brown. Or maybe Johnson.

"Do you mind if I come in, sir?"

I allowed that I did not mind, and he came in.

"I'm Detective Bronson." I was close. "I have some questions for you," he said.

"Before you get started, detective," I said, "I think I legally have to tell you that this conversation is being recorded."

He stopped in the middle of opening his notepad, and let the cover fall back.

"Excuse me?" he said, looking at me as if there was something strange about me.

"It's just... well, look," I said, pointing to the camera, which was pointing at us.

He raised one eyebrow and sighed. He opened his notebook again.

"Now, according to your statement taken over the

phone, you were at Ms. Hope's house two nights ago, when she pushed you out and locked the door." He looked up from his notes, and I nodded. "You went there tonight because she hadn't been answering your phone calls, found the place in a state of violent disarray with the lady in question missing, and you drove back to your house to call the police."

He paused, apparently thinking over his notes, and looked down at my feet.

"Correct me if I'm wrong here," he said. "You also said that the door appeared to have been unlocked from the inside, so she must have unlocked it to let the… kidnapper," he flicked his eyes up to me as he said that, and then back down to his notes, "in the house."

"In the lady's bedroom, Mr. Well, we found signs of forced entry through the chimney. 'Signs' is just a technical term we investigators use, but for your benefit let me explain that there was a man-sized hole in the chimney. We also found a pair of shoes." He looked down at my feet again, and I looked down too. "You're not wearing any shoes, Mr. Well, and your socks look awfully dirty. Is that soot?"

"I…" I wiggled my toes. I agreed that it did look odd. "I left my shoes in her bedroom," I said.

He wrote in his pad for a moment.

"Mr. Well, are you saying that it was you who broke into Ms. Hope's house through the chimney? After she had locked you out of her house two days prior and ignored your calls in the two days since?"

I didn't very much like the way the conversation was going, and I said so. He drew himself up.

"It's my duty to inform you that you're officially a

suspect in the disappearance of Penelope Hope, Mr. Well."

"I'm the one who reported that she'd been kidnapped," I said. "I'm the good guy, here!"

He stepped up close to me, close enough that I could see the pores in his nose, and tapped the badge on the breast of his suit. "No, Oscar, *I'm* the good guy here. I thought I recognized you, but I wasn't sure until I heard the rest of this bullshit story. You're the one who said, 'oh my keys almost didn't fit in my door and I had to buy a different brand of apple juice once so I killed a man.' You're a real piece of work, harassing this girl and then trying to pretend like someone else did it."

"It's not—I didn't—"

"Now I come here and I see you've got cameras set up right in the middle of your house, you're not wearing any shoes, and you're trying to tell me someone else took Ms. Hope. Is she back there?" he asked, pointing behind me. "Have you got a camera on her too? You're some kind of sicko, aren't you? I don't know what technicality your lawyer used to get you free from that charge with the guy you killed, but you're not going to do the same thing this time. Now I'm the one with my eye on you," he rumbled, and poked me in the chest, "and I'll be seeing you back in jail again, this time for good." He stepped out the door, and then turned back to say, "Don't leave town," before walking away into the rain, leaving my door open.

I walked back into the living room and sat down on the couch. I sat for several minutes before I was even able to think about the situation. Not only was I powerless to do anything myself, but the only people who could do something were looking in the wrong place—at me. I ran my hand over my face, and it came away black. I must have seemed like a maniac to the detective, shoeless and covered in soot in my house under the watchful eye of my cameras. I hadn't even thought to explain to him that they weren't actually *my* cameras, but everything had happened so fast I hardly had time to think about anything. With me looking like an obvious kidnapper, I was lucky that he hadn't arrested me on the spot.

Once I could calmly explain everything to the police, he'd see that I didn't have anything to do with it, but he was gone now, and I didn't know when I would be able to see him again. Until I could get it straightened out, it seemed like I was going to be the prime suspect. I didn't worry about going to jail again because this time I truly hadn't done anything wrong, but I was worried that nobody was actually looking for whoever had really kidnapped Penelope.

The only other person I could turn to for help was Dr. Boggs; maybe he would know something. At the very least, he'd be able to contact the police on my behalf and explain to Detective Bronson about my paranoid past and my newly medicated self.

I eventually dropped off to sleep on the couch with the front door still wide open.

Part 3
Chapter 19

MOST PILLS START their life as a vast amount of powder in an industrial-sized stainless steel container. The powder is a mixture of the active ingredient, a light lubricant to help the powder move around during the manufacturing process, neutral filler to bulk out the powder so the pills can be a suitable size but without too much of the active ingredient, and finally a binding agent to keep the different ingredients of the powder together. After mixing, the powder goes into a steel heat dryer, which heats it to about 120° Fahrenheit to evaporate any moisture.

Below the dryer, a machine consisting of a rotating steel ring and a multitude of small pill-sized presses spins into action. Each press comes down precisely as it reaches the right point, and scoops off a little of the mixed powder from a tray where the dryer has first deposited it. Once it passes the tray, the press pushes down hydraulically into the mold with a pressure of about eight thousand pounds. At the same time, a press with equal pressure pushes up from the bottom of the mold, so that the pills are molded in the middle of sixteen thousand pounds of pressure, so much pressure that the ten thousand or so grains of powder which make up the average pill are compacted into a single solid object. This process presses five thousand pills per minute. It happens so fast that the machine appears only as a blur to the unaided human eye.

Every fifteen minutes, five pills are tested. Five pills out of seventy-five thousand. A machine measures how hard they are by smashing them and recording the pressure it took. Another machine checks their color to make sure it matches the desired palette. If the manufacturer has included an identifying stamp on the bottom or top of the pill during the pressing process, the stamp is checked for legibility.

Each hour, or once approximately three hundred-thousand pills have been pressed, a worker loads them by hand into another industrial-sized machine (in an industrial plant, all machines are industrial-sized) resembling a tumble dryer for clothes, but twenty times the size. The drum tumbles the pills and a mister sprays a mixture of water, coloring, and shellac[1] onto them. This misted coating ensures that the pills don't crumble back into powder, helps to conceal the possibly unpleasant taste of the active ingredient from the eventual consumer, and finally allows the pill to dissolve slower inside of your stomach so that whatever medical effect it is supposed to have can be more effective over time. The misting is so fine—to prevent over-wetting—and there are so many pills that it takes about forty minutes to

---

[1] Shellac, for those of you who don't know and have thenceforth enjoyed a life of blissful ignorance, is actually an excretion from the female *Kerria lacca* insect. Most pills are covered with this insect excretion. So are many oranges and apples, although it is called 'food-grade wax' in those cases, because 'some kind of sticky beetle poop we scraped off a tree' doesn't sound as tasty.

complete the coating process. Once the mister has finished, a worker opens the tumbler and inspects a handful of pills out of the hundreds of thousands in there, mainly checking their appearance.

A tube in the bottom of the tumbling unit opens and the weight of the pills leads them down the tube, where a machine weighs them. After weighing, it counts them and moves them into different lines, where they will make their way to bottles. Another machine at the end of each line counts the number of pills that are to go in each bottle, and dumps them in, filling the bottle up.

As the bottles fill, they are pushed off the line onto a conveyer belt that leads them to the packaging machine. A final machine places a child-proof cap on the top of each bottle and screws it on. Humans then place each bottle into a box for distribution to doctors and pharmacies, or to regular supermarkets and convenience stores if they're not made of any controlled substance.

They check only a few hundred pills from the beginning to the end of the process, and at no point in this process do they check the individual pills for efficacy. It's not out of negligence on the part of the manufacturer; it simply can't be done. Billions of pills are made each month around the world, and there are just too many to test. And yet, there are many phases of the process where a contaminant could be introduced. Not an intentional contaminant—that would be exceedingly difficult because most pharmaceutical factories search employees as they enter the plant, and because machines handle most of the process, giving few opportunities for potentially malicious human hands.

But perhaps the powder doesn't mix just right in one

one-thousandth of one percent of a certain day's mixture. Nobody meant for it to happen, but only a tiny percentage of pills are tested, and that tiny percentage is unlikely to have been located anywhere near the other tiny percentage which was affected by the imperfect mixture.

Maybe it never happens. All of the machines are very precise, and the process has been continually refined over many decades. Pharmaceutical companies have a powerful financial incentive to ensure that it never happens, because a hundred-million-dollar lawsuit is very upsetting for anyone. It must happen sometimes, though; the whole process can't always be perfect, even if it can be perfect most of the time, down to the tenth decimal point. Perhaps it happens to two pills out of ten million, or out of a hundred billion.

For the most part, nobody would ever notice. As an example, although we aren't talking about ibuprofen here, the recommended dose of ibuprofen for adults is two at a time, every four hours, up to four times a day. If one of those two ibuprofen out of eight daily ibuprofen was reduced in effectiveness by half, or two-thirds, would anyone notice? Your aches might be slightly less soothed, but you wouldn't think anything in particular of it. You might not even notice, because your body is tricking you with the placebo effect, so you feel fine anyway. Good for you.

Some medicines affect the state of your mind, though, perhaps by hampering the signals your amygdala sends, and if those pills aren't as effective as they should be, then maybe some of the signals are going to get through. However, because it's not possible to have someone suffering from an overactive amygdala testing each pill to see if it works, it isn't done.

And so the very rare less-effective pills make their way through the manufacturing, testing, and packaging process. They make it to a pharmacy. Someone fills their prescription, and when they get home the bottle with the NorCorp label is placed into their medicine cabinet in the bathroom. Maybe the name on the bottle is 'O.R. WELL.' Maybe it's not. It is, though, in this case. The bottle may have a hundred pills or more inside it to begin with, and the few ineffective pills may have settled to the bottom because they weigh slightly more due to the improper distribution of the ingredients, so that person may use nearly a hundred pills out of the bottle before suffering any ill effects.

Chapter 20

I woke up on the eighth day after the police accused me of being Penelope's kidnapper, even though I was the one who reported the crime. On the first day, because Detective Bronson had not closed the door and neither had I, I woke up to find a squirrel on the couch next to me. When I moved my head, he looked at me, surprised to find out that I wasn't dead after all, and scampered out the door. It was the second day after Penelope's kidnapping before I collected enough energy to shut the door. It wasn't because I minded anyone looking in, either; it was because there were two squirrels on that morning and I worried that the number might continue to double each day until after two weeks there would be eight thousand squirrels nesting on me.

Before I shut the door, on the first and second day, I could plainly see a police surveillance unit outside my house. It wasn't marked, but the white van was still very out of place across the street. I was a nice fat suspect for them, and they weren't going to let me out of their sight. It probably didn't matter that I shut the door anyway; they likely had cameras that let them see my heat signature through the walls, so they'd know what I was doing.

I went to the bathroom to take my Psylocybin. I reached into the medicine cabinet for the bottle that said 'O.R. WELL,' and shook it. The meager rattling sound I got in return told me that not many pills were left; I estimated that I had used nearly a hundred so far. I took four pills from the bottom of the bottle. I had been taking a double—and sometimes triple—dose since Penelope's kidnapping. I wasn't paranoid, and that was an unhappy fact, because there was nothing I could do. But at the same time, there was a real danger my amygdala could override the Psylocybin and give my paranoia an outlet, where it would manifest itself and latch onto someone innocent who I would suspect anyway, and might even kill. I wasn't going to give it the chance, so I buried it under as much Psylocybin as I thought was safe. I'm not a doctor, so it probably wasn't safe, but at least I hadn't dropped dead after eight days of it, and my urine was a normal pale yellow. It did mean that I made my way to the bottom of the bottle faster than I would have otherwise. I didn't think anything of it when the four pills I took that morning tasted slightly odd. I didn't think of the long and mostly untested manufacturing process that pills go through, where perhaps a contaminant could be introduced, or the active ingredient wouldn't get combined in the right percentage and render the pills ineffective. I thought maybe it was just something to do with eating too much cold food from a can. I brushed my teeth.

The extra dosage of Psylocybin combined with my depression over my helplessness regarding Penelope gave me an incredible lethargy. I had cut a head-sized hole in a sheet so I could wear it as a robe and not worry about changing clothes or washing clothes or unzipping my pants to pee. Eight days of scratchy beard grew out of my face. I gave the police surveillance team an easy time, because I never left my house. GP&A deposited my first check in my bank account, but they still had not given me any work to do. I assumed they still watched me on the cameras, so I was being watched from inside my house as well as outside. Maybe my job was to be a cam-guy for internet voyeurs to watch as I went about my daily business, and that's why GP&A hadn't yet told me. Maybe the customers who paid to watch me were sexually aroused by the fact that I didn't even know it, like watching someone in the shower through a hole in the wall. I didn't care, and I stood over the sink and let them watch me eat cold Chef Boyardee from a can for dinner. I licked my lips afterwards, for the cameras.

Chapter 21

I sat bolt upright in bed. It was early in the morning the day after I had taken the four odd-tasting Psylocybin from near the bottom of the bottle. My head ached in a way that it hadn't done since I was in room 20 at Maple Ridge. My room was completely dark, and the only sounds were my breathing and the beating of my heart. My hands shook, and I had to concentrate to calm them. I sat in bed until a vague, pervasive light heralded the approach of dawn through my bedroom window. My bedroom door was open, and the camera in the living room was pointed at me. I felt as if I was on the other side of the camera looking at myself, and the room seemed to pull away from me as the camera zoomed in on my face. Right then, I knew *they* were watching me. My stomach filled with terror, and I stumbled out of bed towards the bathroom. My legs wobbled, and I stumbled against the bathroom door, then just barely managed to vomit into the toilet. I kicked the door shut to have some privacy from the unblinking eye of the camera, and curled my arms around the cool bowl of the toilet as I knelt on the floor.

Psylocybin was what I needed. Paranoia extending from the lower part of my brain, spreading dark, wiggly tendrils all through my mind. I stood up and took the bottle from the cabinet. I held it in my trembling hand, but I could not bring myself to open the cap. I wondered if the cops outside could see my heat signature, if they had watched me being sick. Then I remembered how the camera in the living room had pointed quickly away from the bathroom wall when I had left it, two weeks or more before. I realized that the cameras in my house must also have heat-sensing technology. It didn't matter that they were only in three rooms of my house; they watched all the rooms. They watched through the bathroom wall every day as I took my Psylocybin.

Then I suddenly understood. They watched every day *to see that I took my Psylocybin*. Why was it so important that I take it? The paranoia rose up inside me and I knew I should take the Psylocybin to rein it in, but I wanted my mind to be clear and sharp. Finally, this was my opportunity to help Penelope. I removed the cap from the bottle, and shook several pills out into my hand. Four should be enough, and in keeping with the dose I had been taking. I brought my hand up to my mouth and let the pills slip through my fingers into the sink. They each clinked against the porcelain, and I hoped the cameras did not have sensitive microphones.

I stood in the bathroom and looked at myself in the mirror, holding the pill bottle in my hand. In the reflection, the NorCorp name on the bottle was reversed. How could I have missed it? It jumped out at me now. *Ron*Corp.

My mouth dried out. My eyeballs too, because I forgot to blink while I stared at the label in the mirror, while I stared at Ron looking back at me from the bottle of pills. I realized that the cameras were still watching me through the wall, waiting for my next move. I couldn't stand there all day. I gulped a cup of water to moisten my mouth, and also to give the impression that I was actually swallowing the pills as they expected me to.

I had to keep up the illusion of everything being fine, so after I got dressed I made breakfast even though the knowledge the pills I had been taking were from Ron made my stomach uneasy. My hands shook almost imperceptibly as I buttered the toast. I hoped it was completely imperceptible to the cameras. As I carried my bacon, eggs, and toast to the table, my buttered hands lost their grip on the plate and it fell to the floor, shattering when it hit. I stood, frozen, amongst the wreckage of my breakfast. Then I looked up at the camera; it was looking directly at me. I could see the lens adjusting behind the blackness of its eye. I had to get out of my house.

"Oops." I grinned at the camera. I began cleaning up my breakfast from the floor. "Those were the last of my eggs," I said, ostensibly to myself, "I guess I'll have to go out for breakfast."

When I got my keys from the key rack, I saw myself in the mirror beside the door. I looked as if I had been lost on a jungle island for weeks. I ran my fingers through my hair and down over my scraggly, food-stained beard, then went outside anyway. As I closed the door behind me, a cool breeze blew over me and chilled my legs. I looked down and saw that I wasn't wearing any pants. I turned around to go back inside, but I stopped with my hand on the doorknob. All of the cameras were probably watching me through the door. Could I go inside and face their gaze? I took my hand off the doorknob. I was wearing underpants. That would have to do.

Chapter 22

I stopped shaking once I was driving; the cameras couldn't follow me. Out here, I was safe from watching eyes. Then, in my rearview mirror, I saw the white surveillance van which had sat outside my house for the last eight days. The police were still watching me. Was it even the police? It could be anyone. It could be GP&A. Maybe they had grown suspicious of my behavior and had placed a mobile unit outside my house so I truly couldn't get away from their eyes.

I knew the area better than they did; I had lived there for years. My lack of pants made my legs lighter and more responsive to my commands; I was ready. A familiar alley came up the street between houses, and I slowed down as I approached it. I turned in, and the white van followed closely behind me. I accelerated up the alley and the van accelerated to match. I slammed my foot fully down on the gas and turned the wheel at the same time. My car jumped into action, swerving to the left and crashing through a wooden fence onto someone's lawn, knocking aside a child's swing set behind it. The driver of the van didn't have time to react to my unexpected turn and drove past the car-sized hole I had made in the fence. A woman stood inside the house, looking out the French doors at my car speeding past through her back yard as she drank her morning coffee.

I drove out the other end of the fence, onto the next alley and now heading in the opposite direction. I made several more turns onto different alleys and side streets to be sure I had lost them, and when I looked in the rearview again the road behind me was clear.

I had lied to the camera when I said I was going for breakfast, but the chase had given me a large appetite, so I decided to stop to eat. I parked my car behind the dumpster at a restaurant. Inside, I sat at a booth by myself and ordered bacon, eggs, and toast. A man at a nearby table stared at my bare legs as he ate a sausage. I met his gaze and slowly pulled one of the legs of my boxers higher up, revealing the smooth, milky skin of my thigh, and raised my eyebrows at him. He moved to a different table and faced away from me, so I was able to eat my breakfast in peace and think about my situation.

I hadn't been back out of the hospital for very long and I really knew very few people who I could trust. I couldn't go to Winslow, because if he found out I wasn't taking my medication he'd call the police to protect me. And I couldn't bother my parents with it. There was Dr. Boggs, though, I knew he would help. I wouldn't have to tell him that I hadn't taken my Psylocybin, but I could ask him about Penelope, see if he had found anything out from the police.

The woman at the counter spent a long time looking me over when I asked if I could use their phone, but at last she said yes, probably only to get me behind the counter where my lack of pants wouldn't bother the other customers. She went back to cooking, but kept an eye on me, ready to throw a pan full of hot grease onto me if I started any trouble. I would have to get some pants and shave my beard as soon as I could; it wouldn't do to be under the threat of hot grease everywhere I went.

"Dr. Boggs, it's about Penelope—" I started, when he answered the phone.

"Yes, it's a terrible thing, what happened to her," he said. "Would you like to talk about it?"

"It's just that the police think *I'm* responsible. They're not even looking for whoever actually took her. I was hoping you might know something about it."

"I'm afraid I can't help, Oscar. I spoke to her at work the day after we talked last, and she admitted to not using her medication properly. We were getting her started on a program to get her back onto it. That was the last time I saw her."

"The day after..."

He couldn't have seen her the day after. I had been in her house and seen the drinks we'd been having together had been spilled in the struggle. She must have been kidnapped that same night, after I spoke with Dr. Boggs over the phone. After I told him I suspected she wasn't using her Psylocybin, and that she was home alone.

Right then, I wanted nothing more than to not be talking to him anymore.

"Why don't you come in and we can talk about it?" he asked.

"I think I will, Doctor," I said. "That sounds like a good idea."

I placed the phone back on its cradle and leaned against the wall, my face pressing against an OSHA workplace hazards bulletin. Dr. Boggs was behind Penelope's kidnapping. But, really I was the one behind it; what an idiot I had been.

Now who could I turn to? It had to be someone who understood me, someone who understood the mental condition me and Penelope shared. The only people I could think of were all either patients in Maple Ridge or staff there. I couldn't get to any of the patients, and if I did it wouldn't matter since they were nearly all genuinely crazy anyway. I couldn't trust Dr. Boggs, which meant I likely couldn't trust any of the other staff. Penelope was gone. My normal friends on the outside would be no help, because they didn't understand the situation and wouldn't take me seriously. I could no longer stay in my own home because of the cameras there.

Then I thought of Jim the hedgehog guy, who would have been released from the hospital by that time. He'd given me his address, but where had I put the paper? Then I remembered; I had put it in a kitchen drawer at home. My home which was being watched from the inside by the three cameras I had allowed to be installed. As the Psylocybin from the weeks before gradually worked its way out of my brain, I realized more and more what a terrible trap I had gotten myself into. Everything I could use to help myself was at home. Any kind of tools, electronics, or notes was there. Even my pants were there. If I went in then I'd have to willingly let myself be watched by the cameras, which I had done many times over the past weeks but now seemed like an unbearable torture, now that I knew who was watching and why.

A sudden sizzling reminded me that I wasn't alone, and I looked over to see that the cook was watching me as she flipped sausage patties on a grill. Why was she watching me? I had to get home, I had to get there fast, and then I had to get to Jim even faster. My appearance in public with no pants and a week of beard, my leaving the house suddenly, my driving through someone's yard in my car, all of those things were pieces of a puzzle, and if Dr. Boggs and whoever else put those pieces together they would have a very clear picture to show them that I was not taking my Psylocybin in the prescribed manner, and they would come after me just like they had with Penelope. They would do to me what they had done to her, but I could not bear to contemplate exactly what that might have been, both because I didn't want to think of it being done to her and also because it didn't seem like something I'd want done to me either.

I looked back through a window when I was out of the restaurant, and saw that the cook was on the phone now, still flipping sausage patties and rearranging bacon on the grill with her other hand. I went back to my car behind the dumpster, but as I put my hand on the door handle, I realized I couldn't take the car. She hadn't said anything when I left without paying, and that could only be because they didn't want to frighten me further. They'd made a mistake, because getting free breakfast was very unsettling. Whoever she had reported me to would be looking out for the car, and so would the police surveillance team, and probably any other police patrol cars which were in the area. Plus, there were the traffic surveillance cameras, which only a few days before I felt protected by, but now caused me the same fear as the cameras in my house. I would have to go on foot. At least I had remembered my shoes, even if I was pantsless.

The Psylocybin had left an effect on my mind and I could more easily sense the paranoid feelings coming over me, and in a feeble way I was able to separate them from reality. I found out I still couldn't resist them though, as I scrambled into a metal trash can beside the road, hiding from an approaching ice cream van even while thinking how unlikely it was that an ice cream salesman would want to hurt me. Paranoia aside, I had no reason to trust anyone at this point, even if they were selling delicious frozen treats and bringing happiness to all, so I stayed hidden while the van went past.

Being inside a trash can could be much safer than outside. There was an old rubber duck in the trash can with me. Briefly, I considered the possibility of making a new life for myself in the can. The duck could be my friend, and perhaps—in time—something more. The tubular metal shell around me would protect me from the elements and from hostile forces. People would deposit their trash and I would feast on it grandly, king of that cylindrical metal universe. It sounded like a glamorous, easy life, and its call tempted me, but only for a moment. I had to save Penelope, and I couldn't do it sitting on old newspapers cuddling a bath toy. Technically, I *could* do it sitting on old newspapers cuddling a bath toy, but at the very least I would have to leave the trash can.

I extended my legs a bit and raised my eyes above the rim of the trash can, with the lid balanced on my head. I scanned the area. The ice cream van was out of sight on another street now, and the sound of *The Entertainer* playing over its loudspeaker had faded into the distance. I stepped out of the can, and after sharing one last meaningful look with the duck, I lowered the lid on my old life.

Providence had littered the way back home with bushes, trees, and large pieces of litter that I could hide behind. I leapt from one tree to the next, rolled around a bush, and then popped up behind a fence. I kept a constant watch around me as I slinked and snuck and skulked through all the streetside flora, but there were no threats apparent. I sidled along the side of a house at the end of my street and then peeked around the corner of it. The surveillance van was not there. The whole street was quiet. I might have said that it was almost too quiet, had anyone been there with me to hear my movie reference, but in fact it was not too quiet. It was very quiet, which is just the way I wanted it to be. Any suspicious noise would have made my leg muscles unwilling to carry me to my house, so the quieter the better.

I ran across the street and burst in through my unlocked door, shutting it behind me but still ready to burst back out if I met with resistance. I met the single eye of the camera in the living room as it stared directly at me. They could see me, but they couldn't hurt me, so I strode confidently forward.

On the first stride, I heard the door saying "THUNK!" behind me, and I spun around with nervous speed to see a tiny metal dart had embedded itself in the wood. I looked back at the camera and saw that a small hole had opened up in the base of it. As I looked, the pointed tip of another dart emerged through the hole. I ducked and dived behind a chair as that next dart also went into the door instead of into me. I heard the small sound of a tiny hole being punched through fabric and particle board, and the tip of a third dart protruded from the back of the chair in front of my face.

Sitting with my back to the chair, I saw that the bathroom door was open, and several Psylocybin pills could plainly be seen lying on the floor. There was no way that the cameras could have missed them, which explained their sudden hostility. Whoever controlled the cameras now knew for sure that I was no longer under the influence of their drug, and they wanted me taken care of.

I had to get out of the living room and into the kitchen, but the gap from the armchair to the living room door was several feet long, certainly enough space for a dart to fit into and then into me as I tried to run past. The chair was the only cover I had access to; I pulled the bottom of it towards me and pushed the top, sliding in under it as it tipped over. Then I walked, crouching, holding the chair on my back as a shield. Another dart shot into the chair as I crossed into the kitchen, but the darts weren't strong enough to penetrate my protective seating.

I pulled the kitchen drawer open and an unruly pile of papers met me. Among other things, there were expired coupons, notes to myself that no longer made any sense, and potato chip receipts in case I was unsatisfied with the product and wanted to return it. Organizing the drawer had been a top priority of mine since I had come home from Maple Ridge, but I always got stuck on some important decision, like whether expired coupons should be filed under the 'Financial' or 'Food' category, and shut the drawer again. As I sorted through them then, I wished that I had just filed those things in the trash. As I pulled out the old and unnecessary bits of paper, I dropped them on the floor. I found Jim's shoelaces which he had nearly killed himself with, and since I wasn't wearing pants and couldn't spare the time to go find some, I just put the shoelaces in my underwear. Jim would understand that it was an unusual situation I found myself in, and that was the best place for them. The cameras couldn't get to me in the kitchen, so at least I had plenty of time for sorting through everything until I found his address.

Then I heard the sound of a machine drilling, and after a minute I heard the high-pitched 'ting!' of something small and metal hitting the top of the stove. Right after, there was the quieter sound of the same small and metal thing landing on the linoleum floor. I looked and saw that it was a small screw. I had no idea how it had got there, but I would deal with it later, after I had found Jim's address. The same curious sounds repeated a few moments later; another screw rolled on the linoleum next to the first. I risked looking out from under my protective chair to see who was in my kitchen apparently disassembling machinery. The drilling sound started again, and came from high up on the wall. I was surprised to see that the teddy bear camera on the wall was waving two of its legs freely; it had detached them using a small tool and was now busy detaching one of its arms, the only thing still holding it to the wall. The bear stopped drilling for a moment, turned to look at me in as menacing a way as a tiny, expressionless machine inside a tiny, expressionless stuffed animal can, and fired a dart at me through its mouth just as I ducked back under my chair armor.

I had expected a lot of things. As a long-term paranoiac, I was skilled at expecting. I often expected the unexpected. One thing I had not expected, though, and therefore had not prepared myself against, was the cameras in my house being sentient killing machines and detaching themselves from the walls in order to pursue me to my death. I didn't actually have any direct proof that they were killing machines, but I suspected the darts wouldn't be healthy for me.

Even as the bear was busy freeing itself from the wall, a thumping sound came from the other side of my office door. Fortuitously, I always locked that door from the outside to protect the expensive equipment GP&A had given me. Still, the camera in there had been much larger than the ones from the kitchen and living room, and the door was shuddering dangerously with every impact against it.

Knowing now that I wasn't free to investigate the drawer at my leisure while under the protection of the chair, I sorted even faster. Business cards went onto the floor. So did restaurant loyalty-punch cards. Catalog cutouts, onto the floor. Finally, nearly at the very back of the drawer, I found Jim's address, scribbled on a tiny scrap of paper. I shoved it into my underpants along with the laces and hunkered down under the chair, waiting for my chance to escape.

The third screw tinged down to the stove. I launched my chair at the camera, and before that final screw had fallen to the kitchen floor the chair had smashed the camera against the wall. The teddy bear dropped to the stove among a shower of sparks, and feebly kicked its legs in the air while its broken arm flopped uselessly at the wrong angle. I didn't have time to finish it off, because just then a loud chirping announced the camera from the living room as it skittered in, a metallic cross between a Chihuahua and a tarantula. I ran for the back door, punting the second camera as I went and enjoying the satisfying clang-crunch of metal against wood when it hit the wall.

I reached the back door and reached for my keys, but then remembered I usually kept them in my pants. It didn't seem to matter, though, because the thumping at my office door had finally stopped. It seemed that the camera in there had broken itself. The teddy bear on the stove had stopped kicking its legs, and I had kicked the other camera into several pieces.

I only had a moment to relax, because then the high-pitched whine of a circular saw started, and a swiftly spinning blade sliced through my office door. I ran past it for the front of the house, and when I was past my office I heard resumed thumping, now accompanied by the sound of splintering wood as the door finally gave in.

Once I was out the front door, I turned around and saw the large office camera coming straight for me on a set of rubber wheels, led by the still-spinning saw blade. I shut the door before it could get out, but the blade instantly cut a slit through the door. I felt pretty sure that this one was definitely a killing machine.

I had nowhere left to go. I couldn't outrun the camera in the streets, it moved with such incredible speed. I was trapped just outside my house, with freedom nearly in my hand, by a square surveillance machine that only reached to the height of my knees. I had to think fast, and my mind chanced upon one of the few advantages that humans still hold over machines. The camera smashed through the door and I immediately bashed it with a large rock, bending the saw blade into a useless piece of steel and knocking the camera onto its side. I realized then that I actually had many advantages over that particular machine, other than the ability to select unlikely weapons from one's immediate environment. One of those many advantages was that I didn't need to be upright on my wheels to move. Also, nobody had bashed me with a rock. I could experience the wonderful emotion of love. The list was endless, and in a way, I pitied the machine.

The camera had landed with its lens pointed at me, and I smashed that out with the rock too. I was tired of being stared at. I brought the rock down hard onto the machine's body several more times, just to be safe. I left the rock on top of the battered camera and walked away.

Chapter 23

From the outside of Jim's house, it appeared that nobody was home. According to the tall grass and the weeds encroaching on everything, nobody had been home for quite some time. A lesser man may have lost hope right then and dejectedly dragged himself to the headquarters of GP&A in order to throw himself upon their mercy. I was not that man, though, and I went right up and rang the doorbell.

After a minute or so, I heard a stumbling about inside the house. The door opened, and a man who was like Jim but was not quite Jim answered the door. He was unshaved and appeared to have just woken up, but he still looked much better than I did.

"Hello," I said. "I'm looking for Jim."

Not-Jim rubbed his eyes. "I'm not Jim," he said.

"Yes, I can see that. Is Jim home?"

He squinted in the bright sun and looked at me. Then he looked down at my bare legs and asked, "Do you have any idea what time it is?"

"It's about eleven in the morning. Most people are awake at this time. I'm Oscar, by the way. I'm a friend of Jim's."

He looked at me reproachfully, and seemed to be considering me for a very long time.

"Jim isn't here, anyway," he said at last, and shut the door without offering his name in return for mine. Sadly for my foot, one of the immutable laws of physics states that two objects cannot occupy the same space, and the law-abiding door did not quite close all the way. He grudgingly opened it partly again, and looked at me with half asleep eyes.

"Do you know when he'll bc back?" I asked.

"You'll have to ask Dr. Boggs about that, man."

"What?" The anger must have shown in my face, because he took a step back into the house. "Where has Dr. Boggs taken him?"

"Whoa man, relax." He held up his hands. "Dr. Boggs hasn't taken him anywhere. Jim checked himself into the hospital; he's been there for months now. Boggs is just the head doctor there."

So Jim hadn't been released from the hospital after all. He was due to come out just a few days after I did, but he was still in, weeks later. He was definitely still alive, though; his brother would have been notified if he'd been successful at another suicide attempt. I had nothing else to ask, so I decided to let him get back to his mid-day nap. I moved my foot out of the way, and Jim's brother closed the door.

I sat down on the curb and held my injured foot in my hands. Now what? I had nobody to turn to. I couldn't go back to my house. Even though I had destroyed the cameras, those who watched the cameras knew everything now. All my money and my cards were there, so I couldn't get a hotel room or anything. Sitting on the curb wasn't getting me anywhere though, so I stood up.

I looked back at Jim's house, hoping perhaps to catch the sympathetic eye of his brother, and saw that at one window the curtains weren't fully drawn. There was a large glass tank sitting inside the window, and a small animal lying on its back in the sun. I walked closer, and saw its pink underside and four tiny legs pointed up at the ceiling. I walked until I was standing right next to the window. I knew I was looking at Mr. Hodge, the hedgehog that had won him a free extended vacation at luxurious Maple Ridge.

Because I had no other options, a wild plan formed in my mind as I stood there looking at the little brown and pink mammal sunning itself. Without any great hope, I wrapped my shirt around my forearm, and smashed it against the window. To my surprise, the window shattered into several large shards of glass. I felt exultant with this result after the terribly disappointing times I'd had trying to break into various doors and windows recently. I reached in through the opening, into the tank, and grasped the hedgehog around his belly.

"What are you doing, man?" Jim's brother shouted when he came into the room and saw me attempting the hedgehog heist. "That's my hedgehog!"

"It's Jim's hedgehog," I said, through the broken window. "I'm taking him back." And then, realizing that perhaps there should be more explanation, I added, "To Jim!"

Jim's brother seemed to be considering whether he should shoot me or call the police. I deduced that because he was holding a gun in one hand and a phone in the other. Then he tossed them both onto a couch. He reached down, out of sight below the hedgehog's tank, and I heard him opening a drawer. When his hand returned, he was holding a bag of hedgehog food.

"He sleeps ten hours a day," he said, handing the bag to me. "And he likes to be fed every two hours when he's awake. Just put his nose in the bag, he'll stop when he's full. Good luck. Jim needs him." Then he closed the blinds.

I held Mr. Hodge up to my face. He made an unimpressed puffing sound and then scooted around in my hand so he was turned away from me. I put him in my shirt pocket and walked away from Jim's house.

When I was a safe distance away, I decided to try it. I went behind a tree and took Mr. Hodge out of my pocket. I held him up so we could speak face-to-face.

"Alright," I said, "let's talk."

He looked at me.

"I know you can talk. Jim told me all about you."

I shook him slightly. He puffed at me again and rudely moved his spines forward over his forehead so they covered his face. When a hedgehog does that, it's hard to tell which end you're talking to. I reached for him to turn him over on his back so I could see his face while I talked, but when I got my hand close to him he started making a sound which I can only describe as malevolent purring. He was going to get turned over whether he liked it or not, though, and I moved my hand closer. Suddenly, he fluffed out his spines and prickled my hand with them. It startled me more than it hurt, but I decided it was best to leave his face hidden under his spines if that was what he wanted.

At least nobody had seen me talking to him; there was no harm in trying. I put him back in my pocket. His tiny forelegs rested over the edge of the pocket and his delicate curved nose stuck out ahead as if he was a small adventurer eager to go on a journey, facing into the wind. Even if he couldn't talk, I was still going to enjoy having him along.

As crazy as it sounds, I had hoped I could learn something from Mr. Hodge. I wasn't crazy, though, I was just desperate—desperate enough to try having a conversation with a hedgehog. Now the only thing left was to try to find Jim at Maple Ridge. I didn't know how I would do it; there were hundreds of rooms at the hospital and I had no way to find out which one he would be in. Maybe Mr. Hodge knew, but he wasn't talking. They wouldn't tell me at the front desk, because Maple Ridge wasn't the sort of hospital that allowed visitors. If I somehow managed to get past the front desk and not be questioned by any of the staff, I'd surely be stopped at any one of the security checkpoints between wings, put there to prevent the escape of dangerous patients. Since I had no medical ID or uniform and obviously wasn't a patient, I'd be apprehended immediately by hospital security at the first checkpoint, and likely find myself once again as a patient in the secure wing.

If that happened,, Dr. Boggs would surely see to it that I was never considered for release again. I would be labeled a sadly unreformable criminal with an incurable mental illness, and for the good of society I would of course have to remain locked up forever. Sealed court orders would make it all official, and my family and friends legally wouldn't even have to be notified of where I was, or why. The next time one of them went to my house after not hearing from me for days, they'd just see a foreclosure sign with no explanation from me, or maybe they'd all receive letters with my signature forged on them saying that I was leaving the country to pursue a life as a traveling minstrel. As important as saving Penelope was, it was just as important that I not end up locked away in an underground level of Maple Ridge forever.

Maple Ridge was thirty miles out of town, and I couldn't use my car. Probably the police had already been alerted to the license plate number as belonging to a dangerous criminal. If it actually was a police surveillance van following me that morning, then they'd assume I was on the run and then they'd be even more convinced I was Penelope's kidnapper.

I hiked a good distance out of town, staying on back roads and going into the woods whenever a vehicle went by. After several hours had gone by since I had passed any houses, I judged that I was far enough out from town so that there wouldn't be a thick network of spies layered around, and I started looking at cars approaching to select a good candidate for carrying me to Maple Ridge. I stopped at the far side of a hairpin turn, which allowed me a long time to view approaching drivers as they slowed down to navigate the turn.

I expected it to take a long time to find a suitable ride, but the first car that approached was a silver old-model Cadillac driven by an elderly woman who reminded me of my grandmother. She approached the other side of the turn and hardly had to slow down any, since she was already moving at a sedate pace. I moved to exit the woods and flag the woman down, but Mr. Hodge, who had been resting contentedly in my pocket for hours, suddenly made a high-pitched squealing noise and I looked down at him, thinking perhaps I had been careless moving through the bushes and had got him caught on a thorn. His squealing was incredible, and my head ached when I heard it. It was a headache like from before Psylocybin, a warning of something. Maybe a reminder that Jim would certainly not be pleased if I allowed his dear friend to be injured. Mr. Hodge looked fine, but I pulled him out of my pocket anyway and turned him over, inspecting him. By the time I was finished and was satisfied that he was in perfect health, the car with the old woman had gone by. I called Mr. Hodge some unflattering names and stuffed him back in my pocket, resisting the urge to put him in headfirst. To be fair, she probably wouldn't have given me a ride anyway, considering my lack of pants and general unkemptness.

After that, no other cars seemed good for hitching a ride. Something about the color of their paint, or the way the driver was holding the wheel would set my suspicions going, and so I stayed in the woods.

Several large canvas-covered black trucks, of the kind you'd expect military personnel to be riding in the back of, drove by in the other direction, towards town. I wondered what their business was, but only a little—getting Jim's help was the most important thing, and there wasn't room in my mind for much else.

I didn't keep count of all the vehicles passing, but probably a hundred had gone by and I still hadn't felt good about any of them. I supposed that maybe Dr. Boggs & Co. might have had hundreds of cars patrolling those roads, and it *did* seem busier than usual, especially for that time of day. It was so hard to tell for sure, though. Months before, I had felt sure of every thought I had, and I never questioned them. Then, while I was using Psylocybin, it had been the opposite; even though I had no paranoid thoughts, to the point that I let my enemies set up a surveillance system in my home and then helped them kidnap my girlfriend, I had still mentally derided and ridiculed myself for even the smallest paranoid inkling, such as 'what if the mailman rubs his genitals on my door before he knocks?' He does it sometimes, I'm sure of it.

In either state of mind, confidently paranoid or hopelessly naïve, I had felt more or less happy, sure that my thoughts were the right ones, even if they were wrong. I was having paranoid thoughts again but wasn't sure at all whether I should trust any of them. Part of me wanted to get in the first car I saw, and I nearly had, while the other part of me wanted to get in no car ever, which was useless.

Eventually, as I paced, a tractor carrying a low trailer of hay bales passed by. I shoved all paranoia and anxiety out of my mind and leapt onto the truck as it rounded the curve. I crouched down behind several bales of hay so that the driver wouldn't see me if he looked back. Mr. Hodge climbed out of my shirt pocket and onto my shoulder, resting his warm body against my bare neck. After a while he went to sleep, and began to whistle quietly as he breathed.

I tried to formulate a plan while we rode along, but I wasn't able to get much farther than 'get to Jim.' I still didn't know how I was going to get to Jim, and I didn't even know what to do if I did actually get to him. I needed someone who could help me figure out what had happened to Penelope, and Jim was the only person I knew who could listen to my explanation of what was going on without trying to medicate me and put me in a straitjacket, if only because people were also trying to medicate *him* and put him in a straitjacket. He would understand. I couldn't do it on my own; I felt so tired already and I didn't even have a place to sleep now that my house was off-limits to me, nevermind a place to think.

A bump in the road jolted me awake some time later, and I opened my eyes. I didn't know how long I had slept, but it didn't feel very long. It was surprising that I had been able to sleep at all, with the scratchy hay against my bare legs. The road around me looked familiar, and I realized that we were only a few miles from Maple Ridge. I didn't want to get off the trailer in sight of the hospital in case there was anyone watching, so I gently picked up the sleeping Mr. Hodge from my shoulder and slid him back into my shirt pocket, then jumped out onto the road. I pumped my legs as I hit the ground, and since the tractor wasn't going very fast I was able to stay upright with not very much flailing about.

I walked until I reached Maple Ridge Road, which led off the main road and into Maple Ridge. Trees surrounded the hospital on all sides, and that little road was the only way in or out unless you wanted to walk through miles of forest. I stayed in the woods as I walked along the side of the entrance road, still wary of any patrolling cars.

It was late at night by the time I passed the Maple Ridge Mental Hospital sign and approached the parking lot beyond. There were very few cars left at this time of day; there was only a small medical team at night because most of the patients would be asleep. The security team was the same size at any time of day, though, because many of the patients could be dangerous without regard to the rotation of the earth relative to the sun. One of the cars was a silver old-model Cadillac. The car that had passed me on the road with the grandmotherly woman driving it was now here in the parking lot at Maple Ridge; she must have been one of the staff there. Mr. Hodge seemed to have seen it at the same time, because he puffed at me. If I believed a hedgehog to be capable of condescension, I might have been offended by Mr. Hodge. As it was, though, I did not consider a hedgehog capable of such a thing, so I was not affected. I remained above it; I patted him on the head—rather roughly, an observer might say—and continued on.

Chapter 24

The front doors were always locked and the receptionist had to buzz you in, but after 6 o'clock, there was no receptionist[1], so I had no hope of socially engineering my way inside the front of the building. There was a door at the back for late deliveries, but I had nothing with me which could convincingly be a parcel.

I was walking around the building, looking for a way in, when I almost walked into a security guard coming around the corner. He couldn't have been more than twenty feet away when I saw him, and I leapt deeper into the bushes, landing face down.

The guard shined the beam of his flashlight around me. I knew he couldn't see me, because it was a thick bush and I was well concealed within it; years of hiding behind or inside bushes had honed my skills so that I invariably selected the best bush on the first leap. However, nobody could have missed the sounds caused by a hundred fallen leaves as my body crushed them, so I knew that presently he would come closer to investigate, and up close even the most well-concealed person trying to look like a bush still looks very much

---

[1] To be precise, there was a receptionist; she had just gone home for the day. I don't mean to imply that each day at 6 o'clock the receptionist ceased to exist.

just like a person hiding in a bush.

Mr. Hodge wriggled himself out of my pocket and walked away.

"Mr. Hodge," I whispered, "come back." But he paid me no attention. He had already moved several inches, and I couldn't reach for him; if I moved at all in the leaves, even to extend my arm, the noise would surely betray me. If I got caught and had Mr. Hodge with me, at least there was a chance that I would be able to reach Jim inside the hospital and get Mr. Hodge to him. But if Mr. Hodge ran away and I was captured without him, and then I had to tell Jim that it was my fault that his best friend was running wild in the woods instead of safe at home with his brother, I feared for my chances of enlisting Jim's help.

Mr. Hodge trundled steadily forward, right out into the open. He made a soft rustling noise as he waded through the leaves with his round, low body. He walked out of the bushes and into the beam of the guard's flashlight. Once he was in the light, he turned toward the guard. Mr. Hodge blinked in a sleepy way, as if surprised by the bright light from the flashlight.

I realized in that moment that Mr. Hodge was a genius. Nobody would suspect a hedgehog of being a malicious intruder. Even though the noise I had made was much larger than the noise a hedgehog could possibly make, his cuteness would make the guard forget about details. He would believe the evidence of his senses: his ears had heard a noise from a bush, and then his eyes had seen a sleepy hedgehog walking out of the bush.

The guard took a pack of peanuts from his pocket and threw one to Mr. Hodge. The hedgehog considered the peanut, and then, appearing to accept it as a payment for interrupting his sleep, took the peanut between his front paws and stuffed it into his mouth, then headed back into the woods, slogging through the leaves once again. The guard chuckled to himself and continued on his patrol, whistling as he went.

Mr. Hodge returned to the bush, and stood in front of my face. He munched on the peanut, appearing much contented. The small sound of his teeth crunching the peanut was the only sound to be heard. For a while, neither of us moved, and I didn't speak.

"You don't have to be so smug about it," I said to him at last. Then I picked him up, and put him back in my pocket. "And don't get any crumbs on me, this is my good shirt."

I watched the building for another hour, establishing the routine of the guard patrolling. He would walk around the building, shining his flashlight to and fro into the woods and into the windows of the building, doing a pretty thorough job of inspecting. He didn't know that he was up against a master of concealment, though, so I didn't blame him for not finding me even though he walked past me several times in different places. Once he had gone all the way around the building, he would return through a side door using a key card.

A plan presented itself to me, and I acted upon it without too much time wasted considering whether it was a good plan or not. When the guard made another round, I walked up behind him and pressed my only available weapon against his back.

Unfortunately, Mr. Hodge's nose didn't make a very convincing gun barrel, and the guard wasn't fooled for very long. Fortunately, that was just long enough for me to get the handcuffs off of his belt and cuff him to a tree, and by the time he realized he had been duped, and asked, a bit unsure of himself, "Is your gun a hedgehog?" it was too late. I twirled Mr. Hodge in the air and put him back in my holster. He bit me through my shirt, but the pain and the small amount of lost blood were worth it.

I had come very ill prepared. Luckily, he'd had his own handcuffs, but I had no rope or tape to gag him with. My initial lack of pants coupled with my hiding in the bushes may have given the guard the wrong idea about my intentions, and he seemed frightened as I started to undress him. His fears were soon calmed because I only wanted his clothes to disguise myself as him. His jacket had large pockets in the sides, and I put Mr. Hodge in one of them so he would be out of sight. I took off my shirt and put it on the guard, apologizing that I didn't have more for him to wear on such a chilly night. Then I used my undershirt to gag him with, so that he wouldn't be able to shout and alert anyone else to what I was doing.

I waited near the security entrance to see if another guard would come out, if some hidden signal had been sent and an alarm raised. Nobody came. After several minutes, I crept out of the woody shadows, and into the slightly brighter shadows near the hospital wall. I stayed low to the ground and kept an eye out for any cameras that might also be keeping an eye out for me. I pressed myself against the wall and shuffled along until I reached the door. I unlocked the door with the key card I had taken, and let myself into the guardroom.

Another guard was in there at a desk with an array of monitors showing closed circuit television feeds from around the hospital. Most of them were from inside the hospital, only two showed the outside and both of them were from right at the front entrance, where I had not gone. No cameras watched the sides or the back of the hospital. None of the screens had shown when I ambushed the first guard, and none of them showed him handcuffed to a tree. I reached for the baton in my belt. I would be able to take this second guard completely by surprise.

"Hadley," he said, turning around and taking me by surprise, "can you cover for me here while I go out? I know it's not your turn yet, but I need to stretch my legs." His nose was bandaged, like it had recently been broken by a brick.

"Mm-hmm," I assented, hoping that was the kind of noise Hadley might make.

"You're alright, Hadley," the guard said on his way out the door.

I settled down to watch the cameras while he was away. A few insomniac patients were still awake in the low security wings of the hospital; several sat playing poker, a few others watched television, but most seemed content to wander the empty rooms and halls.

In the secure wing, all the doors to the rooms were closed and locked just like they had been when I was behind one of them, and no patients were out in the halls. Nearly half of the cameras all showed the same picture of the secure wing, apparently of the same hallway, which seemed very odd to me, but I couldn't figure out what it meant. The checkpoints between the several wings were manned even this late at night, with a guard located at each one.

I watched the non-secured patients playing poker more closely. As I looked at them more, I didn't think they were playing poker at all. They whispered to each other, and looked around as if they were afraid of someone hearing, like they were planning something. I zoomed the camera in on them. Then I remembered that I wasn't actually Hadley, and it wasn't really my responsibility to keep an eye on the patients through the cameras. I zoomed back out to let them carry on with their poker game/devious plan.

There was a computer on the desk, with a database program open on the screen. It was a list of all the patients in the hospital. I scrolled through, looking for Jim. I didn't know his last name, and there were hundreds of patients listed, with about twenty named Jacob, James, or Jimar, all of which could be shortened to Jim. The names were listed in alphabetical order, with the last name first, and down at the H's, one stuck out. *Hodge, James*. Jim. Good Lord; he had given his hedgehog the family name. He had probably willed all of his possessions to it as well. I pulled up the extended patient information and saw that he was still in the same non-secure wing I had been in with him before I left. The floor schematic showed that he was still in the same room as well. If I could get to that wing of the hospital, it would be easy enough to find him in his room, shake him awake, and explain to him why I wasn't crazy and needed his help.

Just below Jim's name, still among the H's, I saw an unexpected name which made me push the chair back and stand up, unable to believe it.

Hope, Penelope. She was there, in Maple Ridge, right then. I clicked on her name to get her patient information. She was in the secure wing, and she had been there for ten days, the exact amount of time since I had last been at her house. If she was in the secure wing, then that meant she wasn't hurt too badly, even with all the blood I had seen in her house, because otherwise she'd have been in the medical ward.

I still wanted to get to Jim and give him Mr. Hodge, but Penelope was *right there.* I had to get to her first. I didn't know the full internal layout of the hospital but I knew she was probably within two hundred feet of that guard room. It was almost close enough to touch her, providing that I first moved two hundred feet.

I wrote a note for the other guard, 'gone to the toilet' so he wouldn't wonder where I had gone if he came back before me, and stuck it to the screen for him to see. Before I left, I appended '(diarrhea)' to the note, so he would be less likely to ask questions about why Hadley had abandoned his post, or why he was away for so long. Then I went through the interior door, deeper into the hospital.

If you look like you know what you're doing and where you're going, people will assume you do. I walked down the hall with firm strides, keeping my eyes ahead mostly but nodding a greeting at any hospital staff I passed. I went in a bathroom; the door was in full view of several of the late-night cleaning staff, and it would lend credence to the bathroom note I had left in the guard room.

I came out of the bathroom several minutes later, feeling refreshed, and continued on my way. At the end of the hallway, I followed a sign which pointed me to the secure wing. I could see the checkpoint at the end of that next long hallway; my heart began to beat faster as I approached it, and my legs felt shaky. I was ready to attack the checkpoint guard and beat him into unconsciousness if he challenged my business there—although the closer I got, the bigger he looked. In fact, he was huge; he barely fit in the security booth and had the appearance of having been stuffed in there. I could not turn back; to do so would arouse suspicion. I came near, and he grinned a large, toothy grin, giving me the very uncomfortable feeling that he had plans to eat me.

"Comin' through, Hadley?" he asked, extending his head up out of his uniform like a massive carnivorous turtle might.

"Mm-hmm," I replied, with confidence I did not feel. If I went through, then I would be on the same side of the security gate as that monstrosity. He pressed a button, and the gate swung open like the door to a cage.

"Come on in," he said. With sweat pooling under

my collar, I went through. The door shut behind me, but the guard did not come out of his booth. I walked on towards the elevator which would take me to the secure wing.

"Nice beard," he said to my back.

"Mm," I agreed, putting as much nonchalance into that small noise as I could manage. Did the real Hadley have a beard? I couldn't remember, but it was too late for a shave. I went into the elevator and pushed the button to go down. The checkpoint guard continued grinning at me as the doors closed. It was a relief when I no longer had to see his huge mouth, and I felt measurably safer.

The ride down was long, longer even than I remembered from when Penelope had taken me outside so I could see that I wasn't actually being kept thousands of feet underground. She had saved me from myself that day. I had been falling apart mentally, just as I had worried that the whole foundation of the building was falling apart and would cause me to be crushed under a million tons of dirt. Now I was going to save Penelope from the same place that she had saved me.

I had plenty of time to think on that long ride down. Why was it so important for me to take my Psylocybin? Why had they had gone to such lengths to ensure it, including installing killer cameras in my house? And they also wanted to ensure that Penelope was taking it, so much that they kidnapped her when she had stopped. I didn't understand how they thought we could bother them or influence their plans. We had a reputation for being paranoid; nobody would believe us. Besides that, most of the time I was paranoid, I felt sure that it wasn't for anything legitimate, like with the boy on the street, who I thought was trying to kill me but was only playing a game.

It definitely seemed that the Psylocybin was the key to it, though, even if I couldn't understand why. It was only when the cameras in my house had seen my untaken pills that they turned against me. And it was only when I (stupidly) alerted Dr. Boggs to my suspicions about Penelope not taking her Psylocybin that she was captured. While we were using the drug, we were docile. We would let anything pass without a word, even things that a regular person would be paranoid about like having cameras installed in their house by someone else. They didn't seem to care what we did, though, we were allowed to live our lives as normal; other than the cameras there was nothing they did directly to me.

There were other cameras, though, like the ones recently set up at traffic lights. I had felt safe when I went under them, the opposite reaction to what I would have now if I went under a camera. And they hadn't been used for just their publicly stated purpose; the woman who had written to the paper to complain had been arrested only days later, caught by the traffic cameras. Did she have the same paranoia as me? Was there a connection between those cameras and the cameras in my house? Perhaps she, too, was in Maple Ridge, being kept from the outside world. I couldn't find a reason for any of it, and my head was full of too many things right then; Penelope was the most important thing, and the rest would have to wait.

The elevator bell dinged, and the doors opened. The hallway was empty, except for me. Upstairs, the floors were hard tile, but down in the secure wing plush carpet covered them. The walls, too, were soft. Some of the patients had self-harming disorders, and so every hard surface had been padded so they didn't get opportunities.

Penelope was in room 2, one of the first rooms. I had taken a ring of keys from the guard outside, and I went through the ring until I found a key labeled 'Master.'

I would open the door to find Penelope in bed, and I would rouse her from slumber and tell her that I had come to rescue her. We could kiss deeply—but briefly, *there's no time, my love*—and then we would leave Maple Ridge forever, perhaps with me carrying her in my arms. Instead, I opened the door to a room halfway filled with dirt. The far wall had collapsed inward, and a ton of earth had spilled through, carrying furniture and plaster and padding with it. A wheelbarrow and a shovel sat against the wall, and I could see shovel impressions in the pile of dirt that dominated the room.

I closed the door to give myself a chance to clear my head. I knew I hadn't really seen it, and I told myself that when I opened the door it would be gone. Then I noticed that beside the '2' on the door there was the outline of '0'. The second decal must have fallen off recently and not yet been replaced. This was room 20, my first room in Maple Ridge. They actually *had* moved me to a different room after the incident where I'd thought the whole building was going to collapse on me.

I opened the door again, and the room was still filled with dirt. It was real. It had really happened. The day which still lived in my memory as one of the most frightening things I had ever experienced was real, even though they had told me it was not. I had been terrified of being buried alive in that room, of a slow suffocation while worms and other underground creatures used my body as a playground. I had been convinced that my fear was false, that my mind was playing cruel tricks on me, and I had been pacified into taking Psylocybin to 'cure' myself. They had tricked me; my mind had not been broken, it had only been warning me. The collapse I had been terrified of had actually happened.

The dirt filling the room proved another thing as well; I *was* underground. The elevator was not a slow elevator; it was a normal elevator travelling at regular speed. Why, though? Why build this single hallway of rooms so far underground?

I closed the door again. It proved that I was right before, that I wasn't actually crazy, but it didn't matter right then. Penelope still needed my help. I went down the hallway, which had twenty rooms, numbered from 1 to 21. I used the master key again, and let myself in.

Penelope was sitting on the bed, turned away from the door.

"You can't keep me here forever," she said, without looking away from the window, where a thin moonlight shone through. Her words were confident, but her tone was defeated, as if she knew that the opposite of what she said was true, but that she should say it anyway.

"Penelope, it's me," I said.

She jumped off the bed as if propelled by a spring when she heard my voice. Her hands shook. She still didn't turn around. She seemed afraid to, like I was an illusion which might be dispelled if she looked. Then her shoulders slumped.

"So they've got you too, then. But why would they put you in…" her words trailed off, and she turned around at last. I smiled and twirled the ring of keys on my finger.

"How… why…" but she wasn't able to finish any of her questions. She came and put her arms around me, then kissed me deeply, and not briefly. I didn't complain—I decided that there was time for it after all.

After a while, I felt my hands moving over her body of their own accord, and I decided there was not time for *that*. "I've come to get you, Penelope," I said, breaking our kiss. "There are only a few guards between us and the outside, and I'm sure we can fake some kind of late-night patient transport story for you. We can just go; nobody even knows I'm here."

When I said that, the radio on my belt crackled, and out came the voice of the guard who had gone outside to stretch his legs. "We have an intruder," the radio said. "Someone has attacked Hadley and taken his uniform. He's inside the complex, but I don't know where. Stay alert and start a patrol in your zones. Over."

"I know where he is," replied the deep voice of the giant guard I had passed before the elevator. "I'll take care of it. Over and out."

"Alright, now they know I'm here," I said.

Even though there was now an urgent reason for us to leave, I first wanted to show her what I had discovered in room 20. The windows in the rooms were hard plastic instead of glass, and the furnishings in the room had been carefully picked so that anything light enough to lift was not solid enough to damage the window. The guard's truncheon riding on my hip was metal, though. I walked over to the window and smashed it with one blow from the truncheon. The pieces of thick, clouded plastic fell on both sides of the window frame, revealing a single light bulb in a concrete box. It gave off a dim, white light, which through the plastic had appeared to be moonlight.

"These rooms *are* underground, Penelope," I said, when I had revealed the deception, "I looked in my old room and it was filled with dirt, just like I had been terrified of that day."

"I know," she said.

"You… know? What?"

"After you had that vision of being trapped underground, they changed the lights so they weren't mimicking the yellow light of the sun all the time. Before you, nobody had ever questioned the bulbs. Now, at night, they look like the moon," she waved her hand towards the milky bulb, "and sometimes they dim and then brighten again like clouds have gone across."

"But... you said... you said that it wasn't underground." I felt unsteady. "You took me in the elevator. You said there was nothing to worry about. And there really was a collapse in my room, so you moved me to another room. But why are these rooms even down here? It doesn't make any sense. That's why I started taking Psylocybin." I moved away from her, until my back hit the wall. Paranoia saturated my brain. "You're behind all of it," I said, in a fit of sudden realization. She was with Ron. She had convinced me to take the RonCorp pills. "Every time I had worries about Psylocybin, you talked me out of them." I knew I should be leaving, but I felt weak; I couldn't will my legs to move. "I was in your secret entrance, Penelope, I forced myself into it. Now they've used you as bait to get me back here with the faked fight scene at your house, but you don't even need to be rescued. You're one of—"

Before I could finish that sentence and tell her I knew she was one of them, the checkpoint guard tore open the door, popping a bolt out of one of the reinforced hinges. His body filled the frame. There was no way around him. They had trapped me again. They would never let me free from Maple Ridge this time. I would never see my family. All my houseplants were going to die. I had been lured into a trap by the first pretty girl who showed an interest in me, and I hadn't suspected anything. I was a fool. The room swayed around me, and the ceiling suddenly got farther away. My legs had decided that my body wasn't worth supporting any longer and I fell, hitting my head on the floor.

Chapter 25

I was dropped onto something soft, like a pile of fresh earth. I could feel that I was moving forwards in space, and turning. The darkness lifted from my eyes, and I could see a network of lines in the distance, blurry and moving fast. I blinked my eyes and the lines came into focus. They were ceiling tiles. I raised my head with a great effort and looked side to side; I was in a wheelbarrow moving down the hall. I was lying in fresh earth. I leaned my head back and looked up. Penelope was pushing the wheelbarrow. I looked back and saw that the checkpoint guard was lying on the hallway floor outside Penelope's room. She jammed the button for the elevator to open the doors and then wheeled me inside. When she turned to fit the wheelbarrow in properly, I saw that she had my truncheon slipped into her pants at the hip.

I struggled to get out of the wheelbarrow. If I could only stand up, I could resist. My muscles still weren't responding very well, though, and I was only able to raise myself a little bit. Penelope put her hand on my chest and pushed me back down.

"Just rest," she said.

"How could you do this to me?" I asked, knowing how pathetic I must sound to her, now that I knew she didn't care about me. It didn't even matter why they had done it anymore. I wished I could die.

We had only been going up for a few seconds, and the elevator dinged. I thought I must have blacked out again and missed the long journey up. Penelope pushed the wheelbarrow out the door.

"Look down the hall," she commanded. I looked. It seemed that we were still on the same floor. Then I looked at the numbers on the doors; the one right in front of me was room 41. How had the numbers changed? Why?

She pulled me back into the elevator and started it again. I noticed that she pushed the 'up' button more than once, in a certain sequence, but I couldn't follow it. We went up longer this time, but still not as long as the usual time, and the elevator dinged. She pushed me out into another hallway and I looked without prompting. The room at the end of this hallway was number 101. It must be different floors, with twenty rooms on each floor. The floor with room 101 was the fifth floor from the bottom. Why was she showing me this?

"This is why the rooms are so far underground," she said. "It's just not one set of rooms; there are twenty floors on the secure wing. Anyone they don't like is kept here; anyone who knows anything, anyone who could harm them, or anyone who might tell other people what they're doing. If it's actually their mental condition causing it, then some people get a chance with this or that variation of Psylocybin—on a short leash, of course, like with the cameras in your house. The bottom two floors, rooms 1 through 41, are for the intractables, people who have already been tested outside and failed, people who are thought to be incurably violent, or sometimes just people who know too much. In your case, it's because you had the *potential* for finding out too much. I don't know why they wouldn't just kill people like us, but they don't."

"Why are you telling me this? I feel like James Bond, with you telling me your whole plan instead of just killing me."

"Jesus, Oscar, this isn't a movie. It's not my plan. I'm not with them. I convinced you to take Psylocybin, but that was only so you could get *out*. If you were out, then you could help me, you could do good; there's nothing you can do from inside. What could you have done if you were still in one of those rooms down there, refusing treatment? I was going to tell you everything that night at my house, but then you spooked me by talking about cameras."

"Because you weren't taking your Psylocybin," I said, remembering.

"I never took it. I only pretended to, so I could get close to them. I'm constantly paranoid, especially about things like cameras. Even when you were in here and I was your nurse, I was paranoid. Every single time I came to this place—to the stronghold of our enemy—it took an enormous amount of will, and I always left feeling exhausted."

"You have to believe me," she said, "I meant to tell you all about it the next day, but then Boggs showed up. I let him in, because to do otherwise would surely have made him suspicious—although that particular worry turned out to be a waste of time, because he was clearly already suspicious, although I have no idea what I did, I was always scrupulously careful." I would have hidden my face away when she said that, had I been able to, but there are very few places to go when you're lying in a wheelbarrow. "Once I had unlocked the door, a bunch of the guards from here pushed in. I managed to hit one of them in the face with a brick, and I think I broke his nose because of all the blood he left. There were too many of them though, I couldn't get away. They brought me here and stuck me in the bottom floor. They never would have let me out."

I contemplated what I was going to say next. I believed Penelope, if for no other reason than that I was desperate to believe she wasn't involved in this vast plot against me, that we truly were on the same side. If everyone was with Ron, then no one was with me, and I needed someone on my side. I needed friends, and friends are honest with each other.

"Dr. Boggs was suspicious because of me," I said. "More than suspicious. That night after you made me leave, I told him that I thought you weren't taking Psylocybin. I told him about how you were acting that night, and I told him that only someone who was extremely paranoid would have such a variety of locks and bolts and latches like you did." I fidgeted with my hands—my muscle control was starting to come back—and looked steadily at the ceiling as I spoke. "I was using Psylocybin at the time, so I didn't know anything about Dr. Boggs. I worried something bad would happen to you if you weren't taking it like you were supposed to be."

"I understand," she said, after a pause. "Don't worry, I'm not angry with you. I know you did it with good intentions, because you were worried about me. And you also came here to get me. I forgive you for it."

Knowing that she wasn't angry at me for what I had been feeling was a betrayal gave me energy, and I was able to stand. I got out of the wheelbarrow, and we pushed it to the back of the elevator, out of the way.

"I came here to rescue you, but I guess you ended up rescuing me," I said, pointing to the wheelbarrow. "How did you get us out of the room past that huge guard? I felt sure he was going to pull out a bottle of hot sauce and eat us both."

She pulled the truncheon out of her pants and handed it to me with a grin. "One of the most useful things I've ever learned is that nobody likes to have their boys whacked with a metal stick.[1]"

The elevator dinged; we had reached the top floor. When the doors opened, I expected that a cluster of guards would be there to greet us since they would have seen Penelope take out the huge guard, but there was nobody.

"Where is everyone?" I asked.

---

[1] I have also found this is very true, and it is also one of the most bizarre things about the human male's body. His testicles, one of the most pain-sensitive parts of his body, just hang down openly between his legs. It's not so with other organs. His heart, his lungs, and the lower part of his trachea are protected by his ribs. His brain is protected by his skull. Even the less important organs like his stomach and kidneys are protected by several inches of fat and muscle. His testicles, though, which are necessary to pass on his genes—essentially the entire biological reason for his existence—are just *there,* ready to meet any metal stick that comes along for a whack.

"They don't know where we are," Penelope said. "Months ago, I was able to put the cameras for the secure wing on an infinite loop showing empty hallways, so they didn't see either of us down there, and they don't know which floor the guard went to either. Once we leave the elevator, they'll see, but I think we can escape in time because they're spread out over the hospital."

"But can't he just call on his radio once..." she held up a radio, and I stopped. She had taken the guard's radio so he wouldn't be able to call for help. I was very happy to have her with me, doing the things I couldn't.

"We can't leave just yet, though," I said. Before she could ask why, I reached into my pocket and held up Mr. Hodge. It must have been the same pocket that the guard kept his peanuts in, because Mr. Hodge's head was covered with peanut crumbs and they dropped from his face as I lifted him out.

"Squeak," he said, looking very small and deceptively fuzzy in my hand.

"You remember Jim, the hedgehog guy, don't you?" I asked her.

"The guy with attachment personality disorder who thought his hedgehog was his best friend?"

"That's the guy. His name is James Hodge. And this is the hedgehog, Mr. Hodge. I came here tonight to bust Jim out so I could get his help finding you, and it was only coincidence that I found out you were here when I looked in the patient database. I had to get you out first, but now I can't leave Jim here, not now that we're so close. I owe it to him. It's going to be a lot harder now that they know I'm in the hospital and soon they'll discover that you're out of your room too, but I have to try."

I told her what I knew about where Jim was in the hospital, and after she locked the checkpoint gate so the guard from below couldn't follow us, we were off.

She said she would take us the safest way even though it was longer. As we walked, I remembered that I had more to tell her.

"I've figured everything out," I said. "All of it. They only wanted us to take our Psylocybin, but I don't know why. RonCorp, though. RonCorp!"

She just looked at me, without the instant recognition that I had expected when I revealed Ron's clever trick. "Don't you see?" I asked. "NorCorp? I saw it backwards in the mirror; it's RonCorp. The company that makes Psylocybin is owned by Ron, he's behind everything."

"Oscar, NorCorp just stands for Nordic Corporation," she said. "I think it's based in Greenland. Maybe Sweden."

I decided I would explain everything about Ron to her later; she just didn't know as much as I did. "Alright then, Sweden," I said.

We carried on walking until I felt sure we must nearly be there. She walked around a corner and then stepped back.

"Get out of sight," she said quietly. "I'll take care of this."

"What is it?" I asked, but she had already moved out into the next hallway again. I stepped back around another corner but kept my head out so I could see. I didn't know what she had seen, but she knew the hospital much better than I did and was apparently much better with a truncheon than I was, so it was sensible to let her take the lead in any situation she wanted.

I couldn't tell what she was trying to do. She looked from left to right, and appeared to be surprised. Then she leaned against the far wall and briefly put her hands up. She was talking, and I strained my ears to hear what she said.

"Out all on our own, are we?" I heard a man say from around the corner, out of sight.

"Please don't sound the alarm," she said. "I only want to get out of here." She put her hand on her breast. "If you help me, I can... help you." As she spoke, she slowly moved her hand down over her stomach and onto her thigh.

A hospital guard stepped into view and moved close to her. Something about him was familiar, like I had seen him before. He put his hand on her hip, and I felt jealousy seething inside me, burning at the base of my skull; I forced myself to ignore it. I was going to let her handle the situation.

"I'm willing to negotiate," he said, sliding his hand around to her bottom. I could see his fingertips making impressions in the fabric at the rear of her patient's uniform. I changed my mind about letting her handle it, and stepped out from around the corner, leaving the wheelbarrow. As I did, she reached back, pulled a previously hidden truncheon from her waistband and swung it right at the face of the guard. She moved so fast that he had no chance to react before it impacted across his mouth; even from a distance of ten paces, I heard the crunch of metal against his jawbone. He uttered a loud moan and staggered back, moving the offending hand up to his mouth to catch the bits of teeth which were being washed out in a stream of blood, and held his other hand out in front of his face to defend himself. Penelope swung the truncheon back, down, and then brought it up between the guard's legs, and I heard a dull thump and what might have been another crunch. He groaned again, pulled his knees together and bent his body forward with one hand between his legs and one over his mouth, with blood dripping between his fingers. He swayed from side to side, and she used the tip of the truncheon to give him a small push; he toppled over backwards, slowly and without resistance, dripping blood down onto his uniform as he went, and then lay unmoving on the floor.

I went up to join her. The guard's nametag said *Steven*, and the mole to the left of his mouth confirmed that I had seen him before—he was one of the guards that had been there when Penelope took me outside when I was a patient. His face was a mess, and he was going to be in a lot of pain once he woke up. I never liked him much anyway.

At the end of that hallway, there was a young guard moving towards us with uncertain steps; he must have seen everything. Behind him, I saw several faces poking out around the corner, watching. She menacingly raised the bloody truncheon in her fist and he turned on his heel and left.

"Come on," she said. "Jim's room is just up ahead." She dropped the truncheon on the floor, leaving it as a reminder for the unconscious guard with the broken mouth.

There was the sound of a scuffle from the common room. We turned the corner and entered the room where I had sat at a table a month before, when the other patients had unkindly kidded Jim about Mr. Hodge, until he left the table in a suicidal depression. It had been full of patients then, and it had contained ten or fifteen patients earlier when I saw it on the security monitor. Now there were only four patients, the ones I had seen playing poker, who looked as if they were planning something. Two of them were holding the young guard by the arms; one was on the floor and had him around the legs, and the fourth was unbuttoning the guard's shirt. Several pillows were on the floor behind him, as if intended to be a bed for him to rest on, and a tub full of a thick, clear liquid sat nearby.

They turned around when we entered the room.

One of the patients holding the guard's arms whistled at Penelope.

The other said, "Nice moves, Nurse."

She stopped walking and gave them a withering look of medical authority. They quietly returned to their work.

The fourth man now began to undo the belt of the guard. They couldn't have been intending to help us, but it was helpful anyway for them to have gotten this final guard out of the way. I wasn't sure what they were planning to do to him, but I didn't ask. I figured he was getting off easy; they didn't have any truncheons or other dental equipment around that I could see, so at least he would keep all his teeth.

We went to Jim's room, and found the door unlocked. Once inside the dark room, Penelope locked the door behind us, and I roused Jim by gently shaking his shoulder.

"Jim, it's Oscar," I said.

He opened his eyes halfway and looked at me in an unfocused manner.

"Hmmaphmm," he mumbled with heavy lips, then closed his eyes and seemed to go back to sleep.

Then his eyes opened all the way, and he looked at me. "Oscar, you're in my bedroom, in a mental hospital." Then he looked at Penelope. "Nurse, you're wearing a patient's uniform." He looked at his bedside clock, and added, "At midnight."

I reached into my pocket and took out Mr. Hodge. I set him on Jim's chest. Jim put his hands around his best friend and sat up in bed. Tears dropped from his eyes and he looked at us. "I've been so lonely," he said. "It's so good to see all of you. I know this is only a dream," and he sighed, with a happy contentment, "but it's the best dream I've ever had."

"Jim, it's not a dream," Penelope said.

"At midnight," Jim said, shaking his head.

"Jim!" I shouted, shaking him by his shoulders. He looked at me, still uncomprehending, in a daze. Maple Ridge *was* a mental hospital, after all; I don't know what else I expected to happen. For him to be some sort of mastermind who would take us out of the hospital through a secret tunnel he had made through the wall and concealed expertly, and then once outside he would fit all the pieces of the vast conspiracy together for us?

Jim stroked Mr. Hodge's prickly body and continued looking up at us with a silly smile. The hedgehog puffed in what you could almost take for exasperation, and dug his teeth into Jim's thumb. Jim said, "Ah," like someone who has just discovered some small fact he was searching for, stood up out of bed, and walked over to a mirror on the wall. He held his thumb up in front of the mirror; a single drop of blood issued from the wound and ran down his thumb. He turned around to us.

"I'm not dreaming, am I?" he asked.

I thought that Mr. Hodge rolled his eyes as he sat in Jim's unbitten hand, but it was hard to say for sure.

"You're not dreaming, Jim," Penelope said. "Get your things together, we're getting out."

"There's a bag of my things there," he said, pointing to it, "but I'm not allowed to leave. I'm not a voluntary patient anymore; that's what they said."

"That decision has been changed," Penelope said.

The doorknob rattled.

"Nurse... you're not in your uniform," Jim said.

"Jim, we have to get out of here. They're not going to let you keep Mr. Hodge if you stay." When I said that, Jim's eyes lost their sleepy look and he held the hedgehog close against his body. He picked up his bag of things. I got his old shoelaces from my underpants and he laced up his shoes; we were ready.

Someone pounded on the door, making it shake in its frame. I picked up the bedside table and moved to throw it through the window, but Jim put his hand on it and stopped me. He put his finger up to his lips and pulled the bed away from the wall to reveal a secret tunnel he had expertly concealed.

"I've been digging this for a few weeks. I didn't really intend to use it, but it did keep my mind off of things when I was tunneling."

Jim went first with Mr. Hodge riding on his shoulder. Penelope went next. I picked up the bedside table again and threw it through the window, setting off a distant alarm. Then I went through the tunnel as well, and pulled the bed against the wall behind me. I expected to hear the sound of the door falling into splinters or bursting open back in Jim's room, but instead I heard it opening normally; whoever was doing the banging had been replaced by someone with a key.

The tunnel was large, as far as secret tunnels go, but still small enough that we had to go on our hands and knees. Penelope's bottom swayed from side to side in front of me as she crawled forward, and I was amazed by my ability to focus on it to the exclusion of all else, even though we were faced with imprisonment, torture, and probably even death if they discovered the tunnel before we were out. It was a great comfort to me.

Instead of going directly for the outside which was

several feet away—as you might do if you were making a secret escape tunnel—Jim's tunnel took us on a tour of the inner walls and vents of Maple Ridge.

"I really wasn't intending to use it for escaping," he apologized from up ahead, "I was just trying to stay busy."

We had been crawling for several minutes when we passed through ductwork leading beside the common room, and through the vents I saw a group of guards gathered, talking. One, the young guard who had been captured by the four patients, was naked except for a coating of white feathers, almost as if the contents of several pillows had been stuck to him with glue. We moved slowly through there, shuffling on our hands and knees so we wouldn't make any noise, and I watched through the vents as we passed by each one.

"They couldn't have gone far," the feathered guard said. "You got into the room just a few seconds after they went out the window. They have to be hiding in the woods close by the hospital; the guys patrolling out there will find them."

I shuffled past that vent, so I couldn't see them, but I could still hear.

"When we find them, I'm going to show her what this truncheon is really for," another voice said, sounding like someone with a speech impediment. I could hear the sound of metal tapping against flesh; he was hitting his truncheon into his palm for emphasis. Then I heard someone else striding across the room, and then the same man saying, "Hey, that's —"

We passed by another vent just in time for me to see

Dr. Boggs raising the truncheon and bringing it hard against the guard Steven's face. The lower half of his face shifted sideways to accommodate the bar of metal, and he fell to his knees with fresh blood flowing down his chin. He held his hands up in a pleading gesture, and tried to say something through his ruined mouth, but it was unintelligible.

"*That's* what the truncheon is for," Dr. Boggs said. "If you'd been thinking with the head on top of your shoulders, that patient wouldn't have been able to escape at all." The doctor spat in the guard's face. "Get him out of here," he said to a pair of orderlies who stood nearby. They each put one of the guard's arms over their shoulders and dragged him off; his feet didn't appear to work very well.

Dr. Boggs turned to face the rest of the guards in the room. "I don't want that to happen to any of you," he said. "Everything has already started. This town will be mine tonight, and anyone who gets in the way of that is going to get more than a crushed jaw. The escaped patients and their accomplice are somewhere *in* this hospital. They did not go out through that window. You," he said, pointing to one of the guards, "go to the west wing. You," pointing to the feathered guard, "patrol the front entrance. Stay out of sight."

We passed by the last vent and went into a wall cavity, and I couldn't see what was going on the common room any more.

"Doctor," a new voice said. "There's a handmade tunnel behind the bed in the patient's room; I think they might have gone through that."

"Of *course* they've gone through that!" Dr. Boggs shouted. "Find where it comes out. Find them!"

We sped up, as much as you can when you're crawling in a confined space.

"What did he mean about the town being his?" Penelope asked.

I shook my head. I had wondered that myself, thinking about it made my head ache, and it didn't matter anyway. The important thing was to get Penelope and Jim out safely.

"This is the end of it, just here," Jim said, after we had gone forward a few more minutes. We were in ductwork again, at an intersection large enough for the three of us to crawl side by side. I pressed my face to the vent and looked out onto a hallway. There was blood on the floor, and what looked like several teeth. I looked to the right, and saw the wheelbarrow Penelope had carried me in. We were at the hallway intersection where Penelope had taught the guard his first lesson about the use of truncheons.

"Jesus, Jim, we've only moved a hundred feet in the past ten minutes. This is right back outside the common room."

"You heard what bird man back there said about patrols in the woods," Penelope said. "If we hadn't gone through Jim's tunnel we'd already have been caught."

She was right, and I apologized to Jim.

"It's alright," he said. "I know it's not a very good escape tunnel; it was never meant to be."

"This is where we get out, anyway," I said. I turned

around and horse-kicked my leg out behind me, bending the vent. I kicked it again and it clattered out and onto the floor below. Jim went first, with us holding his arms to lower him down to the floor, then I lowered Penelope down to Jim, and then they both received me in their arms.

"Get in the wheelbarrow," I said to both of them. "I'll push."

They climbed in, making the wheel squeak with their weight, and I pushed. Penelope directed me, and we soon came to the hallway which led to the front of the hospital. I could see the glass at the reception area and the parking lot beyond.

"Hold on tight," I said. I backed up several feet, so that I was against the wall, and then pushed as hard as I could.

"Oscar, I don't think this is a very good idea," Penelope said. Jim didn't say anything, but from his face I could tell that he agreed with her. I was picking up speed, and then I was running, pushing the wheelbarrow in front of me like a battering ram.

"Keep your heads down," I said, "it'll work."

"Oscar," Jim said, "slow down. This is a wheelbarrow." He started to get out, but I only sped up; we were committed to my plan. He hunched down in the wheelbarrow and pulled Mr. Hodge tight against his chest.

As we neared the reception area, the feathered guard walked across the hallway. He heard the sound of the wheelbarrow's squeaky wheel and turned towards us. He stood still, like a nocturnal animal caught in the beam of a bright light—he definitely wasn't cut out for his line of work. I didn't slow down; I pushed the wheelbarrow straight into him and he toppled over into it, falling across Penelope and Jim.

I continued at full speed and crashed the wheelbarrow and its occupants through the front window. The shatterproof glass was carried forwards in a single spider-webbed sheet by the force of the wheelbarrow and the several hundred pounds of humans in it, and we rode out over it, sliding down the front steps of the hospital and crunching the glass underneath. I skidded the wheelbarrow to a stop, and the guard rolled off onto the grass in a trail of feathers, dazed but unhurt. Penelope and Jim climbed out of their noble steed, and we ran into the parking lot. We reached the edge of the asphalt; ahead of us I could see flashlight beams moving in the woods near the exit road. Behind us, back at the hospital, guards emerged from the shadows and shone their flashlights on the broken front window.

I put my arm around Penelope and pulled her close to me. We were trapped; at least we were trapped together.

Jim, not having any answers to our predicament, took the opportunity to hold Mr. Hodge close to his mouth and whisper something to him in what might be their last moments together. Then he set him down on the hood of the silver Cadillac which had passed me on the road earlier, and Mr. Hodge trundled under the hood, out of sight.

It was a good idea for the hedgehog, but the rest of

us wouldn't just be able to hide under a car until the guards went away. I closed my eyes and put my free hand over my face. I had to think. Then my thoughts were interrupted by the sound of a car engine starting, and I opened my eyes to see Mr. Hodge running out from under the Cadillac. He sat on the pavement next to the car's front tire, looking very satisfied with himself. Jim scooped him up and got into the car, moving over to the passenger seat. Penelope followed after, sitting in the middle. There wasn't time to consider the fact that Mr. Hodge had apparently just hotwired the car, so I just got into the driver's seat and put that to the back of my mind.

I reversed out of the parking space and then pointed the car towards the exit. Two guards stood barring the way, although I had a strong hunch that a human body—or even two human bodies—is a very ineffective bar to a four-thousand-pound vehicle powered by an internal combustion engine. I revved the engine, but they didn't move, so I let my foot off the brake and moved slowly towards them. I intended to give them every chance to move, but if I had to choose between us and them, I knew that I would choose them: them being smashed by the car.

In the bright beams from the car headlights I saw what looked like a giant, frenzied duck running towards the guards that stood in our path. I pressed the gas down partway and the car lurched forwards. The feathered guard waved his arms to the others and shouted something, which I couldn't make out exactly, but it sounded roughly like "He's a maniac!" It convinced them, anyway, and the guards moved out of the way just a few seconds before the car's steel frame would have been trying to occupy the same physical space as them.

In the rearview mirror, I saw Dr. Boggs slowly descending the steps at the front of the hospital. He wore a red glove on his hand and was still clutching the bloody truncheon in his fist. I had seen that before! It was the red fist I had seen it in my dreams, and I had seen it on the walls. I shook my head. That was months ago; there couldn't be any connection between the things I had seen then and the fact that Dr. Boggs was wearing a red glove now. Sometimes people wear red gloves.

A guard near him got into a car, but Dr. Boggs said something to him and shook his head; the guard got back out of the car. From that distance of a hundred yards or more, the doctor's eyes seemed to meet mine in the mirror and burn into my mind, and I could not hold his gaze. My head hurt and the pain caused me to close my eyes. When I looked again, we were out onto the road and the maples concealed the hospital.

We drove in silence for a while, except for Mr. Hodge who sometimes made a light purring noise as he sat fuzzled against Jim's neck. The first few minutes were tense, particularly when we briefly heard the rapid *tht-tht-tht-tht* of a helicopter passing overhead, but after we had been driving for several miles and no headlights appeared behind us, I felt the air in the car change as we all were able to relax. They apparently did not feel the need to pursue us. Maybe Dr. Boggs had realized that we were no danger to them after all.

Jim moved into the back seat with Mr. Hodge, and Penelope scooted over next to me and leaned her head on my shoulder. Just feeling her warm body against mine and the weight of her head on my shoulder was exquisite. I put my arm around her and drove with one hand; my high school driving instructor would have been displeased, but I felt supremely happy. We had done it.

We continued on in that way, until I brought up the subject of where we would go; the half tank of gas in the car wouldn't last forever.

"Why don't we go to Jacob's house?" Jim suggested.

"Jacob?" I asked. "Who's that?"

"My brother. Didn't you get his name when you got Mr. Hodge?"

"I… no. It didn't come up." I decided not to tell him that I had broken Jacob's window with the intent to steal Mr. Hodge. That was all in the past.

I was against going to Jacob's house. In fact, I was against going back into town at all; I felt an unexplainable paranoia about it.

While we talked, I got a dim image of Dr. Boggs pointing a gun at me. I knew he would kill me if he got the chance; he would kill all of us, so it was important that we get as far away from him as we could, and Jacob's house would be pretty far. I still felt uncomfortable with the idea of going there, but Penelope was with Jim, and since I had to assume Mr. Hodge would be with him on that issue as well, I felt outvoted by a large majority. Jim assured us that Dr.

Boggs didn't know about his brother's house and that it wasn't even listed as belonging to the Hodge family.

My paranoia was eased somewhat by the fact that Penelope's own paranoia was not bothering her about it. I decided that perhaps my fears were unfounded, and relaxed again. I turned onto the road which would take us toward Jim's brother's house, a place where we could rest and talk.

As we came closer to town, we had more to worry about. We drove by a corpse lying beside the road. From the amount of blood on the ground and from the size of the hole in the body, the death appeared to have been caused by some large caliber weapon.

"Did you..." I started, hoping someone else saw it.

"It could have been a hunting accident," Penelope said. I supposed it could have. People do hunt, and accidents do happen.

Closer towards town, we passed a house which was surrounded by a group of police in military-style SWAT uniforms. One in front knocked on the door, and when a man opened the door, the leading police officer shot him in the face without a word. I almost lost control of the car when it happened, but I drove on.

As much as I wanted to by then, we could not turn back. We saw that vans and trucks blocked certain roads as we drove on, mostly roads that led out of town. We had gone around a curve in the road so I couldn't see if they had blocked it behind us after we drove into town, but I felt sure they had. Still, nobody on the street and none of the large number of police patrols seemed to take any special notice of us, and I allowed myself the irrational hope that there was just a higher than usual amount of law enforcement going on. The man who they had shot *had* looked a bit dangerous. We drove on.

Chapter 26

The lights were off inside when we arrived. We all got out of the car, and Jim let himself in through the front door with a spare key hidden under one of those fake rocks. When we were all in the front room, the light came on. Jacob was on his knees in the living room. Blood dripped from his split lower lip, and both of his eyes were ringed with bruises.

"I'm sorry, James," he said. A man in an all-black uniform, with a badge on his chest that was a red fist over a gold star, stood behind him and held a gun to his head.

"Jacob!" Jim exclaimed, and moved towards his brother. Behind us, another black-uniformed policeman came out of the corner and grabbed Jim by the arms before he could advance further. Another came from the other corner and grabbed Penelope, and a third grabbed me. I started to struggle, but then realized it was pointless. We were trapped.

Dr. Boggs stepped out of the shadows from the dark kitchen. Now I realized why he had not pursued us; he had known exactly where we were going, and having a helicopter means you don't have to rush.

He held a gun in his red-gloved hand, just as I had seen. I had been trying to get far away from him, but we had gone right where he wanted us, right where he knew we would.

"You've caused quite a lot of trouble, Mr. Well," Dr. Boggs said, smiling a doctor's broad, benevolent smile. "All I wanted was to make you better." He lowered the gun. "I wanted to help you."

"I've seen how you help people," I said, pointing to Jacob and his injured face. I told him of the dead man we had seen on the side of the road, and of the murder of the man who was only opening his door to a knock. I told him I knew about the multiple floors underground at Maple Ridge where he kept the people who were inconvenient to him.

"Those are sad things," he said, appearing to consider the murders, the kidnappings, and the imprisonment in an academic way, with a far-off expression in his eyes. "But sometimes sadness is necessary. Pain cannot be helped, not when it's for the good of us all."

"It appears to have been all for nothing, in any case," the doctor continued. "Perhaps I underestimated the danger you posed to me. After all, you've still walked right into this. Your considerable paranoia has been no help to you."

I noticed Mr. Hodge had gone down Jim's back and was now working his way around the edge of the room, using the thick 70's-style carpeting and the shadows of the furniture as cover.

"Why are you doing this?" I asked, trying to buy time for Mr. Hodge.

Dr. Boggs laughed a short, sharp laugh; a single expelling of air from the lungs.

"You can ponder that on your own in the next life, if

there is one," he said. He pocketed his pistol, nodded to one of the men, and turned to leave the room. Then he stopped, and turned back around slowly. "But then, what's the harm of it?" he asked himself. And then, to me, "You'll have a bullet in what's left of your brain soon enough; I don't begrudge throwing scraps to someone who is dying. I'm not a cruel man, Mr. Well."

"You'd think someone with such a prodigious paranoia would have figured it out by now, but you haven't. You and the others like you are all that stood between me and having this whole state in my hands," he said, raising his hand up and making a fist. In the light, his fist matched almost perfectly with the badge the black-uniformed soldiers wore. "Of course, because of you I've had to put this plan into action sooner than I intended. A few people have become collateral damage because of that." He moved his arm in the direction of Jacob, and in my mind the image of the man being shot inside his front door slid into view. "It didn't have to happen this way, you know," he said. "If you'd both taken your medicine the way you were supposed to, you'd have been oblivious to everything. It would have all been put in place peaceably. However, I've had to rush, and that's when accidents happen. I apologize for this regrettable accident."

Mr. Hodge exited the cover of the couch and pressed his body low against the floor, moving slowly through the plush carpeting near the wall.

"As it was, Mr. Well," Dr. Boggs went on, "you were apparently still oblivious, so I needn't have worried. The outdoor tracking cameras which you know about were one of the first public steps in my plan which has taken years to set in motion. Still, even after you were off your medication you didn't give them any of your mental attention. If you had, we might be standing on opposite sides of these guns tonight. Your noble efforts to rescue the lovely Ms. Hope have blinded your mind to the bigger things going on around you," as he spoke, my mind flashed back to the military-style trucks which had passed me as I was on my way to Maple Ridge, "and I was able to get it started without any meddling from you, which was a welcome change."

"I never interfered with anything you were doing," I said. I could see Mr. Hodge's nose poking out from under the armchair from the far corner; now he was behind Dr. Boggs.

"Haven't you?" he said, shaking his head. "Oh, Mr. Well, I truly have overestimated you. You have done much more than you think. The man you killed months ago, the one you've since convinced yourself was just a man leaving his house after breakfast to go to work, that man was my lieutenant in this city. He helped organize everything for us here. It was through his skill that we discovered Ms. Hope here suffered from paranoia, and got her started on her own Psylocybin prescription."

Mr. Hodge now crept cautiously out from under the armchair.

"At some point, she has obviously stopped taking it," Dr. Boggs continued, "but for years she was a subdued and happy member of the hospital staff causing no bother to us. The 'shadowy organization' you spoke of to the detectives and prison doctors was mine. You felt that you were being watched and followed, and it's because we were watching you and following you."

He paused, and seemed to be waiting for some response from me. When I didn't give him one, he shrugged and said, "But I tire of this long explanation. You are obviously not the mental opponent I thought. Goodbye, Mr. Well. Goodbye, Ms. Hope." He turned to go back through the doorway, and Mr. Hodge leapt onto his pants and skittered up his leg. Dr. Boggs looked down in surprise, but the hedgehog moved with such speed that he was instantly on the doctor's face and had bitten him on the nose. Such was Dr. Bogg's consternation at the situation that he swung his fist at Mr. Hodge without considering where the hedgehog was, and the little creature leapt away so that the doctor hit himself in the face with his red-gloved fist and stumbled backwards. Mr. Hodge landed on the shoulder of the Red Fist soldier holding the gun on Jacob, and bit him on the neck. The hedgehog's knowledge of human anatomy was astounding; blood squirted out from the soldier's punctured jugular vein and splattered an arc on the wall. He grabbed Mr. Hodge and flung him hard to the floor, where the small hedgehog then lay, unmoving.

The soldier clutched at his bleeding neck, and Jacob grabbed the gun from him. The men holding us reached for their own guns. When they released us to go for their guns, we dropped to the floor. Although one was able to get his gun unholstered and fire off a single shot, Jacob was too fast for them; all three went down under the heavy weight of a bullet. The one who fired the shot had been lucky (as lucky as a man who has just been fatally wounded can be); even though he had no time to aim and had fired wildly, his bullet had struck Jacob.

Dr. Boggs stood in the kitchen doorway, astonished by the scene. Jacob's stomach was bloody, and his shirt was torn by a single hole. The soldier Mr. Hodge had bitten had collapsed on the floor, in a red circle of glistening carpet. He moved, but weakly and slowly; his blood coated the walls. The other three lay on opposite sides of the front door, against blood-streaked walls. One was dead, shot in the heart; another in the head; the third was struggling to breathe through a punctured lung and would soon be dead without medical attention.

My head ached, and an image of Dr. Boggs leaving, unharmed, through the back door of the house flashed into my mind.

The doctor, seeing that the tables had turned and all his dinnerware had spilled onto the bloody floor, turned and ran through the doorway into the kitchen.

I grabbed a gun from one of the fallen men beside me and fired into the darkness, and Dr. Boggs screamed in return, followed by the sound of breaking glass. I reached through the doorway and turned on the light. A trail of blood had dripped across the floor and out the broken window; he was gone.

I turned my attention back to the room. Penelope was holding Mr. Hodge, and he stirred in her hands.

Jim knelt next to Jacob with his arms around him. Then I realized that he was holding him up; Jacob didn't have the strength to remain upright.

"I'm sorry, little brother," Jacob said.

"You don't have anything to be sorry about," Jim said.

"I'm sorry this is the last time I'm going to see you, James."

I picked up the phone and tried dialing for an ambulance, but the line was dead. Jim looked at me, and I shook my head.

"Don't say that, Jacob! You're going to make it. Oscar has called for an ambulance, they… they'll be here soon."

Jacob shook his head. "You know I can tell when you're lying." He smiled, weakly. "Thanks for trying, though."

"At least Mr. Hodge is safe," Jacob said. "You'll have him when I'm gone."

"Please don't say that. I can't take it. Don't leave me. Tell me you'll never leave me!" Jim pressed his face against Jacob's shoulder and began to cry. Jacob lifted one of his arms up and put it on Jim's back to console him.

"I'll never leave you, little brother," Jacob said. Then his arm slid down Jim's back, and his head sagged forward. Jim held his dead brother in his arms, and wept.

Penelope looked at me and motioned towards the front door.

"We should go, Jim," I said, laying my hand on his

shoulder, which shook as he sobbed.

"I can't leave him," he said. "He said he'd never leave me."

"Jim, if we don't leave this room now," I said, softly, "we're never going to get another chance."

I gently loosened his arms from around Jacob's body, and helped him to his feet. Penelope handed Mr. Hodge to him, and he put the hedgehog in his pocket. Jim seemed barely able to walk, and I supported him as we walked out the door. Penelope followed, after collecting the guns from the dead men.

Our car was still outside, untampered with. Dr. Boggs must have not thought it necessary, since he wasn't expecting us to be coming outside again.

A searing pain shot through my head accompanied by the image of all three of us lined up against a wall with our hands cuffed behind our backs, and I pulled Jim and Penelope down behind the car with me, just before a van drove down the road, slowly. Once it had passed, we got in the car and left Jacob's house.

I found a road out of town that they had missed blocking, and we took it. We passed a burning house. Behind us, the night sky was lit up by more burning buildings deeper in the heart of town. It seemed that Dr. Boggs was taking out his anger on everyone else. We sat in the car in silence, speeding away. Mr. Hodge snuffled quietly inside Jim's shirt. Jim looked ahead with a blank expression. I didn't say anything to him; I knew only time could help.

Penelope moved over against me and leaned her head against my shoulder. It was just like on the ride away from Maple Ridge, but everything had been different on that ride. We were riding to freedom then, but now we were riding away from death.

I put my arm around Penelope, and we drove on.

Epilogue

I AM AT the end of this journal. If you're reading this now, then you already know of the things that have happened, because *they have happened*. That is the most important thing for me. I now know that I do not have a mental disorder. I was not crazy. I was being followed. The man I killed was not an innocent citizen as I was led to believe by the court and the prison and the hospital and even my friends; he was the architect of my town's demise, which went on to happen even after his death.

Somehow, my mind led me to him, and it has led me through all the tribulations since then. Instead of a mental disorder, there is something else different about my mind. I don't know how to explain it, for I don't yet know what it is. In the end, it has helped me escape, and helped my friends escape with me. I am learning to trust my mind.

It is true that we suffered losses in the course of our escape, but so have we inflicted losses on our enemies in turn. Their losses were greater in number, but ours were dearer to us.

You don't need any proof, though; you don't need this record of the things that have happened, because you have lived through them. I don't know how you got this journal. Perhaps you are now living in the abandoned lot where I intend to bury these pages. Or perhaps you were digging a grave for a loved one, killed in the early days of the occupation of the Army of the Red Fist. On the radio, I have heard of the jailings and murders which happened during the occupation protests that necessitated those graves.

After that, there was nobody left to protest, not even when the Red Fist started grabbing the mentally ill and holding them without any kind of trial or charge. I've heard of all kinds of experiments and torture being carried out by Dr. Boggs, but I don't know what is true or false. For now, we can't go back to the town, it's too dangerous.

It's even possible that you are our enemy, and that this journal has somehow fallen into your hands. In that case, it hasn't told you anything you don't already know. I know you are searching. You will not find us—we will find you.

I have started making my own orange juice. I am not powerless as you imagined me to be; I am powerful. I have adapted. Every day, I tip back a cold glass of juice and let the pulpy liquid pour into my mouth. I drink it up. It tastes sweet.

The Quest for Juice

From the Author

Thank you for reading my book! If you enjoyed it, please leave a review or rating on Amazon or Goodreads, tell your friends you liked it, or even email me to let me know. I'm a self-published author, which means there's no publishing house behind me, no limousines, and no marketing dollars. I'd love to hear from you, and my contact info is below. Thanks again!

JD Jackson

Say hello to me:

JonathanDavidJacksonWrites@gmail.com
Facebook.com/JonathanDavidJacksonWrites
JonathanDavidJacksonWrites.com

Check out the next book in the Paranoia Trilogy, *The Quest for Truth*, available as a paperback or ebook wherever books are sold online.

Oscar's orderly paranoid world has been turned upside down by the Red Fist Army and he now lives in exile. With the help of Penelope, Jim, and Mr. Hodge the hedgehog, he must free their hostage town, take on the Red Fist, and discover the truth about Dr. Boggs.

However, when things go wrong and Oscar loses his closest friends, he has to rely on an unlikely group of refugees with surprising mental abilities. As he continues on his journey to freeing the town and himself, he finds out more of his own truths than he ever imagined, and absolutely nobody shoots lasers out of their eyes.

"LOVE LOVE LOVE ... one of my best reads this summer"
- 5-star Amazon Review

"...you won't think twice about staying up waaaay past your bedtime to finish it."
- 5-star Amazon Amazon Review

"...as bonkers and wonderful as the first."
- 5-star Amazon Review

The Quest for Juice

Made in the USA
San Bernardino, CA
18 July 2018